A. Texan

The Yankee Slave-Dealer

Or an Abolitionist down South - A Tale for the Times

A. Texan

The Yankee Slave-Dealer
Or an Abolitionist down South - A Tale for the Times

ISBN/EAN: 9783744714853

Printed in Europe, USA, Canada, Australia, Japan

Cover: Foto ©Andreas Hilbeck / pixelio.de

More available books at **www.hansebooks.com**

THE

YANKEE SLAVE-DEALER;

OR,

An Abolitionist Down South.

A TALE FOR THE TIMES.

BY

A TEXAN.

"Prove all things ; hold fast that which is good."

NASHVILLE, TENN.:
PUBLISHED FOR THE AUTHOR.
1860.

CONTENTS.

PREFACE.

THE following story was suggested by reading a popular work of fiction, abusive of Southern slavery, and the more recent and bitter attacks of the system on the part of a blind partisan and fanatical press. Though the subject has been ably defended by others, it occurred to the author that something on the plan here offered might present a phase of the question perhaps before unnoticed, and, while not devoid of interest, still prove an auxiliary in the propagation and defence of correct principles.

In conformity with the plan prescribed, nothing has been said as to the *right* of slavery, socially or politically, and but little morally—the author contenting himself by introducing into a story designed mainly to entertain, a few points bearing on the general question.

Should it be thought that too liberal an expression of views has been allowed the abolitionist, a perfect confidence in the truth of the position defended must be considered a good excuse—the author wishing, in all fairness, to place the chief character of the tale in such a position as an *honest* abolitionist might be supposed to occupy.

Whatever merit the work may possess, is its sole dependence for popular acceptance: from critics of a certain class the author neither asks nor expects favor; but to the candid he commits the result of his labors, hoping his well-meant efforts, though not entirely faultless, may yet accomplish something in the mission on which it is now sent.

TEXAS, May 21, 1860.

YANKEE SLAVE-DEALER.

CHAPTER I.

THE ABOLITIONIST AVOWS HIS PRINCIPLES.

"I am a man,
And all calamities that touch humanity, come home to me."

"'SLAVES cannot breathe in England: if their lungs receive our air, that moment they are free.' Noble, glorious, happy country! Most happy people! 'Slaves cannot breathe!' 'That is noble, and speaks a nation proud!' O! my country, wanting but this to render thee the most favored, the happiest land on this fair globe! would I could thus speak thy praise! But no—alas that such should be the case!—the curse of slavery stains thy bright escutcheon, and must inevitably prove thy ruin!

"Yet, O that thou wouldst see thy peril, and, by purging thyself from this black crime, avoid the coming evil! For surely the vengeance of Heaven will sooner or later fiercely fall on a people that dares thus violate the sacred principles of justice!

"O! my poor, injured, down-trodden fellow-beings, would that I could alleviate your woes, or lighten your sufferings! For though it has pleased your Maker, in his wisdom, to create you with 'skins not colored like theirs,' you still have souls as pure, and hearts as true, as those of your despotic, inhuman oppressors, and as much deserve the blessings of freedom."

This grandiloquent tirade was uttered by a fiery young abolitionist, Mr. Carolus Justus, a passenger on board a New Orleans-bound steamer, who sought by this means to relieve his surcharged feelings on the subject of Southern slavery; performing, the meanwhile, sundry corresponding flourishes with the newspaper which, up to the time of the *explosion*, had evidently engaged his whole attention.

The immediate cause of this unusual and unexpected rhapsody, was cause of no little wonder to his sole auditor, a young Southerner, of whose presence even Justus, in his philanthropic absorption, seemed to be utterly unconscious, or entirely forgetful. The stranger, it is true, had been informed that this fellow-passenger had but recently returned from a visit to England; but, from the earnestness with which he perused the paper before him, could not suppose his mind was running on what he had there seen and heard. It had, however, been hinted that the gentleman was an abolitionist, and this speech, so indubitably confirming the suspicion, led him to conclude that his paper had furnished the *humane* man a well-served dish of the peculiar atrocity of some "*brutal* slaveholder."

Desirous of something to break the tedium of the voyage, and feeling, withal, rather humorously inclined, he resolved, let the cause be what it might, to improve this opportunity, the first yet offered, to draw out his companion on his favorite theme. He accordingly remarked:

"Perhaps, my dear sir, were you to become intimately acquainted with the structure of society, both in that *England* of which you boast, and among our Southern planters, you might undergo a change of mind. Your examination of this matter has, no doubt, been altogether *ex parte;* you would do well to turn your attention to the other side. You abolitionists do not——"

At this point, Justus, who, with dilated optics, had been gazing at his interlocutor, could contain himself no longer.

"Other side, indeed!" he interrupted. "Why, sir, there *is but one side* to this subject. Slavery is

an evil, an unmitigated evil, and a gross wrong—
an utter violation of every right of man; and, you
may depend upon it, this iniquity, though it may
prosper for a time, will yet be visited with merited
punishment. Only think, sir, that you are engaged
in the unholy work of buying and selling human
beings! And to talk of '*one side of the question!*'
Ah! buying and selling! But that is not all, nor
the worst; but, as the beautiful author before
quoted says, to

'Exact their sweat
With stripes that Mercy, with a bleeding heart,
Weeps when she sees inflicted on a beast.'

"O, sir, I feel on this subject, and—*you* may,
perhaps, sneer at it, as a pusillanimous weakness,"
at the same time brushing away a tear—"I never
speak of it without having the fountain of my feelings stirred to its very depth. I observed, sir, the
contempt denoted by your manner of enunciating
the word *abolitionists;* but this does not affect me.
I am one: I *glory* in the name. With *me*, it is a
consuming passion; and there is nothing that I
would not undergo for the sake of carrying out the
grand plan we have devised for the relief of the
Negro. Indeed, my sympathies are at times so fully
aroused and enlisted in their behalf, that had I the
power at those moments, I should most assuredly
cause them and their inhuman masters to exchange

conditions, as a compensation, on each hand, for the wrongs suffered and inflicted. I have heard the so-called arguments by which they who thus sin attempt to sustain themselves; but it is all pretence. There is not, there *cannot be*, any sincerity in them. It is personal *interest* that influences them; and this *alone*, without any regard to justice or right, upholds the diabolical system. Were they to speak honestly, they would say, *It suits us* to have it so, regardless of the wrong connected with its personal benefits."

This was rather more than the Southerner had either expected or desired, and there is no divining what might have been the result, had he not, at the outset, prepared himself to listen to discourteous remarks. As it was, however, he found himself unable to smother down his ire during the utterance of the last few sentences. He had risen to his feet in no amiable mood; but a second thought enabled him so far to subdue his wrath as to prevent any outburst of passion, remembering the cause of his engaging in the discussion, which was simply a spirit of mirthfulness, being at the same time aware of the entire unreasonableness of the *class* to which the gentleman belonged. He replied, with great apparent indifference,

"Conventional civility, or a decent regard for the

sensibilities of others, should restrain you from the use of such insulting language, especially where the application is so readily made as in the present instance. Let it pass, however, for the present, in consideration of the source whence it emanated.'' Then, assuming a tone of pleasantry: ''But that would be a novel way of alleviating trouble, to simply transfer the misery from one to another; though I suppose you would have the satisfaction of knowing you had given the supremacy to the more worthy race, contrasting yourself and friends, perhaps, (for I presume you have had no acquaintance with any other class of *white* men,) with the *noble race* of free negroes at the North, in making your estimate. However, you need not give yourself much uneasiness on the subject, as we do not intend you shall have the *power*, for many days yet to come. But, if it is not assuming an unwarrantable degree of familiarity, will you suffer me to inquire whether or not I have been correctly informed, that the object of your present voyage is a temporary residence in a portion of that devoted land, the South? I mean in Texas, my adopted home.''

''Yes, sir; that is my purpose; though, if influenced by any other motive than that actuating me, I should feel ashamed to avow such a design.''

''Doubtless!'' answered the other. ''But do you

not know you are exposing yourself to the influence
of the general curse hanging over that land of iniquity, and that you are yourself liable to suffer with
the rest in her doom?"

"I must acknowledge," replied Justus, "that it
has some appearance of temerity, thus to venture;
yet I have not undertaken it rashly or without due
consideration. I am influenced by powerful motives, and though I will be *among* the guilty, I will
not be *of* them. The leading cause of this procedure is, I am engaged in the preparation of a work
on the horrors of slavery, and wish to observe the
working of the despotic system at the fountain-head,
or, at least, where it holds full sway."

"Well thought of, too; and if those of your
school had always adopted the same plan, there
would have been less ill-feeling on this subject, and
less unfair dealing on your part. But let me now,
for your own sake, inform you, or rather suggest,
that, if you are not very discreet, your plan may lead
you into trouble.

"To avoid this, it would be well for you not to
have too many confidants in your movements, to
depend on your ears and eyes, and to talk or question sparingly. But I will propose a problem for
your solution: How long a sojourn in Texas, think
you, will it require to subvert your present princi-

ples, and to place you in connection with the nefarious business you seek to expose?"

It would be a fruitless task to attempt to convey an adequate idea of the emotions of the other, induced by this interrogatory; but, restraining his indignation, with an air of offended dignity he hastily answered:

"If it be not your deliberate intention to insult me, I am at a loss to conceive your meaning; for I cannot imagine that to be a sober question, in reality arising in your mind; to harbor the mere thought would be to impeach the soundness of your judgment."

"O," replied the other, "you may enjoy all the benefit of the belief in my insanity. I proposed the question seriously, and I would at no time be surprised to learn that you had become a real *slaveholder*, as monstrous a matter as you now seem to imagine it. And more: As I deal in the article at times, I hope to supply you a few. One caution, however. When you do make up your mind to join the inhuman crew, do not entirely lay aside *your* humanity, but let your present zeal for the poor negro measurably burn in you *then*, and do not forget that, though your property, he is still your brother, or, at least, a human being."

This was spoken in a half serious, half jesting

manner, with a meaning smile, that it was impossible to repress. During its utterance, Justus had retreated to the opposite side of the cabin, gazing on the speaker with an expression of manifest abhorrence. After a prolonged look of utter disgust, he thus relieved himself:

"O shame, where is thy blush? Is it possible such language should be addressed to me! That *I* should be expected to own *slaves!* *I*, who, on account of my uncompromising love of the helpless and oppressed, and my exertions in their behalf, have been designated 'The Slave's Friend!' *I* join the inhuman crew!—well named, too. No!

'I would not have a slave to till my ground,
To carry me, and fan me while I sleep, and tremble when I wake,
For all the wealth that sinews bought and sold have ever gained.'

To what cause I am to impute your unwarrantable and unprovoked outrage, I am at a loss to determine, unless it be that *your* connection with the impious crew has blunted your perceptions of the demands of courtesy in your intercourse with others. But I will not expose myself to a repetition of the same treatment by further conference with you."

"Very fine, indeed, thus to talk about courtesy! Of course it is very courteous to apply the terms lying and hypocrisy to others; *but you must be handled very delicately*, or you are grievously outraged.

Be assured, however, that nothing but a knowledge of the ignorance which influences you has enabled me to bear your language; considering it idle to take offence at the ravings of a monomaniac, in which light—if the information will in any wise enhance your own good opinion of yourself—I certainly view you. Yet," assuming his former manner of pleasantry, " recollect I still have a few choice hands in reserve for you."

A look of mingled rage, pity, and contempt was Justus's only reply, as he abruptly left the cabin; and the short-lived acquaintance, begun under auspices so unfavorable, as suddenly terminated. Our hero has, in the foregoing scene, given pretty much all the information in regard to himself that we deem necessary, at present, to lay before the reader. A native of Boston, Massachusetts, it is, perhaps, almost superfluous to add that his mind was fully imbued with the principles of abolitionism, reflections on the " concomitant horrors" and inconceivably evil results of Southern slavery constituting no inconsiderable part of his earthly troubles and perplexities. Urged on by such thoughts, and incited, furthermore, by an innate, unbounded love of humanity—*bronze humanity in particular*—he had, as already made known, been engaged in writing a work on slavery, which he had little doubt would for ever settle this vexed question, and cause the horrible evil, so faithfully exposed, to hide its head in shame, without even an *inclination* again to vindicate itself. And often, while engaged in this holy work, had his great heart swollen vehemently, and beaten tumultuously against its ribbed enclosure, sending the blood more hurriedly along its channels, and his laboring fingers with greater energy athwart the fair pages destined to convey his burning thoughts to posterity, as an immortal fame loomed up before him in the dim future, when the glory of every thing hitherto undertaken in this line would be dimmed in the superior effulgence of his own great work.

He had not felt himself driven to the South for the purpose of confirming himself in the faith, and satisfying his own mind on the subject of abolitionism: there was not a shadow of a doubt with him. Neither did he feel impelled to this course on account of the paucity of material at hand; nor yet for the lack of means by which to operate on the sympathies of his readers. Yet, while amply furnished with all these things at home, he believed the present movement would open up extensive fields, in which he might have unlimited discretion in *choosing* his " select incidents."

It was by no means his intention to practice upon

his peculiar articles of belief in regard to slaves and their owners, but merely to observe and study the workings of the system of slavery; and, more particularly, to form a choice collection of those atrocities which his education had taught him were inseparably connected with Southern slavery. Established in some favorable section of the chosen State, discarding his abolitionism outwardly, he would conduct his observations as opportunity might offer, expecting a few months of toil to be amply repaid by enabling him to return home enriched with invaluable notes, sufficient to bring his work to a speedy issue—observations made in person—truths none would have the hardihood to call in question.

To end all preliminaries in this place, and bring up the history to a fair starting-point, we will pass over the occurrences of the intervening time, and simply state that the trip was accomplished, and Justus installed in the desired post, in one of the new counties of Texas.

CHAPTER II.

PRINCIPLES DEVELOPED.

"A chiel's amang you takin' notes,
An' faith he 'll prent it."

FOR a time Justus pursued the "even tenor of his way" in this new field of operations, conducting his observations with so much prudence, in conformity with his projected plan, that his associates entertained no suspicion of his purpose. It is true, his progress in collecting material for the great work on hand was not so rapid as he had anticipated; but this did not discourage him. Fully satisfied as to the daily perpetration of those acts of barbarity he had come to witness, it was only a question of time when they should fall under his own observation. He had arrived at a strangely inauspicious time; or if indeed the place of his selection was an exception to the rest of the South, he had, at worst, but to seek a more favorable situation.

But while casting in his mind the propriety of this latter measure, an event occurred which, in its results, had a material influence on his subsequent actions. Preparations were in progress for a camp-meeting in his vicinity. It was a fixed purpose with him to neglect no opportunity that might be improved to the furtherance of his great design. Knowing that the colored portion of the population would be largely represented on that occasion, he hesitated not in determining to be in attendance on the meeting, feeling a strong presentiment, no doubt greatly influenced by his wishes, that the time for important revelations was near at hand.

But here, too, he was disappointed. The meeting proved to be a dull affair—that is, so far as his business was concerned—and he was not long in making up his mind that "here is to be found nothing to suit my purpose."

"Can it be possible," thought he, "that my coming has been covertly made known, and thus its effects guarded against?"

What he had already seen of slavery would have fully satisfied himself, had not the perfecting of his book, according to the plan laid down, so engrossed his mind. He had been a witness of the thing called slavery; had seen, as he expressed it, numbers of human beings so degraded as to consider themselves the property of another. Was not this sufficient? But it was not for this he had placed himself in his present position; for, while in Boston, he knew there was such a state and such beings; and he knew further, or, at least, fully believed, that those slaves, besides the degradation of being such, were subjected to evils untold, and almost unimaginable; and to investigate these cases of unparalleled wretchedness was his chief design in visiting the South. It was natural, then, that he should be perplexed at a state of things so different from that expected.

It had not, indeed, been his opinion that a religious meeting would furnish the proper place or circumstances for witnessing those cruelties of which he had read; but he fondly hoped it would afford a very favorable opportunity for observing some of their results. And, then, how much might it subserve the cause of humanity to picture an assembly of those wretched beings! But the first two days of the meeting had passed, and he had found nothing answering to his expectations. He could scarcely realize that these persons, so gayly dressed, so cheerful, and apparently as much interested as their mistresses in the affairs of the tents, and as much concerned to make a fair show for the accommodation of visitors, were the same whose interests he had so much at heart.

He had come to the conclusion that his hopes in regard to the camp-meeting were illusory, and that other means must be resorted to for the accomplishment of his cherished purpose. His flagging zeal was revived by the public announcement, at noon on Saturday, that there would be "preaching to the blacks, in the afternoon, at the ground appropriated for this purpose."

To most persons, perhaps, who read these pages it will be unnecessary to state the reason why this effort for the especial advantage of the negro was deferred until this particular time, namely, that the Saturday afternoon holiday had given freedom to the servants to attend generally; whereas there were before this time but few in attendance.

"Preaching to the blacks at the ground appropriated to that purpose!" repeated Justus—mentally, however. "Here is an opportunity that must not pass unimproved;" and he at once settled it in his mind to be one of the listeners to that sermon; at the same time soliloquizing, in utter forgetfulness—"An anti-abolition lecture; nothing more nor less!" But observing that this was heard, (though, as it happened, too indistinctly to catch the import of the words,) and that the eyes of more than one were fixed on him, he very prudently restrained his thoughts, or concluded in silence the comments he might have to make.

The thought now first in his mind was, how he should proceed in his design of hearing the sermon to the negroes. So far as any views of propriety were concerned, he would not have hesitated to take his place among the *sable* worshippers; but important considerations determined him to preserve as great a degree of secrecy as possible. In the first place, he would have the minister entirely at his ease, and entertained a fear that he might be led to mollify the lecture to be delivered, were he aware of the presence of a reporter, by whose instrumentality his discourse, in whole or in part, might be transferred to the page of history. And, more than this, he wished to have no suspicion whatever excited against himself.

It only remained to decide how he might dispose himself so as to hear, and yet avoid the consequences to be feared on both these grounds; and, to this end, a reconnoissance of the premises was necessary. With no little gratification, he found the situation conducive to the success of his plan.

The camp-ground was located on a small creek, in an open space at the upper extremity of a considerable body of brushwood, or bottom-land, in which, and at the distance of a few hundred yards from the encampment, was the preaching-place for the blacks. This had been prepared by clearing the ground of undergrowth, and furnishing it with seats; these consisted of split logs, with each extremity resting on others, unsplit, lying firmly on the ground parallel to each other. On the opposite side from the tents, and on the border of the surrounding thicket, was the stand for the minister. The interval between the camp-ground proper and this place was partially cleared of brush, so as to afford convenient passage to and fro. But to the back of the colored people's meeting-place a dense undergrowth of brush and briers still remained; and but a few feet from the stand a large fallen tree offered a very convenient place for concealment. Here he selected his station, and, placed in such a position that, with a slight movement, he could bring both the preacher and congregation into fair view, with little or no danger of discovery on his part, he calmly awaited the opening of the services.

Justus felt disposed to exult over the opportunity about to be afforded of exposing a preaching to slaves; but the introductory services had a decided tendency to diminish this pleasure; so much so, that he even felt his faith shaken in the correctness of the judgment he had so hastily and decidedly passed. The announcement of the text rendered the case almost hopeless; for it was evident that the words employed—"Behold, I stand at the door," etc.—furnished a very unbecoming foundation for a lecture of the kind he had anticipated. Still, he derived a faint hope from the "known ingenuity of these slaveholders in distorting things to answer their own purpose."

It is not our province to say any thing in regard to the exercises, further than this: Justus was entirely disappointed in them—so much so, that at the conclusion he had but few "*notes*" entered.

However, there was yet one resource left, and to this, though contrary to his proposed and more prudent plan, he determined to apply; for he was brought to the point of desperation, and "items" *must be obtained*. Hitherto he had spent his time and energies to no purpose; and the prospect of succeeding in his benevolent undertaking, unless he could devise some more available means, was really alarming.

The mode of procedure now suggested was, to select from the congregation, after dispersion, some one whose appearance might proclaim him sufficiently intelligent, both to understand what might be said, and to return sensible replies, and endeavor to learn from him the manner of his treatment, as well as his views of the system, and his feelings under "the galling bondage."

He would be very guarded, however, not forgetting the critical position in which a rash expression of opinion might place him, and would be careful to say nothing that could give offence to the most easily alarmed owner of slaves; unmindful of the fact, that to be found in private conference with a servant, under the circumstances, would, of itself, excite suspicion.

Cautiously looking from behind his covert, for the purpose of making the selection, he observed an aged negro approach the minister, to whom he seemed to be communicating some important intelligence. Though unable to hear the words, he perceived that the information, of whatever nature it might be, caused the preacher, together with all others in hearing, to direct his eyes toward his own retreat.

Though fully satisfied of the propriety of his conduct, his discovery placed him in a very humiliating posture, on account of the light in which his behavior would be viewed by those around him. His first impulse was to advance and explain the cause of his suspicious movements, putting on the matter the best face possible; but fear and hope together deterred him—fear that his explanation would not be well received; and hope that he was, after all, undiscovered, and consequently not suspected of any improper act. At all events, he determined to abide the result, and, with wonderful composure, retained his position. Yet he did not trust himself to look toward the stand for some moments; but, drawn down to his smallest dimensions behind his breastwork, with eyes fixed on the ground, he could only meditate on the probable result of his enterprise.

When he did again venture a look, the prospect was most gratifying: the ground was entirely deserted, except by a solitary, venerable negro, apparently engaged in reärranging the seats. Without further hesitation, and entirely forgetful of his late perplexities, he approached this occupant of the premises, retaining only so much thought of prudence as to embarrass his mind in regard to the manner of opening the interview. But the manœuvres of Uncle Moses, as he drew near, entirely removed his embarrassment, and scattered to the winds his caution.

Beholding the stranger, the negro started in evident alarm, casting his eyes around as though he had thoughts of a race. And, indeed, the appearance of the white man at the place, and under the circumstances, might well excite in the mind of Uncle Moses suspicions that his designs were not

strictly honest. Seeing this movement on the part
of the slave, and also observing his manifest uneasiness, Justus familiarly accosted him with the customary salutation of the day, adding—"Why, my
dear sir, you seem to be somewhat alarmed; but
there is no occasion for it, I assure you: I am not
at all dangerous."

"I don' 'no dat, suh! Duh's been some black
folks stoled about heah, lately; and once or twice
dem folks dey calls abolitioners has been roun',
tryin' to puhsuade 'em to run 'way. Now, you see,
dis's de black people's preachin' groun', and as
you's a stranger, I don 'no dat you's got any
'ticlar business 'mongst us, *ef you aint no notion of
doin' nuffin wrong.*"

Justus was ready to observe the sagacity of the
slave, as displayed in his reasoning, so logical and
conclusive, though constructed rudely and without
rule; but he paid no attention to the reproof contained in his remarks, or, indeed, did not seem to
regard it as such. His mind was employed in instituting a comparison between the negro and some
man of his own imagining, his master—noting the
superiority of the former over the latter, and reflecting on the probable consequences of giving way to
his impulse in conversation with Uncle Moses. Re-
solving on a prudent course, he replied, after a

brief silence: "Why, sir, you must have but a poor opinion of me, to imagine either that I would come in this way to steal you, or that I would attempt to display abolitionism *here*, were I ever so much disposed in that way."

"It might do, mastah, to talk to *some* in dat way; but I happen to know dem kin' o' folks 's mightily set in dur own notions; for one tried to git me to go 'way wid him once, from dis very campground."

Justus was fast losing the cautious reserve he had imposed upon himself, owing partly, no doubt, to the long-continued disappointment he had experienced; and he now felt himself unable to act the part he had resolved on during this interview. He had sought a meeting with the negro for the furtherance of an end dearer to him than personal ease; and there was no probability of attaining that object, unless he should, in a measure, reveal his true character; and *this*, a fresh attack of enthusiasm inclined him to do; simply designing to learn the views of the other in regard to the condition of servitude in which he was held, and his treatment in that state. He again addressed Uncle Moses:

"Well, sir——"

"Don't talk so to me, mastah; my name 's Moses.

Ef Mas' Jeems 'as to heah you talk dat way, he'd t'ink you abolitioner, *shoah nuff*, or dat you was n't smart, one."

"Well, Moses, then! Do you not think you would be far happier to-day if you had yielded to his entreaty, and gone with him to freedom?"

"No, suh! I do n't nigh b'leve so. I's a heap bettah off heah, dan ef I 'as to go Norf."

"You do not look at the matter rightly, my dear —Moses."

The negro winced during the slight pause that occurred; but as his own name ended it, he regained his composure, as Justus continued:

"You are a slave now, Moses, belonging to another; you have no will of your own, but must submit entirely to him, and be whipped like a brute at his pleasure."

"No, suh; not dat 'zac'ly, nuther. Mas' Jeems neber strike me yet, an' he lets me do 's I please in a heap o' things; and very often he axes my 'pinion about things he knows I have a right to know sumf'n about. I does s'mit to him, and so I oughter do: it 'ud be wrong if I didn't. And, mastah, I do n't b'leve any servant who does right's ever whipped like a brute, as you says."

"You say, Moses, you are allowed to do as you please in some things; but recollect, these are only

very unimportant matters. And, at best, you are
not free: to say your master allows you is an acknowledgment he has the *right* to prevent it; and
that you are not whipped—*most degrading punishment!*—is not that no one has the right to do it, but
you obey all orders, and do not put his authority to
the test. But only think of the glorious privilege
of being independent of any one, of doing as you
please in *all things!* And this priceless boon, Moses,
was intended by God to be enjoyed by every child
of Adam. It is a great sin not to endeavor, by all
the means in our power, to secure this greatest of
all blessings. To run away from a master is a righteous act; and not to do so, when occasion offers, a
sin. Can you really be in earnest when you say it
would be wrong not to obey your master? If so,
you are laboring under an entire mistake. No doubt
they take especial pains to have you believe so; but
there is no shadow of authority to be found anywhere, except in the wills of masters, and the law
that might makes right, for one man to hold such
control over another."

Justus had now become warm, and all thoughts
of consequences were forgotten. To all this, however, Moses replied:

"I's learned to read a little, mastah; and de Bible
says, 'Servants must obey dar masters in all things.'

Now mebbe you's so larned, you find some better
meanin' for it; but I's jis' got to take it for
what it *says*, and 'taint *right* to run away from mastah."

"You entirely mistake again, Moses. The great
apostle could never have thought of giving any encouragement to such a thing as *slavery ;* and, believe
me, you are grievously wronged. But if you would
gain your own consent to be a *man*, Moses, a happy,
free man, I might give you instructions that would
be of advantage to you, or, perhaps, aid you otherwise."

Uncle Moses's eyes were opened wider than ever,
and he shrank back instinctively, replying: "I
must n't heah dis kin' o' talk, mastah: I must go
to camp now. I stayed too long, anyhow. But,
mastah, I's boun' t' tell Mas' Jeems all 'bout dis,
and I 'spec' you'd best to leave while times is
good."

"Well, Moses"—as the words of the slave brought
to his mind a thought as to what might be the effect
of his rashness—"I am sorry you will not view the
matter in its proper light, and that I must abandon
all hope of seeing you escape from your wretched
state. So, with a heavy heart, I leave you, expecting to become a martyr myself to the cause of humanity; for nothing short of my destruction, I

suppose, can atone for the heinous offence of trying to alleviate the miseries of the helpless and oppressed." And at that moment came rushing on Justus the memory of all the atrocities of which he had either heard or read, under which persons engaged in similar acts of mercy had been made to suffer and to expire. For a moment a sense of his extreme danger overwhelmed him; but, recovering most heroically, and in the true spirit of a martyr, he continued:

"But be it so, Moses: it is a privilege even to perish in a good cause, and in *this* cause thrice happy! yea, glorious! Farewell, Moses: I can freely sympathize with you, though you will not appreciate my kind and merciful efforts, but will rather join with an inhuman master to persecute me."

"I don't intend to persecute you, mastah, but only to do my duty. Good-bye! and I'd be mighty glad if you'd leave, and quit all dese ways."

Upon the departure of the negro, Justus subjected the above conversation to a strict examination, in order to learn what he might be able to gather therefrom suitable to his purpose. But, view it in what light he would, it still seemed rather unfavorable; and he had well-nigh come to the conclusion that Boston itself was a more favorable field for observation than the one now occupied. But no! A bright

2

idea strikes him, and he suddenly exclaims, with exultation:

"I see through the whole affair. This slave has been tutored to talk thus. He is not, he cannot be, better satisfied in his condition than I would be; and I fully believe that, had he not been made to think such a thing as escaping impossible, he would gladly avail himself of the first opportunity to do so. Barely to report this conversation will be worth a great deal. For who can believe that any person, however degraded, could utter such a sentiment as really the conviction of his own mind—that, as a servant, it is right for him to obey his master; nay, wrong to disobey! In what light, then, will this matter appear, when it is shown how slaves are made to dissemble in the presence of strangers? And what measures must of necessity be resorted to, to bring them to this state! Humanity shudders at it."

This great discovery, with sundry reflections thereon, and so much of the conversation with Uncle Moses as suited his purpose, was speedily entered among Justus's items; and complacently running his eye over it, he inwardly congratulated himself on the imposing show which, when properly elaborated, it would make in his forthcoming volume. Yet it is true he could not forget the fact that this was merely a surmise, and rather an improbable one at that, seized on as a drowning man will catch at straws. So, notwithstanding the confidence expressed, he was far from being satisfied with this case; for even had he collected a sufficiency of such items to fill his book, he would have required a little confirmation before sending them to the world, being, with all his humanity, not quite so gullible, or so scarce of common sense, as the sage item-hunter who invented for the occasion the story of the negro coachman chained by the neck while driving his master to church.*

Having no doubt that this, if indeed a case true to appearances, was a very rare one, and that there were many slaves in attendance on the meeting who would render a very different report from that of Uncle Moses, he determined, as he had committed himself so far already, to seek, during the continuance of the meeting, for some more pliant subject, on whom to operate, without relaxing, at the same time, his vigilance in other quarters.

---

* A Northern newspaper some time since published an account, by some verdant correspondent travelling in the South, of a family being driven to church by a negro chained by the neck, which said correspondent seemed to consider but an ordinary occurrence.

This will at once be recognized as a part of the regular staple from which affecting anecdotes are manufactured for abolition use.

CHAPTER III.

RENCOUNTER AND REBUFF.

"A man convinced against his will
Is of the same opinion still."

AFTER his interview with the negro, it seemed to
Justus that he was looked upon with an eye of suspicion. This he at once, very naturally, attributed
to the report Uncle Moses had given of the affair
between them. However, determined not to be
deterred in the prosecution of his great work by
any thing short of actual compulsion, he diligently
continued his quest of some one in the colored portion of the assemblage, from whom he might learn
something more definite, with which at once both
to grace his work, and more intensely to excite the
minds of his Northern friends.

Not that he was at all pleased with the course he
had taken, but circumstances had driven him into
it; and *now* was no time to pause. His purpose in
visiting the South—to form a collection of the revolting and shocking scenes incident to Southern

slavery—was so far from being accomplished, that he had become somewhat uneasy. So far from the evils he had expected, he found that many things, before regarded as settled facts, were merely exaggerations of matters in themselves harmless. Yet, even thus enlightened, there remained sufficient credulity in his previous information to more than condemn slavery. Aware, however, of the fact that accounts such as those he sought to lay before his readers would create a more exciting interest, of such scenes he must have details. If not fortunate enough to witness them himself, he must apply to those whose unhappiness has consisted in being forced painfully to participate in them. Being unable to accomplish this in or about the precincts of the camp-ground, there remained but this, that he should betake himself to the scene of yesterday's adventure. Even this, as fearing watchful eyes were upon him, he thought it not prudent to attempt openly, and that he had better seek a round-about way to that locality. While performing this movement, he chanced to meet with Uncle Moses again.

Justus had regretted the length to which he had gone in committing himself before the negro, and had entertained thoughts of another interview, to counteract, in part, the impression he had previously made. His present good fortune, however, was beyond his hopes.

As he found himself in something of a dilemma, and was, consequently, confused, we shall not attempt to repeat his explanatory remarks, which were, in part, to the effect that Uncle Moses must not suppose his friend had any design, in his remarks of the previous day, further than to test his fidelity.

Uncle Moses, however, did not appear to put a great deal of confidence in his explanations, but was willing to let it all pass, being not particularly concerned in that matter. He too, in consideration of some expressions made by the " gem'n" on the previous evening, and the new light that had broken into his own mind in cogitating on the subject, was anxious for another interview; so, without seeming to notice the remarks of Justus, so soon as an opportunity was given him to speak, he began as follows:

" *You b'leve, mastah, dat no man dat owns slaves can be good man,* does you? Seems to me you said so t'other day."

Justus thought of returning an evasive answer; but not being skilful in dissembling, the words of the slave, so appropriately expressing his views, threw him off his guard, and, oblivious to his late fears and resolves, he replied, with emphasis:

"*Yes, sir;* such is indeed my opinion. *I would as much expect to enter heaven with the knife in my hand, still reeking with the blood of my brother, as with the stain of this accursed thing on my soul.* No, my— friend, no righteous man *would* own slaves : it is too great a crime for him to *think* of committing."

"I wish, mastah, you'd jis' call me Moses, or Uncle Moses, ef you likes : I's bin used to dat, and white folks 's not used to call me nuf'n else."

Justus had barely completed his last-mentioned reply before he regretted it, and determined to stand, guarded by prudence, firm against any temptation to give expression to his views, happen what might. But as the "Ethiopian cannot change his skin, nor the leopard his spots," so Justus could not lay aside his philanthropy, which was, in fact, a part of his being; and this speech of Uncle Moses called into instant and full play every latent spark thereof, opening beyond all hope the fountains that he had even just now determined should remain sealed; though one less benevolent might have found nothing exciting in Uncle Moses's remarks, or aught connected with or growing out of them.

"And what right have they," he exclaimed indignantly, "to disregard all the conventionalities of life in your case? They must be Mr. So-and-so, or

A. B., or What-not, Esq., or have A. M., D. D., or
M. D. appended to their names; while upon you,
in common with their dogs, their oxen, and their
horses, they bestow the appellations, Mose, Dick,
Jack, etc., merely for the sake of distinguishing
one piece of property from another. O, it is a
shame, Moses—as thus *only* I must call you—though
even this is a trifling matter, and, indeed, a shining
spot, compared with the darker parts of the inhuman system!"

"Well, mastah, ef I 'as jis' smart 'nuff to tell
what I knows or thinks, like you can, I might lead
you to talk diff''rent.   I had chance to be free once.
Mas Jeems tuck me to New York to let me have
freedom; but I tell you, mastah, before I'd been
dar two days, I wanted to come back wid him.   I
do'no how to tell it, but de good slaves *heah's* more
'spectable dan de mos' ob de colored folks *dar*, or
dan a heap o' de pooh white folks.   I noticed dese
tings, mastah, and I talked to some o' my own
folks 'bout it. Day know day ain't more'n half
free, and not thought nothin' of in s'iety; and
none but de few who happens to git property are
noticed 't all. If I could git to be white, it might
be some use to be free. Now heah, dar's not a
man knows Uncle Moses meets him widout shakin'
hands and talkin' friendly, and answerin' all de

queshuns he axes. And when I gits sick, all de black people around comes to see me, and wait on me, and set up wid me; and no matter how busy de times is, I's certain to have plenty company; and Mas Jeems and missus, and other white folks, often comes to see me and talk wid me. I think, mastah, slaves dat knows it, is a heap better off dan some ob your folks at de Norf. Your own 'sperience 'll tell you more about dese things than I can."

"Ah, Moses, you are entirely in the wrong! A person with right views would prefer freedom, with any conceivable state of wretchedness, to slavery, attended with all comforts, save that alone of freedom, that could be desired; and yet you know your mode of life is not attended with many comforts. For my part, had I the choice of being a free man, in a land where I should be totally isolated, treated with contempt by all; or as a slave, with all the blessings of friends and friendly associations, such is my estimate of freedom, that I would unhesitatingly choose the former situation."

"Ah, mastah, gib me frien's and 'sociates; mebbe you think *now* as you talk; but I b'leve you'd change your mind ef you 'as to try it. But, anyhow, you *must* know, mastah, dar's a diff'rence 'twixt white folks and black ones. Youah people's s'perior to ourn, and dis 's de bes' way we kin git 'long togeder. Sometimes it does seem to me it 's hard an' wrong, an' that it could n't a been intended for us to be treated so; but don't you have white servants in youah country? Day is free; but what good is it to 'em? Day has mastahs jis' as well as we. Dur little wages is all day gits, an' when day 's sick an' old, nobody cares for 'em; money soon goes, an' den no frien's. We has de care ob our mastahs, an' when sick an' old, neber wants for frien's."

"Ah, Moses, I discover you are well schooled; but your reasoning is very transparent. Though our white servants—hired persons, or *helps*, you should have called them—have no claim on their masters, further than their 'wages, and can claim nothing of them in sickness or old age beyond this, yet you must recollect they have the disposal of their own time; and, should they ever be brought so low, we have comfortable poor-houses, where they can be taken care of at the public expense."

"Ah, mastah, to be put in poor-house 's sorry comfort arter a life ob servin'. De diff'rence, in fact, I can't see. We labors for a mastah while we 's in health, and hab a right to a livin' when old an' sick. You works jis' 's hard, an' den are altogether 'pendent on others. Ef you's purvided fur, its charity. Now I'd ruther be in a way to hab a *right* to dat I needs, an' not hab to look to folks dat don't care for me, an' dat, too, whar dar's so many needin' help, an' so few ready to gib it. An', besides, you know, at de bes', we can't be equal to de whites, and I'd sooner be a slave heah. Ef slavery's *wrong*, we's been under it so long we would n't know how to behave if we 'as free."

"I perceive, Moses, your intellect has become dull; your perceptions in regard to this matter are confused, and your prejudice too strong. You will not be enlightened, Moses."

This sentence Justus intended should end the conference; but Moses, who had been led away from his subject, did not feel like giving up his point. He rejoined interrogatively, reverting to his first proposition:

"Well den, mastah, I s'pose you can't b'leve Abra'm was a good man?"

"I must confess I do not understand you, Moses; what had the patriarch, Abraham, to do with this question?"

"Why, was n't Abra'm a *slaveholder*, mastah?"

"Now do not display your lack of discrimination so plainly, Moses! The servitude in the time of Abraham was, doubtless, a far different thing from our slavery of the present day; perhaps they were merely hired for a term of years. Though, be the condition of his servants what it might, from this we know that he was no slaveholder: he was undoubtedly a *just* man, and no man of that class, you know, can own a slave."

"I don'no dat, mastah, for I knows *good* men dat does own 'em. I dunno whah you gits youah knowledge, but I can't see nothin' in de Bible looks like day didn't own dar slaves, jis's much as our mastahs owns us."

"O, well, we will not contend about this, Moses; for it makes no difference, one way or another, what may have taken place in those barbarous ages. Recollect, the things connected with this man in the Scripture history transpired in the infancy of the world, and cannot in any wise be an example for us in this enlightened age. The times have changed very much, Moses, even allowing your supposition to be correct."

"Now dis don't soun' right, mastah! Wasn't it de same God ruled den dat dus now? An' if dis ting was *wrong*, den wouldn't it 'a been spoken about as sumf'n wicked?"

"Another evidence, Moses, that your instructions have all had respect to one side of this subject, and that you have entirely failed to study the other.

But do you not perceive that it is owing to the plainness of the case that it has not been animadverted on? the inspired men who wrote the Scripture, perhaps, thinking it too clear to require warning. Though, depend upon it, Moses, you need not think to strengthen your position by such reasoning; yet, I doubt not, you are well drilled in it, and the Bible diligently searched for arguments to render you satisfied with your state, by those who do you the occasional favor of reading to you."

"You forget, mastah! I can read myself; an' I read de Bible t'rough more 'n once."

"True, you did tell me you had learned to read. So they have not that advantage over you; and I think, Moses, you are not convinced of the great criminality of the thing, only because you *will not be*."

"Well, heah's sumf'n else, mastah: we read in the book of Leviticus dat de child'n of Isr'l was told day should buy slaves. I marked de place, an' I'll jis read it to you; doe I s'pose you's seed it many a time. It's in de twenty-fif' chapter, de forty-fif' and sixt' verses." We will take the liberty of rendering it for him: "Moreover, of the children of the strangers that sojourn among you, of them shall ye buy, and of their families that are with you, which they begat in your land; and they shall be your possession. And ye shall take them as an inheritance for your children after you, to inherit them for a possession: they shall be your bondmen for ever."

"Now, aint dis slavery?"

"This is only permitted, Moses," replied Justus, "as if God had said: 'If you must buy bondmen, do not seek your brethren, but strangers.' Though allowing to this language all the force it can in any wise claim, you should not lay too much stress on it; for the words were spoken at a time when men's minds were not prepared to receive any thing better; when society was in an unformed and chaotic state. Therefore, even though this buying were in any manner similar to what is here practiced, we are now too enlightened to receive an example from such an age."

"I'm boun' to think, mastah, it's you dat won't be pervinced. Now you knows jis before dis dey was 'low'd to buy one anudder till de jubilee, when da must be set free; but strangers could belong to 'em, an' d'scen' to dar child'ns. But was'nt de good Bein' givin' his people laws to be governed by, an' aint day a sample for us too? And if dis ting is so fur wrong *now*, wouldn't it 'a been too much so *den*, for Him dat knows ebery ting, to command his people to do it? He wanted 'em to be *holy*, an' couldn't he 'a said: 'Thou shalt not *own* servants,' as well as, 'Thou shalt not *kill?*' an' ef it's wicked, wouldn't he 'a done it too?

"If dem *was* barb'rous times, I reckon he wus as wise *den* as he is *now;* for it's said: 'He's de same yesterday, an' to-day, an' for ever,' an' he could see what de command would lead to. An' he didn't say any ting 'bout ' ef you *will* hab 'em;' but you *shall* buy. But what he even 'lows, as you says, can't be so bad."

"There is another thing you seem to forget, Moses. Those strangers, by their wickedness, had forfeited all their rights, and were doomed to destruction; which seems to have been commuted, in the case of those who by any means escaped, to perpetual bondage."

"Do you reckon, mastah, dese strangers is de Cana'nites day was commanded to destroy?"

"Most assuredly, Moses! I cannot believe that a merciful God would condemn to hopeless slavery any but those who had fully forfeited all rights to life. And here, Moses, at this particular point, modern slaveholders are left without their model or example."

"Mebbe not, dough; mebbe we's in de same state. I know I'm jis' guessin' *now*, but wasn't you a guessin' too? For aint dese de same strangers dat's spoken of as bein' made pros'lytes, an' comin' under de same law as de Jew hisself? Dis do n't look much like da was to be destroyed, anyhow. Besides, dar chil'en was to be bought too, an' da had n't sin'd; an' ef *da* was so wicked as to d'sarve to be killed, mebbe da could do pooty near's much harm bein' servants as any oder way. I's got de idees, but do n't know how to 'spress 'em; but you know what I mean, mastah."

"Alas! alas!" sighed Justus, "how obstinately you will defend this iniquitous thing! and that, too, notwithstanding you are so deeply injured by it. And to endeavor to press the Scriptures into service! But, sir"—entirely thrown off his guard—"could I ever be brought to believe that the Bible gives the least countenance to slavery, I would repudiate it. I would trample on it and its unhallowed teachings, and exert myself to the utmost to destroy it from off the face of the earth. *I never could recognize as God a being who represents himself as so manifestly unjust.*"

In blank astonishment and utter horror, the negro gazed in his face for a moment, and then, turning on his heel, abruptly left him. Glad to be relieved of his presence, Justice continued his course.

CHAPTER IV.

SUSPICIONS AROUSED.

"How now!   What do you here alone?"

IT chanced that Justus's concealment on the previous day, while listening to the sermon to the blacks, was not so perfect as he thought; and he had been discovered by an aged negro who was wending his way to the place of worship. This negro was not able, by any mode of reasoning he could employ, to satisfy his mind as to the meaning of a "white ge'man" being in such a situation alone; and, indeed, was at a loss, under the circumstances, to imagine what particular business he could have there at all. He was fully convinced that it boded no good; and as, from time to time during the service, he cast his eyes toward the stranger's place of concealment, the display of the note-taking operations—by the way, rather infrequent—tended in no way to allay his suspicions. Immediately after the completion of the exercises,

he reported the case to the officiating clergyman.
This person, who already had an eye of suspicion
on Justus, chiefly in consequence of his comments
in regard to the announcement of preaching to the
blacks, was at once ready to conceive an idea of a
plot forming for the abduction of slaves from the
camp-ground.   His first impulse was to accost the
stranger, and learn the motive for his singular conduct; but this he declined, considering it better to
suffer the plan, if such thing there might be, to
work its own way to light.   Yet, in order to hasten
its development, having seen the congregation retire, with a strict injunction of silence on the subject to those in the secret, he left alone on the
ground his faithful Moses, who, he well knew,
would be proof against all arts of persuasion; believing that, if his suspicions were well grounded,
this would be a lure not to be withstood.

This arrangement made, he betook himself to the
tents to await the result in patience.

The interview between Justus and the negro was
faithfully reported by the latter, agreeably to promise.   The master, Mr. Blanton, was well acquainted with the peculiar views of abolitionists,
and he knew the excitement occasioned by the
known presence of one of Justus's stamp on the
ground would be intense, and the danger to him

of ill-usage quite imminent. He further knew that even a general *suspicion* of a person being of this character, would be deemed reason enough for demanding at least his abandonment of any locality in which he might be found. It was these considerations that influenced his actions in the affair from the commencement. Though not apt to use any means to screen the guilty, or to connive at the escape of offenders from punishment, it was abhorrent to his feelings to cause any excitement against one not known to be an evil-doer, or in any wise to injure him. He, therefore, determined to preserve strict silence in regard to his suspicions until they should be confirmed.

For this reason he chose to meet his servant on his return in an unfrequented place. "Well, Moses," he began, "did you receive a visit from our attentive listener behind the oak?"

"Yes, sah; and a visit indeed! He's a bad man, Mas' Jeems; he's not doin' no good heah certain, an' he may do a heap o' harm."

There chanced to be a third person in hearing, of whose presence neither Mr. Blanton nor Moses was aware: whose curiosity being excited by the rather singular interrogatory and reply, he silently listened, while Uncle Moses made his report.

"Did he seem disposed to listen to your advice,

Moses, or do you think he will be apt to make another attempt there?" asked the master, after the slave had ended his account.

"Well, I dunno sah, indeed," replied Moses; "when I told him what I did, he said somef'n 'bout bein' a martyr, an' a heap more dat I did n't understand; but he did n't talk nuf'n like he was goin' to leave, an' I would n't wonder if he's dar agin."

"Very well; say nothing about it, Moses. He shall be watched; and, if blessed with any regard for his own welfare, will not delay his departure many hours."

The recent developments had placed Mr. Blanton in a rather unpleasant state of mind in regard to his dealings with the visitor from the North. He could form no other conclusion than that he was some inexperienced youth, just let loose from an abolition society, with his mind, in all probability, recently inflamed by a characteristic speech from some choice leader. On no other ground could he account for his madness in exposing himself to risk, where there was no hope of accomplishing any thing, and no probability of receiving aid or sympathy in case of detection.

Reflecting on these things, and believing that a few weeks' observation would reveal to him a better view of the subject, he felt an inclination to allow him to continue his operations uninterrupted; and, in pity to him, he did not wish to be instrumental in procuring the infliction upon him of the penalty due to an outraged law, if it could be avoided by any honorable means.

But, on the other hand, notwithstanding he was too far removed from headquarters to be able to accomplish any thing in his peculiar line, there was yet danger that his representations might lead some of the more excitable slaves to abscond, causing no little inconvenience and loss to their masters in their recovery. He hoped to be relieved of all responsibility by the sudden departure of Justus; but in case he should again be found in a suspicious position, circumstances, and the views presented thereby, should determine the mode of treatment to be resorted to.

This point arranged in his mind, the next consideration was to find assistants, to whom he could reveal his suspicion and his plan, without stirring up a spirit of persecution against the abolitionist. This, as he had anticipated, was found to be no easy matter. But at length the thing was settled, the whole conduct of the business being left to Mr. Blanton, the others to aid him in the performance of whatever might be determined on as the final measure.

Apprehensive that the stranger might not be disposed to take the kind advice of Uncle Moses, as the time for service drew near, Mr. Blanton and company proceeded to reconnoitre the ground in the vicinity of the negroes' meeting-place. The object of their solicitude was found at his post; on discovering which, the guardian trio were speedily concealed, calmly awaiting the course of events.

Far different were the feelings of the two parties at this stage of the proceedings. Justus, having learned that the pulpit was to be occupied by one holding views slightly different from those of the minister of the previous day, congratulated himself on having secured so favorable a position for hearing what might be said. He had taken care to conceal himself more effectually than on yesterday. He did not doubt that matters were approaching a crisis in his case; yet, happily, ignorant of the manner in which the stroke was to fall, or the direction whence it was to come, he exulted in the thought that, happen what might, he would at least enjoy the rare opportunity of exposing to his brethren a slaveholder's sermon to the negroes.

The watchers, on their part, were solacing themselves with the reflection that, whatever danger to their interests there might be from the presence of

the abolitionist, they themselves were at hand to
counteract it, and that they would speedily have the
proof before them, whether or not this was really
his character.

CHAPTER V.

DETECTED AND EXPOSED.

*"Do not, for one repulse, forego the purpose which you resolved
to effect."*

Upon being so abruptly abandoned by Uncle
Moses, Justus's first emotion was one of pleasure
at the riddance. But a reäction suddenly took
place, of which we will suffer him to explain the
nature and the cause in the soliloquy indulged in
on the occasion:

"Is this one of the persons whose miseries have
so strongly operated on my mind as to lead me to
suffer all I have undergone in the hope of bettering
his condition? And can he be so well satisfied
with his lot? If so, he surely needs no sympathy
from me.

"But I cannot believe it. He either sees the
hopelessness of his condition, or has been duped
until he believes it to be the one designed for him;
in the former case thinking it useless to seek any
thing better; in the latter, sinful. Yet does not

this case clearly prove that the task I have imposed on myself, by the advice and assistance of my friends, is a work of supererogation? If the poor slaves will not see the evils surrounding them, or feel the miseries which *I* so deeply lament, why should I longer incommode myself for their relief? And if one so enlightened as *this man* cannot be convinced, what hope is there for the mass? The cause had as well be abandoned." Then, after a pause of a few moments, he added, emphatically, "*I will return home!*"

Overcome by the emotions thus excited, he seated himself at the foot of an ancient tree, his face buried in his hands, in deep meditation. At length his whole being seemed to undergo a change, as, rising to his feet, he exclaimed:

"Humanity demands it. What though my exertions are not, at present, appreciated by those for whose benefit they are put forth? What though their minds are too much benighted to understand my kindness? I labor for the good of my race; and though I may effect nothing immediately, in the behalf of these oppressed beings, by my own intercourse with them, I will at least furnish to my friends a true statement of their condition, and the means by which they can hereafter accomplish the great object we have in view."

His soliloquizing was interrupted by the unexpected presence of an object which would have driven away his late despondent feelings, even though his better nature had not already achieved this triumph. This was a negro, bearing in his outward appearance a nearer approximation to that state of degradation which Justus had ever delighted to picture to himself as the condition of the slave; and, for this reason, it was the most pleasing one, to him, that he had encountered for some days, possibly since leaving Boston.

The negro was illy clad, and his whole outer man seemed to indicate that he was rather low in the scale of moral being—far from possessing the intellectuality of Uncle Moses—and, withal, in no very amiable state of mind, as shown by his sullen and discontented demeanor.

"Ah!" thought the man of pity, "here is a poor, degraded wretch, who will thankfully receive any instruction or suggestion calculated to improve his hapless lot. And how many thousands are there in the same condition! No, Carolus, it will never do to yield to a slight discouragement. Success now begins to dawn; and here, no doubt, is a whole treasury of items to be acquired, of wrong, injustice, and oppression."

The one idea now present to the mind of Justus

was, to gain an insight into the cause of this slave's apparent trouble, the manner of his treatment in general—to learn any thing, in short, in the power of the other to communicate, bearing in any manner on his own peculiar calling. He did not for a moment reflect on the circumstance of his being a free man, one of a superior class, about to address an inferior, a slave, who knew nothing of the refinements of polite society. He merely, as a philanthropist, saw before him a suffering fellow-being.

"My dear sir, may I be so bold as to ask what cause of discontent sits so heavily at your heart? It is true you may think it rude and unbecoming in me thus to accost you, an entire stranger; but let an ardent desire to alleviate the woes of the suffering plead my excuse for this breach of decorum. And be assured, sir, if your trouble is of such a nature that the aid or sympathy of a friend can avail any thing, you may command my services."

At the commencement of the salutation, darkey raised his head, to observe to whom the gentleman was speaking; but, seeing no other person present, he was bewildered, not imagining himself to be the one addressed as "*My dear sir*," and comprehending very little else of what was said. There he stood, with open mouth, gazing at the stranger, at a loss for his meaning, and wondering if it were not some madman, from whom it might be as well to make his escape. Nor was Justus himself less confused than his sable friend. What did the man mean? Why did he not answer his kind interrogatory? Or had he not heard? No, he must be deaf. But why did he not *speak?* Justus was forced to the conclusion that the poor man was mute; and, this settled in his mind, he was in the act of turning away, at the same time exclaiming, "Poor fellow!"

Then darkey found the use of his tongue:

"What for massah make fun of puoh nigga dis way?"

Justus was now in his turn at a nonplus. Totally ignorant of the negro's meaning, he replied:

"O, sir, you mistake very much: nothing is farther from my thoughts than to make fun of you."

Another very awkward pause succeeded—darkey waiting to hear what the stranger had to say for himself, and Justus wondering why his kind question was not answered. The negro having discovered that Justus's designs were friendly, broke the silence by asking—

"What you want, masta?"

All Justus's former address was entirely lost, and he was compelled to renew the effort to gain the desired information.

"I simply asked," said he, "what is the cause of the gloom that is settled upon your brow?"

Darkey hung his head for a moment, his fingers busily engaged in the wool thereof; then, raising his eyes to the face of the questioner, replied:

"I dunno what dat is."

"What is the matter with you?" said the abolitionist, who now heartily wished himself in Boston, or almost anywhere else, and who was, for the moment, well-nigh freed from all desire to learn any thing in regard to Southern institutions.

"Dur aint nuf'n de matter of me: does I look like dur was?"

"There are indications of despondency or melancholy in your air, the cause of which I could not fathom."

"Sah?" with still open mouth.

Justus was now fairly disgusted with the negro, and scarcely less so at himself; yet he resolved by one more effort to satisfy himself whether or not darkey could understand English in any thing more than its rudiments.   He rejoined:

"You have a moody, downcast expression of countenance, which led me to suppose there was some grief preying on your mind; and I would consider myself as under obligations to you if you would make me acquainted with the cause."

"Ef you 'll jis' tell me what dat means, so I can understand it, I 'll tell you all 'bout it."

"You look mad or sorry, one: what is the matter with you?"

Justus hoped he had at last reached the capacity of the slave; and, in so far, he was not disappointed. But darkey had never known his variations of humor to excite so much interest on any former occasion, and was at a loss to comprehend the meaning of the gentleman's solicitude.

"Does I?" he asked, after due reflection. "Well, I dunno as I can tell what's de matter. Nuf'n 'tik'lar aint de matter."

"You are not well treated by your master, are you?"

"Well, I dunno, mastah; 'bout's good's common, I reckon."

"You are abused, are you not?—whipped?"

"O no, sah, nebah whipped!"

"Are you well fed? Do you get plenty to eat?"

"Plenty, sah."

"But I see your master does not treat you well in one respect: he does not allow you a sufficiency of suitable clothes." But observing the vacant stare of the negro, indicating his lack of understanding of the language employed, he continued: "He dresses you very badly."

"Mas' Willum gib me plenty o' good ebery-day clothes, sah; but you see he want to git rich, an' he's right savin'. So I don't git's much time to work for myself's some niggas does. He aint's good 'bout dis as ole mastah was, an' sometimes I gits mad 'bout it. But in ebery ting else he's bery good to me; an' I don't know as I oughter be mad: he works hisself's hard 's I does."

"Would you not like to be free, my friend—to be able to have *all* your time to yourself, to employ it as you please?"

"Yes, indeed, sah! ef I could on'y do it, an' be's good 's anybody else; but dat, you know, 's what we can't do 'mongst de white folks."

"Well, would you not like to go North, to a free State?"

"Does white folks live dar, massah?"

"O, yes! I'm from there."

"Well, ef I 'as dar, could I be good 's dem?"

"Surely you could; or, at least, you would be a free man, and no one could have the right to tyrannize over you."

"I 'spec' I couldn't git dar, dough; an', anyhow, I b'lebe I'd rather stay heah: it suits me better dan to go Norf."

Without committing himself any further, Justus, being satisfied that this was not a person suited

to his purpose, passed on to his place of concealment.

The sermon was a warm and fervent discourse
on the practical duties of religion, and differed
from the best efforts the concealed listener had
heard in other places only in its plain and unaffected
simplicity, which, judging from the intense interest
of the auditory, reached at once their understanding and their hearts.

At the close of the regular services, the minister announced that he would hold a class-meeting,
and those who did not wish to remain were now at
liberty to retire. This information was received by
Justus with great satisfaction, as he felt assured he
would now hear in the rather private instruction of
the preacher what he had in vain looked for in his
pulpit ministration. The greater part of the congregation remained, and the proceedings began by
the preacher informing them that the object was to
have a religious conversation with as many of them
as the time allotted would allow. After some general remarks on the benefits of such a course, and a
few words in regard to his own experience, he interrogated a number as to their knowledge and enjoyments of religion. Their replies were sensible
and direct, and, though evincing an ignorance of
language, displayed a knowledge of that which is

far better—the peace and comfort enjoyed as the benefits of the gospel. And whatever former views the abolitionist may have held in regard to the contentment and happiness found in slavery, the fact was now unquestionably before him, that some at least enjoyed these blessings in a large degree.

The faithful preacher had a kind word for every individual. To the careless, the great importance of spiritual concerns was earnestly urged, while the earnest, humble Christian was affectionately exhorted to continued faithfulness.

Despite his prejudices, Justus for a while forgot his immediate object, and felt himself carried away by the spirit of the scene before him. The warm and fervent manner of the minister for the good of the slave surprised him; for he had never before conceived that, in his degradation and bonds, any one cared for the spiritual benefit of the poor Southern negro; but he learned, in the course of the proceedings on hand, that the present and kindred exercises were in regular and constant use, and the well-instructed and carefully guarded morals of the present assemblage could not, in his estimation, fail to secure the best practicable results.

The minister himself, from education, had once been an abolitionist, but proper experience dissipating false principles, he esteemed it his happiest

3

privilege to offer to the slave, whose pastor he was, the consolations of religion.

The services over, Justus did not lose sight of another motive in attending the negro meeting, which was to find some slave more tractable than either Moses or Darkey, whose benighted mind he might enlighten, or from whom receive valuable information touching the object of his quest. And now fortune for once seemed to favor him: the slave he at this time encountered having fresh in his memory a recent correction for his misdeeds. From this cause he was found by Justus in a proper state of mind to render him pervious to any attempt on his fidelity.

Justus was not long in acquiring a knowledge of this fact.

"The inhuman wretch!" he indignantly exclaimed. "I suppose you were unable to perform the onerous task assigned you, and must for this reason be brutally whipped!"

"Hah?" queried Sambo, with vacant stare and open mouth.

"Did your master whip you because you could not do the task he gave you?"

"O, no, sah! Mas Tom neber do dat; I don't much like to work, 's true, but he neber whip me for dat."

"What other paltry offence may you have committed, then, that he should visit upon you such unwarrantable and atrocious punishment?"

"Sah?"

"What did you *do*, that caused your master to punish you in this manner?"

"Why, mastah, you see I did n't do nuf'n, but jis tuck a little bit o' meat."

"O, yes! he will starve you, and if you help yourself to a little of that which is justly your own, it is a crime worthy the most degrading punishment he can inflict."

"No, no, mastah! he no starb me; Mas Tom gib me jis 's much 's I wants to eat."

"Why did you take your master's meat, then, Sambo, if you are so well fed?"

"Not Mas Tom's meat, sah; it was Miss Polly's."

"And who is Miss Polly?"

"Why, de Widow Hill, dat libs close to Mas Tom's."

"Why did you take the meat, Sambo, if you did not need it to eat?"

"I jis wanted de money I could git for it, mastah. I reckon I done wrong; but dey need n't a whipped me 'bout it."

"No, indeed, not at all. You did wrong to take the meat in that way; but why could not your master pay for it, and give you the money you need, or buy such things as you require, that you may not be subjected to such temptations? This would surely be as little as he could do."

"Mas Tom does buy me ebery ting I needs; but sometimes I wants to git some little extry tricks for Sunday, or somef'n else. Mos' on us has a little patch o' taters, or watermillons, or somef'n o' de kind; but I has to work 'nuff anyhow, an' I'd ruther git de tings I wants some easier way dan dat."

"Well, Sambo, would you not like to leave your master, and be free—to be out of reach of any one, and have all your time to yourself, to do just what you please?"

"Yes, indeed, sah! ef I could jis *do* it; but dat's wot I can't do, no way 't all."

"Yes, you might even do *that*, Sambo; and if you will only listen to me, and be governed by what I say, I might be able to render you important aid in the matter, and put you in a way to gain your freedom."

In his excitement, Justus had gone far beyond his original designs; for when the conversation with Sambo began, he had not the remotest intentions of making such a suggestion, being wholly unprepared at the time to carry out any measure of this kind. But he was urged on by favorable omens in a cause in which his inclinations led him to improve every opportunity of accomplishing what he considered good to the slave. To his speech, however, Sambo replied:

"How I gwine to do dis, mastah? I might run away; but den dey 'd catch me 'gin; an' even if day did n't, w'at kin' o life 'd I lead? No, no, mastah; I 'spec' de bes' ting 'ud be for me to stay heah, an' do better."

"No, Sambo, you need not necessarily be taken, even though you should run away. You could make your way to a free State, where they will never be able to find you, or where, at least, should they do so, we can find means to evade their infamous fugitive slave law, and secure you in the possession of your freedom."

Here he indulged in a short tirade against the aforesaid law, which would be no more interesting to the reader than intelligible to the negro.

"If," he continued, "you will only consent to accompany me on my return home, I will conduct you to freedom and happiness."

"Well now, mastah, ef you jis promises to do *dat*, Sambo 's ready to go wid you, any time."

This seemed to be accomplishing something definite; but as the time for Justus's return had not yet arrived, some concerted measures must be taken by which each might regulate his conduct.

But ere these preliminaries were arranged, their deliberations were very unceremoniously interrupted. The sensations of the unsuspecting plotters may be imagined, when Mr. Blanton and posse confronted them. Mr. McMinime, Sambo's master, first spoke, addressing that worthy:

"So you are tired of your situation, and intend to leave us, hey? Well, good-bye, and success attend you." Then regarding Justus with a searching glance, he thus addressed him: "And as for you, sir, I would be glad to know by what authority or right you are acting, and on what ground you justify your conduct in thus unjustly seeking to deprive me of my property? I presume you are aware you have been taken in the commission of a heinous offence against law?"

The sudden appearance of his visitors very much disconcerted Justus; but he had now regained his self-possession. Proudly drawing himself up, as though fully impressed with the nobleness of his calling, he answered:

"Were you an impartial judge, sir, I would leave it to yourself to say which has committed, or is committing, the greater wrong: you, in subjecting this man to hopeless slavery; or I, who have simply instructed him that there is a state of freedom to which he may aspire. But I would simply ask you, by what shadow of a right do you take it upon you to make property of your fellow-beings—enslaving them, both soul and body?"

"Your insolence is equalled only by your villainy. But such language will not bear repetition. You have been more closely watched, perhaps, than you expected, and we desire no better knowledge of your character. In regard to my boy, Sambo here, whose mind you have corrupted, and whose discontent so much increased, I know not how to act; but we have merely to inform you that we cannot tolerate such a man in our midst; and if you have any regard to your own well-being, you will immediately leave, not only the county, but this portion of the State. We give you a half hour; and if, after that time, you are found within the limits of this camp-ground, expect to be roughly handled."

Thus speaking, he, with his companions, turned to depart, when all were surprised to hear a voice, from the bushy top of an oak near by, exclaim:

"Yes, and will give him a pretty strong argument in favor of that move now!"

Then several figures were seen swiftly gliding down a grape-vine depending from the limb of said tree; and some half dozen young men surrounded the now half-stupefied man of humanity.

"We will find means to evade the infamous fugitive slave law!" said one, mockingly; while each, in chorus, saluted him with a quotation from his recent conversation with the negro. The leader of the newly-arrived party then addressed the victim in a tone of mock respect and gravity, lauding his disinterested philanthropy, and eulogizing the magnanimity of his conduct.

"But," continued he, "it is a pity such generous behavior cannot meet with proper appreciation; for, notwithstanding our exalted opinion of your merits, we are forced slightly to differ with you in opinion. Yet," changing his tone, "this disagreement may prove a serious matter. You have heard the sentence pronounced by these gentlemen, and we fully agree with them. Only, considering their verdict too mild, we intend to affix some present penalty; and, as the most appropriate we can devise at the moment, you may prepare yourself for a ride on a rail and a plunge in the creek. Allow me to call your attention to the arm of yon oak: it is lofty, and a fall from it might endanger your neck. From this hint, understand that it will become you to hurry your departure so soon as you shall have gone through the proposed ordeal; for, should you be found here after the expiration of the allotted time, your descent from that limb will not be quite so pleasant as that you have just witnessed. In justice, you would not have the privilege of getting off so well; but in courtesy to these older gentlemen, who have dealt so mildly with you, we will suffer their judgment to stand."

Justus had no reply to make. He did not oppose any objection to the measure they had determined on. Seeing the utter hopelessness of influencing their minds, and believing himself a real martyr in the cause of humanity, he scorned to exhibit so much weakness as to plead to his "tyrannical oppressors."

Though his former assailants undertook his defence, the young men were inexorable. "Allow me a few words with him in private," said McMinime; after which remarking, "Perhaps he may be the better of such a lesson, boys; but do not be needlessly rude," he, with his company, returned to the camp.

Their departure was the signal for the youthful party to throw off all restraint, and the mirth indulged in at Justus's expense was quite boisterous.

Leaving them to the completion of their undertaking, we will accompany our returning friends.

CHAPTER VI.

THE COMPACT.

"Weel, weel, says I, a bargain be't."

THE silence maintained by McMinimc and his friend, as they wended their way back, joined to their abstracted manner, would have been evidence to a *stranger* that they were not entirely at ease in their minds. It was plain, however, that McMinimc was more anxiously concerned than the other. His last interview with Justus may perhaps have some connection with this state of feeling. However this may be, before he had reached the encampment, his trouble was at an end, and he moved on with the air of one who has just settled a long-debated and perplexing question.

Sambo, at the earliest opportunity, had deserted his new friend, leaving him to bear the brunt of the incensed master's ire as best he might; and, should we chance to meet with him at the present time, we could not decide whether his distress were chiefly on account of the frustration of the well-devised plan of escape, or apprehensions of personal indignities that might, in all probability, be offered him, in the way of punishment for what he had attempted.

Some of his thoughts on this subject he thus abstractedly embodied in words:

"Well, dat be one nice man, anyway. He feel for poah servant. He don't mean no harm, foh he can't make nuf'n foh hisself by it, and he's runnin' heap o' risk too. But wouldn't I like to go 'long, dough! But dat's all done broke up now. Wish I *could* go, anyhow, *shoah—I does*. I'd like to know what in the worl' Mas' Tom's a doin' dar. Mebbe he 'spected somef'n."

It was during the afternoon of the same day that two gentlemen might have been seen proceeding from the camp-ground, in the direction of the preaching-place for the blacks, followed by a negro carrying a small bundle.

The object of the party may be explained by the conversation in which they were engaged.

"I know, Mac, you're of sufficient age to conduct your own affairs, without the aid of my instruction or advice. Still, if you will pardon the familiarity of an old friend, I must tell you that, in my opinion, you are about doing a very unwise thing."

"Well, 'Squire, I suppose it does seem foolish, and may perhaps be so; yet I think not, under the circumstances. You are well aware I long since wished to be rid of some of my slaves, who, from the first, have only been a source of trouble, and have not done so only because I thought I could *not*, and do either myself or them justice. My experience has convinced me they need a protector; and, fearing they might fall into bad hands, I have shrunk from the very thought of selling them. But here is an opportunity to experiment on another plan. You well know the worthlessness of Sambo, and of his dishonesty I need not speak. You, as well as others, have received many proofs of that fact, by the peculations made on you personally, or, rather, in the person of your meat-house, hen-roost, etc., if you will allow me the use of such a figure."

"All this is true enough. But do you not think there would be more probability of the fellow doing some good by being restrained, under proper authority? Turn him out in the world without control, and the first thing he does may be to get himself disgraced and punished for his depredations on the public. Apart from his propensity to appropriate to his own use things on which he has no claim, he is utterly incompetent to take care of himself. And more than this, how do you know that Mr.

Abolition means to do the thing that is right about him ?"

"I am very well aware of the truth of what you say; and as for Mr. Abolition, as you call him, I do not intend to put Sambo under his charge without binding him pretty strongly to act honestly, and to see that his wants are provided for, to a certain extent. But the boy, with the aid of this gentleman, has taken a notion to want to be free, and I have determined to gratify him for once, and let him make trial of that state with which he has so fallen in love. This, I think, is the best I can do with him."

"Perhaps," said the other; "but I cannot think so. And by the way, I do not like the idea of letting Mr. Abolition off so easily: he has been guilty of an offence against the laws, and we might be charged with complicity, which would be rather an ugly affair."

"So it might; but I have taken it into my head that to let him off thus is the best thing we can do for ourselves, as well as for him. He has done no real harm yet, and, if allowed to escape now, will soon acquire a better judgment, for which he has not hitherto had opportunities. I know we might inflict on him the penalty he has so justly incurred, had we suffered him to proceed further in his design;

but he can do us no harm, and I wish to see what will become of him."

The other merely replied, "So be it;" then continued, "Here is the place."

They had reached the spot from which Justus had been taken but a short time before by his unexpected visitors. Here they found him again, with no visible traces upon him of the ordeal through which he had so recently passed. Yet deeply fixed in his heart was the remembrance of what he considered his unjust and cruel usage; and upon his tablets had been duly inscribed an account of the "infamous transaction," as a most convincing proof of the demoralizing nature of "Southern slavery." So deep and so bitter were his reflections on the subject, that the approach of the others in nowise disturbed him, though it was evident he was only waiting their coming.

The voice of McMinime roused him from his revery. "My business with you at this time, sir," he began, "is of some importance. I presume your feelings are very much enlisted in the welfare of this boy of mine?"

"It is true, sir, I did commiserate his hapless lot, and would have considered myself amply repaid for all I have suffered, yea, and much more, could I only have succeeded in improving his condition.

But you need be under no further apprehension; I am ready to carry out your orders, and have only awaited you here, in accordance with your request."

"Yes, sir," replied the other, not noticing the concluding sentence of this reply; "and do you not know that, in the attempt to accomplish this purpose, you have made yourself liable to suffer the penalty of the law? But this is foreign to the matter in hand, and has been discussed long since. And now, to come to the point at once, as you are willing to undergo *so much* for Sambo, and as I wish him to have a taste of that freedom with the thought of which you have inspired him, how can you satisfy me that your intention is or was to act in good faith toward the boy: in other words, what pledge are you willing to leave with me that you will do with him according to agreement, if I should put him under your care, to be conducted into a free State, and assisted into a business of some kind?"

Being unprepared for such a proposal, and not entirely satisfied as to the manner in which it should be received, he replied—

"I know not what pledge would satisfy you; yet if you are sincere, and——"

"You need not doubt that," interrupted the other; "I mean just what I say; I want the discontented rascal off my hands, and if we can only agree

on the terms, he is ready at once to accompany you
to freedom and happiness."

"The opportunity of performing so benevolent an
action I would be happy to embrace; and if I can
give you any assurance that he shall be properly
cared for, it shall be done. But I suspect the conditions of his accompanying me entirely preclude
the thought of my undertaking the pleasing task,
for I have it not in my power to offer any thing as
security. I have been long from home, and have
received no remittance up to this time, and our
travelling expenses alone would be as heavy a draw
as my present resources would bear. It is with no
ordinary degree of sorrow I find myself thus cir-
cumstanced; for such a charitable act I cannot hope
again to meet with the opportunity of doing."

"Do not mistake me, sir. I do not demand any
thing like the value of the boy; but simply wish
to retain something valuable as a spur to your dili-
gence, which you can recover when you shall have
performed your contract. And though I do not wish
to barter him, yet were I to receive a pledge of his
full value, I would feel satisfied that you had a
powerful motive, independently of your humanity,
to act uprightly.

"Have you no articles of jewelry you prize,
which you would yet be willing to leave in pledge

of your good conduct?   You have no right to complain of my want of implicit confidence in your word; you are a stranger; and were I entirely to forget the occurrences of the day, I would not be justifiable in trusting you too far, though not doubting your honesty.   What say you?   Can you think of nothing?"

"Here is a watch," replied the other, at the same time exhibiting a costly article of the kind named, "that I value very highly, and would not suffer out of my hands under any other circumstances.   But if this will satisfy you, let me hear the terms with which I am to comply."

"So far, so good; that is a valuable watch, no doubt; but you are very well aware of the disproportion existing between the price of the boy and this timepiece, and should you be disposed to make other use of the transfer I intend to make to you, this would be no obstacle, as you could vastly more than save yourself.   But my aim is to give to Sambo the freedom that he covets, and at the same time secure you from the effect of whatever temptation you may be exposed to—either to appropriate him to your own use, or to fail in properly providing for him; for I not only wish to give him his freedom, but to place him in a situation to support himself decently.   Here, however, is the proposal I wish to make: leave the watch with me, for which I will give you a receipt, and on your presenting evidence that the contract has been complied with, I will return it. But, as I hinted before, that the intrusting of so valuable a piece of property to your hands may not be a lure to you to depart from a course of rectitude, I shall demand from you the strongest assurance a man of honor can give, that you will carry out my wishes. This is nothing more nor less than to bind yourself under a solemn oath; for which purpose I have secured the services of this gentleman, who is an acting Justice of the Peace."

Strong in conscious honesty, Justus, not at all disposed to shrink from the test, unless the conditions should be too onerous, simply asked, "Will you be so kind as to inform me of the terms? I shall surely comply if I am not expected to perform any thing unreasonable."

"By no means; but judge for yourself. You are required to conduct Sambo to a free State; to see him established in some mode of business by which he can gain a support. For this purpose you will lay out the money I intrust to your care. In any contingency you are of course clear; as, for instance, should either die—yourself or the boy; yet in the former case it is expected you will make such provision for him as circumstances may permit. After discharging this duty, you are to present or send to me a certificate, signed by at least three publicly known and responsible men, to the effect that the agreement has been fulfilled, or equally satisfactory evidence of the death of the boy, should such an event occur. This will cancel all obligation on your part, and secure the restoration of your pledge. Further, to secure you from all danger of molestation on your journey, I will execute to you a bill of sale of this slave, which you are to bind yourself to destroy, or return to me with the other documents when the occasion for its use ceases. Should the boy's feelings on the subject change, the return of him, with every thing else received from me, will release you from your obligation, and entitle you to the pledge. If you can agree to this, our matter will soon be arranged preparatory to your departure."

Justus remained silent and deeply meditative for some time; at length he replied: "It has ever been my opinion that the word of a man of honor was as binding as his oath: such at least I have always held mine; and to be thus put upon my oath in regard to a matter of mere charity, does not well accord with my views and feelings. Still, as you demand it, I cannot see but that I may safely take the obligation; though under no other circumstances than for the relief of the distressed would I assume such a responsibility."

"Just as you think best about it; I wish to impose no burdensome task on you, but thinking it would be a source of gratification for you to render such a service to the cause of humanity, I could not, on my part, be satisfied with less than I have demanded. The matter is now at your disposal."

Signifying his assent, the preliminaries were speedily arranged, and the oath administered by 'Squire Brown, with due solemnity.

CHAPTER VII.

ESCAPE FROM FREEDOM.

"The best-laid schemes o' mice and men
Gang aft aglee."

THE sun was low in the western sky when Justus, bidding adieu to the scene of his late benevolent efforts, and of his "wrongs," addressed himself to his homeward journey, attended by the now liberated Sambo. Two hundred miles of horseback travel lay between him and the point of embarkation; and difficult as such a mode of journeying is of necessity to one scarcely ever before in the saddle, the hardship seemed doubled when he remembered that but one horse remained for the two travellers. Sambo's master, wisely thinking a better conveyance than the sturdy legs of the athletic negro a useless luxury, had made no other provision for the journey of that individual than to place in the hands of Justus funds sufficient for the expenses of the trip.

Deprecating the necessity for the inequality be-

tween them, and determined it should not long exist, Justus hastily mounted and led the way, his
protégé briskly following, relieved of his pack,
which had been transferred to the capacious saddle-
bags of his new master.

From sympathy with the toiling negro behind,
the mind of the abolitionist went back to the incidents connected with his present position. Closely
was his conduct reviewed, and he could not but
condemn the hasty zeal which led him to violate
his own originally formed purpose, frustrating his
well-laid plan, involving him in disgrace and punishment, and forcing him from his field of observation.

This materially affected the prospects of his forthcoming book, and the conclusion was forced upon
him that, for the present, it must remain unwritten.
Still, he reflected, "Though nothing has yet been
gained in regard to that particular matter, the
present movement is merely an episode in my great
measure, and, Sambo disposed of, I will return and
prosecute the work to a speedy issue."

Deeply absorbed in these reflections, he continued
his course, utterly forgetful of his charge, and also
of the fact that his steed was moving at a rate
with which no footman could well keep pace.

Gradually he regained the ascendency of his despondent feelings, and began to scan the matter in another light. He congratulated himself on the fact that he had at least rescued one human being from thraldom. This, arousing him from his revery, recalled to his mind his companion, Sambo.

"The man has had a weary tramp," he said, "and must need rest sorely. It would hardly be fair for me to suffer him to walk any longer at this time: though I shall myself suffer by it, we must exchange situations, at least for a while." Turning for the purpose of carrying out this resolution, no Sambo was at hand. At the moment, he felt some misgivings as to the cause of absence; but one moment of calm reasoning assured him he had been riding too rapidly for his friend to keep in view. It was necessary to return and seek him. As he passed back, a diverging road in the direction in which he had before gone, previously unnoticed, now arrested his attention. In doubt whether his charge had not pursued the newly-discovered road, Justus paused in perplexed uncertainty; but the accidental observation of footprints in that direction decided his mind, and induced him to rein his horse in pursuit. Rapid riding soon brought him to a dwelling, where, to his question whether "a colored man" had been seen to pass, a negative answer was returned. Nor did the question, together with the manner of the question, fail to excite suspicion in regard to the nature of the gentleman's character.

Justus was now at a loss how to act. Night was fast approaching; and, for aught he knew, Sambo might be either behind or in advance. There was, then, a probability of missing him either way. But as no time was to be lost, his determination was, to advance while any daylight still remained. The dusk of the evening was giving way to darkness, when Justus, checking his horse, exclaimed despairingly:

"He certainly has not gone on: I must seek him in the opposite direction."

At that moment a dark object, a short distance in advance, attracted his notice, and he continued:

"Ah! there he is now, perhaps."

"Dat you, Mas' Justus?" at this moment saluted his ears. "Whar in the worl' you been? I 'spected you'd gone off and left me clar; an' I 'as jist thinkin' about goin' back to Mas Tom's. Mighty glad you's come, dough; for I's run myself most to def, tryin' to cotch you."

"Why did you not keep up with me from the start, Sambo?"

"Goodness knows, Mas' Justus, I can't walk's fast as that hoss kin pace."

"But could you not follow the same road I did, by the horse's tracks?"

"No, sah! dar was so many tracks in bof of um, I could n't tell which one you tuk; but that gemman you axed 'way back yondah said dis was the road to take; and I 'spected you 'd come this way."

"Well, have you ever been along this road, Sambo?"

"O, yes, sah, once or twice."

"How far do you suppose it is to a house?"

"Dun no, 'zackly; mile or two, mebbe."

The journey was resumed: Sambo—who complained of his feet being excoriated in his long walk—in the saddle; his guardian sturdily trudging in advance.

An hour had passed, and yet the gleaming light from no friendly habitation met the eye; while Sambo's nodding had more than once menaced him with a fall. Again they exchanged situations. Another hour passed with like result.

"Le 's stop heah, Mas' Justus," said Sambo.

"Why, what shall we do? There are no accommodations for us here."

"Well, we can't find no house, nohow, 't don't look like, and we can *rest* heah, and Pompey kin find some grass to eat."

"Halloo, Sambo, as loud as you can: perhaps some one may hear you, and reply."

The negro complied. Again and again. Justus joined, and both shouted in concert: the echo of their own voices was the only sound returned.

Sambo's advice was now taken, and they prepared for their bivouac. "Pompey" was turned loose, to pick what herbage he could find—the riders taking such measures as necessity would allow for their own comfort.

Justus had read and heard of bivouacs in the woods, but had never anticipated the enjoyment of such a camping-out as this; nor was the present privilege very highly prized; and no wonder, under the circumstances. He was lost—having no idea of his whereabouts, further than that he was in a wild, lone-looking wood, and in a totally strange country. One thing was evident, however: it was inevitable, and repining would do no good. He therefore made up his mind to endure it philosophically.

Stopping in the woods, the preparations for their lodgings seemed to have taken away all desire of sleep, even the drowsy Sambo forgetting to doze.

Each one now appeared to be busy with his own thoughts. Suddenly Justus spoke:

"Sambo!"

"Sah?" answered he, startled almost to his feet by the abruptness of his address.

"I have just been reflecting, Sambo, on the happiness in store for you; but now, in the first place, as you are a free man, you must have a becoming name. I will, therefore, call you George Washington; and for a surname you can adopt that of your late master: George W. McMinime, then, will be your style of address."

"Yes, sah," replied Sambo; but the manner of speaking was without enthusiasm or energy, showing that his thoughts were running on other matters. This was observed by his guardian with sincere regret, for he had expected and desired that exultation in his freedom, and reflections on the glorious consequences to result from it, would fully occupy all the negro's time. However, he could not but indulge the hope that time, and the change of condition to be experienced, would work a corresponding change in his disposition. Nor could he wonder much at his present conduct, after viewing the matter in its proper light.

The "man" had never enjoyed the privilege of acting in a man's place; and whatever he may have suffered in his former state, he had tried it, and knew it to be endurable, while the future was dark and wholly unknown; being, on this account, well calculated to excite gloomy foreboding.

Neither one being disposed to carry on a conversation, they again lapsed into silence, and soon G. W. McMinime, enveloping himself in Justus's cloak, which his friend had kindly placed at his service for the occasion, extended himself on the grass, and forgot for a time all toils and cares in slumber; which fact was announced to Justus by heavy snoring, when, adjusting his saddle-blanket to the best advantage, he speedily followed this example. On the following morning, Mr. G. W. McMinime had a variety of questions to propound to his kind conductor relative to his future prospects. He was not fully satisfied of the propriety of his present movements.

"Do you t'ink, Mas' Justus, that white folks'll treat me like I 'as 's good as them, when I gits to Massychoosetts?"

"Why, sir! they dare not treat you otherwise; you will be a freeman, and the law will be open to you for the enforcing of your rights; you need not subject yourself to any uneasiness, as such trouble *will* be superfluous on that ground, Sambo."

"Yes, but won't they *sota* push me aside, and say, *Get out 'o the way heah, you nigga, you don't 'long mongst wite folks!* I's been told dis is de way da does dar to de poah black uns."

"It is true, perhaps, Sambo, there may be some with whom you meet that will act thus; these, however, will only be the rude and ignorant; and then you must recollect that this will be vastly better than it is here, where *all* push you aside, and you are held in estimation by none."

"Yes, it might be; but heah we aint free, but jis know dis is our place; dough to have de name of bein' free, and not be mor'n half free nuder,'s a heap wus dan 'tis heah. If we only acts like we know we oughter heah, we are 'spected as good servants."

"O, my dear sir! you ought not to talk so; you should accustom yourself to think and talk differently on this subject. But I must make allowance for you: your former condition, as well as your education, has been of a nature calculated to blind your perceptions of your rights, and to degrade you below your true level in the scale of being. I entertain no doubt but you will view things in a different light after having acquired experience in the school of freedom. And for the present, let me entreat you to harass yourself by no gloomy forebodings."

Whether convinced or not, this *silenced* him on

that point; but another difficulty rested on his mind: should he not be pleased with his new situation, would there be any " chance to git back agin ?" Being at length satisfied in regard to this also, he announced himself in readiness at once to resume his journey.

The experience of Justus on the preceding day, in the line of walking, had completely convinced him of his extreme need of another horse; but as the want was one impossible at that time to be supplied, nothing remained but to proceed as before till fortune should throw in their way the means of bettering their condition.

Notwithstanding the bitterness of this experience, Justus arranged the order of march as before: he himself preceded on foot, Sambo in the saddle. It is not likely, at all, that Justus would thus have favored the negro for any desire of effecting an equality between them: his memory was too keen for such a motive to exert much influence; but he saw the negro's mind was beginning to waver, and that some stimulant was needed to keep his resolution up to the proper pitch. To effect this, Justus, though at great personal sacrifice, insisted on his taking charge of the horse, at least to take his turn at riding first. Mile after mile was thus traversed, and the pangs of hunger began to be seriously felt, and, as yet, no human abode appeared in view. Unused to such a procedure, Justus was overcome with fatigue and vexation. He was entirely disheartened; but, to better his condition as far as possible, he determined to exchange places with " George," alias Sambo, who, with all the dignity of a judge, closely followed his footsteps. The resolve was scarcely formed, when a sudden turn in the road revealed to sight—most cheering prospect!—a dwelling near at hand. Without dismounting the negro, he continued on to the house.

Though previously so anxious to reach a human dwelling, and though the necessity was imperative, he now felt an involuntary shrinking from that interview which must so soon occur; and, had he not been *compelled* to call, no halt would have been made. It may seem strange that he should be thus affected by what ought to have been simply a cause for joy. But a very natural reason may be assigned. He was about acting in a capacity for which he had had no preparation, and in which a slight error might exhibit him in a very ludicrous light, even though unproductive of any worse result; and to conduct the affair in the proper manner was the identical thing at which his mind revolted. However, the time intervening between coming in sight of the house and entering it permitted him the opportunity to collect his thoughts for the emergency; and yet he fairly started with fright at hearing himself calling for refreshment for "myself and boy."

The desired hospitality was readily extended, and the application for a horse was met by an invitation to the stable, where he might suit himself. There was no other alternative with the traveller—a horse he must have; consequently, there were but few words passed, and a satisfactory purchase was soon effected.

His want thus happily supplied, "George" was called on to receive his charger, and prepare for a start. But "George" responded not to the call, nor to any subsequent ones, which were neither few nor gentle. "Where can the fellow be?" said Justus. But as nothing of this kind could make him appear, it was necessary to institute search; and for this purpose he directed his steps towards the kitchen. He was not found there.

Returning, he was accosted by his host with, "Why, stranger, he has run away, and taken your horse with him." A hasty examination too truly verified this statement, and disclosed the startling fact that his equipment and saddle-bags were also gone.

A predicament of this nature is not easily described. Should we say Justus was taken entirely unawares, and sadly disappointed, this is no more than the reader will know, naturally, without the intervention either of prophet or historian. But, on the other hand, should we say he was *thunderstruck! overpowered!* his *indignation knew no bounds!* or equivalent expressions, it would not be strictly true, for he was a philosopher. But while acknowledging our inability to do justice, we forbear an allusion to his sensations; his actions we may describe. For some moments he reflected, as if doubtful in what way he should account for his loss; but this uncertainty seemed to pass, and he exclaimed, "The ungrateful wretch!" and, after another pause, he added, musingly, "No doubt he has gone back to his master."

"Of whom did you buy the boy?" asked his host. But this question, though quite a natural one, disconcerted Justus, and threw him quite off his guard. So great indeed was his confusion, it was noticed by his host. At length he replied, "I obtained him of a gentleman named McMinime."

This strange conduct on the part of Justus excited in the mind of "mine host" suspicion of foul dealings on the part of his guest. "I suppose you have the papers to show," he added, with seeming carelessness.

"O yes," said he, feeling for his pocket-book.

But his alarm was now more clearly manifest than before, as he exclaimed, "Alas! it too is in my saddle-bags. O, sir, cannot I secure your aid in his recovery? I am a stranger to this business, and know not whether I can succeed in finding him; yet, without the documents he has, I am a ruined man."

The evident sincerity of this appeal wrought a change in the feelings of the landlord, and, though unable to comply with his request, he felt no disposition, as he had previously done, to present any impediments to his movements, or to trouble himself in any way about the matter, as it was evidently no affair of his; and, even though the stranger had obtained the boy by foul means, it was now very clear he was at liberty to return to his master. Justus could afford to lose no time. He therefore set out at once and alone, in pursuit of the fugitive, for his property must be recovered, even though his ward should have decided on abandoning him. And the bill of sale! Ah! what should he do were that lost?

He had paid but little attention to the country over which he had passed, and very soon had the mortification to find he had missed the road, and was lost. This was annoying under any circumstances, but doubly so at the present time.

Long did he wander in this uncertain state, unable to gain any information in regard to his point of destination, and consequently bewildered, on account of his want of knowledge of the locality. From this cause he was unable to designate any place in the neighborhood of or on the route to that place at which he was aiming. The residence of Mr. McMinime was the only one of which he had any idea, and the few persons whom he chanced to meet being as little acquainted with the gentleman sought as himself, he had no means of ascertaining whether or not he was gaining any thing on his journey.

At length he hit upon a plan to gain the desired information. There was a camp-ground near the place he was seeking. He was informed there were two such institutions, at about equal distances from where he then was. His hopes were again dashed to the ground. Yet there was still another hold: "But there is, or was very recently, a meeting in progress at the one of which I am speaking."

"O, well, then, I can put you in the road;" and he was furnished with explicit directions.

This good fortune had come none too soon; for his wanderings had well-nigh consumed the day, and he began to feel no little concerned in regard to a shelter for the night. On this occasion, fortune

favored him, and the gathering gloom of despondency was driven from his heart, and the darkness
of early night enlivened by the cheerful blaze
gleaming through the open door of a contiguous
farm-house.   Though furnished with comfortable
quarters, there was yet a serious drawback to his
enjoyment: previous to entering the house, he
made the discovery that this was the identical
place at which he had inquired for Sambo the
evening before.   It seemed to him at the time that
the question excited some "unnecessary emotion;"
whether it was the interrogatory itself, or the manner of propounding it, he was not prepared to say;
and the suspicion, too apparent for concealment, of
his late host, taught him he was now occupying a
critical position, in consequence of the loss of the
bill of sale.   Still he did not know *all*, or he would
have chosen to remain one other night in the
woods.

Rumors had spread from the camp-ground, of the
movements at that place of the young abolitionist;
and this was the subject of the conversation to
which Justus was compelled to listen.   He was
regaled with an account of the doings of a "poor
fool."   We will not repeat any more of the particular epithets used on the occasion in question: how
he tried to induce the slaves to abscond from their

masters; was watched, and caught in the very act; and, finally, how he was dipped in the creek. Then the "Ha, ha, ha!" that burst from all present, himself excepted, was almost enough to cause his hair to stand on end, and the cold sweat on his forehead. Nor was even this the end of his torments. His entertainers went on to state, "They had no doubt that the same chap passed here yesterday evening." Then the impression he had made at the time was fairly described to him:

"But that's one time he missed it, though. He got hold of a nigger that time harder to steal than he thought for, and he's left afoot now somewhere. The women folks say the same nigger passed back this afternoon, riding the very horse the fellow was on."

Here ensued another boisterous fit of merriment. The concluding portion of this speech, at least, contained some comfort for the puzzled Yankee, inasmuch as it satisfied him of the fact that his escaped ward had returned to his old home, of which he had been previously in doubt. Thus cheered, and thus tormented, at the earliest pause in the conversation he took occasion to withdraw for the night.

CHAPTER VIII.

THE CHASE.

"Now, do thy speedy utmost, Meg,
And win the key-stane o' the brig."

ALTHOUGH Justus retired, it was not to sleep for long and weary hours. It is true, he felt the effect of his protracted fatigue and exposure; but this was forgotten in the ordeal through which he had just passed. To escape further torment, and to prepare himself for a more trying time, anticipated in the morning, or to devise means for escaping it, were the motives for his sudden withdrawal; for, to his mind, a discovery seemed inevitable when he should confront the family in the open light of day; and what might be his horrid fate if apprehended under present circumstances, he could only imagine. It was now a matter of regret that he had not made known the exact nature of his business when the subject was first introduced, and taken the consequences; but surprise, and an undefined apprehension of evil results, had kept him silent at the time he should have spoken; and now nothing remained but to endure in silence.

The fear of being recognized when exposed to daylight, as the "chap" that inquired for the black man, was a matter in regard to which he could not satisfy himself; for this, after affairs had taken the present turn, would be inconceivably worse than to have made the confession himself at the commencement. He might prevent such a result, however, by a very early start in the morning; and this plan, after full deliberation, he determined to adopt. The matter thus settled, he soon sank to forgetfulness.

A heavy hand was laid on his shoulder, and a rough voice sounded in his ear, "Stranger! stranger!" He aroused himself. The sun was casting his early beams into the chamber. "You sleep well," continued the same voice. "I called you repeatedly, and could get no answer. It is our breakfast-time, and I supposed you would like to be travelling."

"Yes; thank you. I should have been up long ago, but I have lost rest lately, which caused me to oversleep myself."

To his great joy, breakfast passed, and he was not recognized; nor was there even so much as a suspicion of his real character. Yet not until he had received the necessary instructions, and was fairly on the way, did he feel himself at ease.

Released from the scene of his late tortures, he again breathed freely, and, for a brief space of time, was comparatively happy. But other reflections presenting themselves, speedily marred his joy. "What if George should rob him, or the paper should be lost?" And he spurred on with renewed energy.

It chanced that the horse he was riding was not perfectly well broke to the saddle, and was subject to sudden starts, by which he had narrowly escaped being thrown on several occasions. And, while passing a house, he took an affright at the barking of a dog that flew out at him, and set off at full speed. Inexperienced as a rider, he had but little control over the beast, whose fright and speed increased with the distance, leaving the rider in doubt as to the propriety of securing himself from danger by falling off, rather than have his neck broken, or being dashed out of the saddle by the first opposing object. Drawing near to a farm on the roadside, he observed a horseman a short distance in advance, who, attracted by the sound of his furious gallop, suddenly turned and looked back.

Justus's surprise may be better imagined than

described, when that look revealed the person of his late ward, G. W. McMinime. One hasty look, however, was quite enough to satisfy the negro, and in a moment his horse was careering down the road as if in emulation of the speed of his pursuer.

It was to no purpose that his master vociferated, "George! George Washington!" for the only visible effect it had was to give his own horse a fresh start, causing him to redouble his efforts. Away went the negro, leading the chase, and headlong followed Justus, shouting alternately, "George! George Washington! You need not run from me."

But the only answer he could elicit from George was the more energetic belaboring and kicking of his steed, and a stolen glance behind occasionally, as if to discover how the chase was going. Yet, in spite of all his exertions, his pursuer gained on him.

The chase now became exciting, Justus one while calling on "George," George on "Mas' Tom." The negroes in the field abandoned their cotton-picking for the nonce, and, almost bursting with laughter, took their stations along the fence, shouting, "Hurrah for de ole Gineral Washington! You's got to beat dat, boy, or de boss 'll catch you, shoah. Don't ole Gin'ral do it brown?"

On down towards the house they swept. The

pursuer had ceased his calling, but the fugitive was crying at every breath, "Mas' Tom! Help! Mas' Tom, Mas' Justus' goin' to kill me."

The cause of such an uproar was matter of no little surprise at the house, which they were now fast approaching, the negro but a short distance in advance; but Sambo's well-known voice—for it was the residence of his late master—being soon recognized amid the other din, the wonder became still more intense. The entire household was speedily collected at the yard fence, to be able to avail themselves of the earliest opportunity of learning the cause of the outbreak between Sambo and his new master, as denoted by such an unusual uproar from the negro, and the grounds of their unexpected return.

That worthy had no sooner brought his horse to a partial halt, than, throwing himself from his back, he rushed through the gate to his master, exclaiming, "Save me, Mas' Tom; I 'spec' he 'll mos' want to kill me. I left 'im, and took all his things off. I do n't want to go away and be free, nohow."

"Why, you worthless puppy! what right have you to run away, and come to my premises? Go to your old cabin, and do not stir out till I call for you to start again."

This he spoke with difficulty, on account of a

disposition to laugh. And the ludicrousness of the scene would have justified one less humorous than himself in an outburst of mirth. The words of the negro had fully explained the matter to his late master; and, though he was scarcely less angry than surprised at his return, he loved a good joke too well not to reap from the occurrence an excellent harvest of fun.

The pursuer was soon at hand, borne on, without any regard to his own volition, by his panting charger, which, however, manifested no disposition to proceed any farther than his leader had done; and, much· to his rider's relief, he came to a halt. The appearance of Justus was by no means calculated to allay McMinime's risibilities, and it was with the utmost difficulty he could so far control himself as to calmly ask, after the usual salutation, "What in the world has happened, that you ride at such a headlong gait? Has Sambo seen enough freedom already?"

"I do not know what is the matter with him," moodily replied Justus. "He left me yesterday morning, taking with him my all. But as my saddle-bags are here, I will examine them, and see if every thing is safe." He nervously proceeded to the task, while McMinime, entirely overcome, fairly exploded with laughter. Justus looked the indignation he did not think it prudent to express; and the other, recovering himself, apologized for the rudeness, but added: "You could not blame me, I know, did you see and hear the matter in the same manner I do."

"That may be, but the subject is in no way mirthful to me. It may, on the contrary, prove a very serious matter," replied Justus, still busily engaged in overhauling his effects.

"This is the thought that excited my laughter," replied McMinime, in further explanation: "I have read and heard of fugitives of various descriptions, as from battle, from labor, from justice, but a fugitive from freedom is something, to me, at least, entirely new."

"Rather a strange idea," replied he, in any thing but a mirthful mood. "I would prefer fleeing from any thing else."

By this time one department of the treasury had been emptied, and the contents examined. But he did not seem to have been very successful in his search; for, with an agitation plainly manifest, he began operations on the other side. This, too, failing to reveal the object of his solicitude, his distress was really pitiable. "Alas!" he exclaimed, "what shall I do? I am ruined."

"Have you lost any thing?" asked McMinime.

"Lost *any thing!*" echoed he. "Alas! sir, I have lost *every thing.* My pocket-book, containing all the money I have in the world, with the exception of some small change, as well as that received from you; the bill of sale, and I know not what else, are gone. I am reduced to penury, sir; and not only so, my character is at stake on account of the loss of the paper."

"Where or how do you suppose you could have lost them? It is a strange thing to lose articles of the kind from saddle-bags, unless, indeed, they were stolen. Perhaps you have overlooked them."

"No hopes of that," he mournfully replied. "But as to how I lost them, it is hard to say; though I fear George has stolen them. At any rate, they were lost while the saddle-bags were in his possession."

"Who is this George you speak of?"

"I mean Sambo." He then narrated the events of the last two days, concluding with, "I know I have not lost any thing myself, for I have had no opportunity to do so; therefore he must have it, unless he has lost it, which is by no means probable."

"A bad business," remarked McMinime; "for if *Sambo* has robbed you—of which I have no doubt—it will be next to impossible to get it from him. However, we must see what can be done.

"Sambo!" but Sambo responded not to the call; and each repetition of the call met with the like result.

"Pa, I think I saw him go in the parlor a little while ago," said a little flaxen-haired child standing by.

"O no, daughter, I reckon that must have been a mistake; he has no business there." But there could be no doubt of his being somewhere; and as he could not be made to hear, a messenger was sent to seek, and bring him in.

This was at length accomplished, when his master observed to him, in a matter-of-course way, "Sambo, Mr. Justus thinks you have been troubled long enough with his pocket-book, and would be very thankful for you to deliver it up, as he feels fully competent now to take care of it for himself."

"What you mean, Mas' Tom? How I gwine to git Mas' Justus's pocket-book? De Lord knows I *aint* got no pocket-book o' Mas' Justus's, nor nobody else's."

"Why, I mean you must deliver up what you have stolen from those saddle-bags, and tell no more *lies* about it, or I will just whip you to death. I see no use, anyway, of suffering such a thievish, lying rascal to live any longer. So, if you value your life, let us know where it is immediately."

"I swah to the Good One, Mas' Tom, I aint stole nuf'n, and don't know nuf'n about no pocket-book nuder."

"Bring me a cord here," said his master; "it is useless to waste time with him; he is tired of living, I presume, or else he thinks because I never have whipped him to death *yet*, notwithstanding all his wickedness, I never *will;* but he may, perhaps, find he has presumed too far." The cord being brought, he continued: "Bind the villain hard; and here, Billy, run and cut me about a dozen good hickory sprouts," handing an open knife to his little son. "I'll break him from stealing, and teach him to tell the truth, before I am done with him. Never mind it, either: nothing short of death will cure him, and he had as well just be put out of the way at once. Go bring me my gun—*that* will be the best way of getting rid of him."

From the earnest asseverations of the negro, Justus fully believed him to be innocent. He had, when the binding was effected, a strong inclination to intercede for him; but the order for the gun completely horrified him. He could not help indulging the hope that there was no intention of using so murderous a weapon; yet he was aware that "slaveholders were wont to perpetrate great atrocities on the persons of their helpless victims." Then, as the image of the mysteriously blackened trees about Legree's farm arose to his mind, he very reasonably concluded that this man could shoot a human being as easily, and with as great impunity, as another could burn him. What could he do? Should he stand by and see the atrocious murder committed? His agitation was so open and violent, it was observed by both the master and the servant. With the latter it proved to be contagious. He had thought that the threat in regard to shooting was only intended to scare him; and, so far from being disturbed at it, he was glad to be released from the whipping which he fully expected. But seeing Justus so much disturbed, his conclusion was that he was further in the secret than himself, and that possibly there was more danger than he anticipated. The sight of the gun increased the alarm of each, and of Justus especially, to such an extent, that McMinime saw it needful to use some means to allay his fears, in order to prevent an interference. Taking the gun in his hand, he observed:

"She has been loaded so long, she may be damp. I will discharge and load her afresh, as I do not wish to make any blunder when I begin the business."

Turning his back on Sambo for the purpose, he

gave Justus to understand, by very significant winks and gestures, that he must keep quiet, and no harm should be done. At the same time he could scarcely restrain a smile at Justus's woe-begone expression of countenance.

By the time the gun was reloaded, Sambo's concern was quite apparent; and as his master confronted him again, he begged most piteously:

"For goodness' sake, Mas' Tom, do n't shoot: I dunno where nuf'n is you wants."

"Stop, Sambo;" adding in a mournful voice, as he fitted the cap on the tube—"*This* is no time to be lying; but say whether you intend to inform us where the money is, or are you determined to die for it?"

"You do n't think I 'd tell you a lie about it, do you, Mas' Tom?"

"Well, Sambo," was the only answer, "I suppose it must be done;" and the gun was raised to the shoulder.

"Stop, stop, Mas' Tom," said the negro, his ignorance suddenly vanishing. "I 'll tell you whar 't is: it 's sewed up in the tick of my bed. Le' me go and git it for you. Mas' Tom, I know jis the place to find it."

He was released; and very soon the cause of all the trouble was in Justus's hand. An examination satisfied him that every thing was just as he had left it, with the exception of the bill of sale, which was missing. Sambo could give no account of it; and though neither of the gentlemen had a very high opinion of his veracity, yet, as the nature of the lost article precluded the possibility of his converting it to any use or profit, they admitted his assertions. This they felt the more ready to do, from the improbability of succeeding again with him in so desperate an experiment. It was concluded to overhaul Justus's papers, to ascertain if the document might not be among them; but before this was effected, the dinner-bell called for a suspension of operations.

CHAPTER IX.

STRANGE OCCURRENCES.

"The man who pauses in his honesty
Wants little of a villain."

NOTHING could induce Sambo willingly to go "Norf wid Mas' Justus," he being, according to his declaration, "as far Norf and as near free as he cared about bein'." In consequence of this declaration, the contracting parties were placed in an awkward position, and one that seemed likely to lead to a serious disagreement. The loss of this paper put it out of Justus's power to comply fully with his obligation, while the other appeared determined to come to an arrangement on no other terms than according to the very letter of the agreement. His intention was not to be finally obstinate, but only to trouble the other party for a time. However, Justus felt himself in his power, and there was no remedy for it; and how the matter could ever be settled while McMinime would take no other assurance from him than the bill of sale, he was at a loss to imagine. For himself, he felt that he had done every thing that could honorably be asked of him, and felt no little hurt at the suspicion of the other.

"I think, sir," he said sharply, becoming irritated, "this is an unnecessary and unreasonable scruple. The bill of sale is gone, and I cannot replace it, nor perform my obligation in accordance with the exact words; but as to the intention of the contract, I can, by an instrument of writing, secure you from all fear of trouble by the transfer being hereafter brought against you."

"Possibly you might do all that too; but bear in mind that this would not be doing what you obligated yourself to do. And more than that, it may be that, after your instrument of writing is lost or detroyed, the bill of sale will turn up. As strange things as this have happened; and it is safe to exercise a little caution, that we may not be overreached."

"Though you will not make a full restoration, I presume you will have no objection to return my obligation and my receipt for the money. As for the watch, though highly prized, I do not much regard losing it."

"I really do not know whether to admire or to be aggravated at your presumption. I must deliver to you the only authority by which I hold your pledge, while I feel myself bound in self-defence to retain that pledge!—in other words, acknowledge myself to be acting dishonestly with you. I would have taken a request for all with much better grace. The obligation is the very thing I wish to retain until it is discharged. But we can make nothing at this kind of proceeding: let it rest till morning, and we will then see what can be done. Meanwhile, you may call to mind something of the lost document; and I would suggest that you study about it: you may, perhaps, not have put it in the pocket-book, and it may yet be found."

Justus's only reply was a doubtful shake of the head; and so the matter rested, with but little probability of an adjustment at its resumption, should McMinime press his present demand. But, during the interval, circumstances occurred which rendered each one willing to accede to the demands of the other.

To calm the perturbation of his mind, and exorcise the evil spirits struggling within him, Justus betook himself to a ramble in the woods. He was soon lost in the contemplation of the scene around him, which was well calculated to withdraw his thoughts from his personal embarrassments. The sun, now midway in his descent, was shining in unclouded glory; while the coolness of early autumn tempered the heat of a Southern clime. The wind sighed softly through the forest, the green apparel of which had begun to assume a russet hue; and, as if to impress him with feelings of solemnity, occasionally a leaf, faded before its fellows, loosening its hold on the parent stem, as shaken by the gentle breeze, would, fluttering, fall to the ground at his feet. The majestic forest trees, the relics of past centuries, well fitted to call up emotions of sublimity, with the music of the birds, preparing for their departure, and the numberless other attractions to be found in such a scene, could not long hold enchained the spirits of the woe-stricken Bostonian. His thoughts reverted to himself and his distressing situation; revolving in a maze, and ever returning to the starting-point, the unfortunate bill of sale. Most heartily did he curse the delusion that had led him to leave his own quiet home in search of a mere chimera, as he now almost feared. Particularly did he reproach himself for having been drawn away from that silent plan of observation he had marked out to follow, thus bringing all these troubles on himself. He contrasted the facility with which, on a certain occasion, he, assisted by others, had liberated the servants of an unsuspecting Southerner, stopping in his city, with the difficulty and danger attending his late inefficient effort in the same line.

His mind was not clear on the subject; but he felt an inclination to return home, and either abandon his work, or collect the material for its completion *there*, so soon as he could get clear of this unfortunate affair. "Ah! should he ever effect that object? Had he not sworn to do that which it was now impossible for him to perform?" Something manœuvring in a manner he could not account for, at a short distance, through the forest, caught his eye. He was able to distinguish neither what it was nor the nature of its employment; though it was his opinion it belonged to the order "man." Influenced by this belief, and that he might no longer remain in his present state of ignorance, he drew near. As he did so, it became evident he was correct in his surmise; and a clear scrutiny revealed his ward, George Washington, whose motive for present action seemed to be to conceal something in the earth. He, hearing the sound of approaching footsteps, hastily sprang to his feet. The "Gineral," as he had now been dubbed by his sable compeers, after gazing for a moment in utter consternation on the intruder, bore himself away in a very unsoldierly manner.

The first thought of Justus was, that the negro

was concealing the lost paper, and he did not delay a moment in instituting a search. The precise spot, owing to operations not having been completed, was readily found. The first indication of the work carried on was a portion of loose dirt, the former resting-place of which he was at a loss to determine; but soon found a small sod that had been taken up unbroken, and afterward replaced. Removing this, he found a small hole well-nigh filled with earth that had been dug from it; and still beneath that, in a bed of grass, carefully placed for its reception, was—surprising sight!—not the bill of sale, but his own watch! which, till that moment, he had thought safe in McMinime's possession. After congratulating himself on his good fortune, he found time to devote a few thoughts to matters connected with Sambo. They were something on this wise: "What an unaccountable villain that Sambo is! And can it be possible that this is the selection for an associate I have made in this new State of Texas? Fortunate, indeed, is it for me that our connection is ended!" How he came in possession of the watch, was a question more easily asked than answered, though this was matter of but little concern, as it had now found its way into the hands of its proper owner.

Then came a sudden damper over his joy, in the

thought that perhaps, under the circumstances, it would not be proper for him to keep the treasure; for did it not in reality belong to Mr. McMinime until there should be a fair settlement between them? Was there not a certain condition yet to be performed, in agreement with a solemn obligation, before he could claim the restoration of his pledge? And had not the other party refused to release him from his contract?

Still there was another light in which the matter could be viewed: it was not through any misconduct of his own he had failed to comply with his engagements. He had been robbed by the very person for whose sake he had entered into the contract—for whose acts the master should certainly be responsible. A further consideration was, he would cause no loss to any one by retaining what *he* had come honestly by. He had returned Mr. McMinime's servant, and was ready to refund the money; and though the bill of sale was out of pocket, being lost, it could never be presented to the injury of any one, even if he were capable of harboring such a thought. So, every thing duly considered, he persuaded himself he would be doing nothing but right to keep the watch, making no disclosures.

Meanwhile, a somewhat similar event had transpired at the house. McMinime was sitting in the piazza, with an open book in his hand. But, though his eyes wandered over the page, his thoughts were not engaged with its contents: they were on the transactions of the last few days. The wholesome advice of his friend, 'Squire Brown, occurred to him. "What shall I do now?" he exclaimed. "I expect the fellow intends to act honestly, and has really lost the paper. He must be released from his suspense." Then, in spite of his perplexities, he could not restrain a hearty laugh at the thought of the ludicrous adventures of Justus. The laugh was interrupted by his little daughter, who came running to him exclaiming, "O Pa! what is this? I found it where the gentleman emptied his saddle-bags;" at the same time holding out to him a folded paper. Eagerly opening it, it proved to be the document, the loss of which had been so much lamented.

"Now I am safe," he said. "And knowing that Mr. Abolition has no evil design, I will hesitate no longer to comply with his wishes. But I will say nothing about the finding of this paper until a settlement is effected; for he has, by his criminal meddling, deserved all the mental suffering its loss could bring."

At this moment, a neighbor, with whom he had a business settlement to arrange, called on him;

and putting the paper in the book, he placed it away, intending, at his leisure, to secure it more carefully. The arrangement was effected, and the neighbor took his departure ere Justus, the tumult of his mind partially quieted, joined McMinime at the house. He was ready, on his part, to agree to aught the other might propose, provided he could only be freed from his obligation. But as the matter had been deferred to the following day, and as it was not in his power to offer any more favorable terms than he had already presented, he disposed himself to endure the suspense until the time should have arrived. McMinime, however, was not inclined so long to afflict him.

"I have been thinking, Mr. Justus," he said, "of this case. I cannot believe it is your intention to deal unfairly with me; and knowing you must feel some inquietude about your bond, I have concluded, if it suits your convenience, to make an even exchange, saying nothing about the bill of sale."

"The very thing, sir, that *will* suit my convenience! Not only so, but I will feel myself under obligations to you for thus freeing me from so great a trouble." He debated the question in his mind, whether to disclose the finding of the watch, or to keep it a secret; but not looking sufficiently into the future to see what might grow out of it, and thinking only of an offset to the lost paper, he said nothing.

"I will bring the articles at once," said McMinime, proceeding at the same time to perform his promise. Justus nerved himself to hear with as much surprise as might be the announcement which he knew was to be made. He soon returned, surprise and vexation depicted on his countenance. "Mr. Justus," he exclaimed, "we are strangely beset— the watch is gone! I have kept it locked up in my secretary, and no longer ago than to-day I saw it there. Surprised by your approach, I left the secretary unlocked, and, as the consequence, the time-piece is gone—stolen, of course. Here are the documents I received of you. You can give me my receipt for the watch, which is all I ask in case it is not recovered."

Justus was not so well prepared for this ordeal as to endure it with any thing like the calmness he desired. And the natural surprise he wished to assume degenerated into open confusion, unobserved by the other only in consequence of his own. But having commenced acting a part, it must be sustained. He replied:

"Not particularly for its intrinsic value, but for association's sake, I could hardly meet with a loss more to be regretted; yet, if it is out of your power to return the watch, I must be content. I might with reason object to such a settlement, yet, in emulation of your generosity, waive the point. Here are your receipt and money; the bill of sale so strangely lost must stand in lieu of the missing watch."

"The receipt will do at present," answered the other; "retain the money until morning, when, if your pledge is not found, I will return you its full value. Being last in my possession, it is but proper that I should sustain the loss."

CHAPTER X.

DIAMOND CUT DIAMOND.

"Lead us not into temptation."

THE eventful day had closed, and as the hour for repose drew on, Justus was shown to his apartment. Not feeling inclined to sleep, he took up a book with which to amuse himself, and while carelessly turning the leaves, a loose paper fell out. Picking it up, it presented a familiar appearance, when a hasty glance proved it to be the mysteriously missing bill of sale.

"What on earth can that black scoundrel mean!" was his sudden ejaculation. Then a light broke upon his mind—he had not put the paper in his pocket-book, but had placed it inside of a small blank-book, carefully laid in his saddle-bags. And how he had managed so entirely to forget this circumstance was beyond his comprehension. He now concluded the negro had in all probability never seen it, and the only solution he could offer for the question of its present whereabouts, was that it must have been dropped while making his examination. There McMinime himself had undoubtedly found it.

Anger at the palpable duplicity of his host banished every other emotion. "Very generous, no doubt, to compromise, with every advantage; but we shall see who is the winner," muttered he.

Without troubling himself to reason on the morality of his course, as a matter of retaliation, he took possession of the document; yet it is but doing him justice to say he had no intention of using improperly the power given him by its possession.

He now felt that, as an act of mercy to the suspected and really guilty negro, the finding of the watch should be disclosed; but the "flagrant double-dealing" of McMinime deterred him.

Early on the following day, Sambo was called upon for information respecting the missing watch, of which, as a matter of course, he expressed profound ignorance. Nor could either persuasion or threat draw any thing else from him than that "he had n't *seed* no watch, an' did n't know nuf 'n 'bout it nudder."

His baffled master seemed in inexplicable perplexity. That Sambo was the thief he did not doubt, for there was no one else to whom it could be reasonably charged; but how to make him acknowledge, and reveal the place of its concealment, seemed beyond his power. It was true, he had gained his end on the previous day by a desperate resort, but such remedies would not answer when too frequently applied. There was, then, but one hope: if the prospect of a severe chastisement should not frighten him into a disclosure, it must be inflicted, and that failing, it would be useless longer to contend.

"Sambo, this is the last time I will ask. Tell me what you have done with the watch, or you may regret it. I do not wish to whip you, but must do so, and that severely too, unless you at once tell all about it."

"I dunno, Mas' Tom, wah no watch is. I haint *seed* no watch."

At this moment, McMinime received a message from his wife, requiring his immediate attendance at the house. He obeyed the summons, remarking, "Here, Mr. Justus, take charge of this fellow till I return. Possibly you may be able to learn something."

He found the lady highly excited, who, holding something in her hand, exclaimed,

"Just look here! Is not this strange?"

"Why, what can be the matter, that you are so earnest?" Then, as he drew near, he saw the *watch*, the identical article for which Sambo was now in duress.

"Where in the world did you find that, wife?"

"Betty, while arranging the room in which the stranger slept, heard the ticking of a watch in his saddlebags, and, knowing the circumstances connected with that gentleman's pledge, without stopping to consider the propriety of the act, brought it at once to me."

"The villain!" he exclaimed, taking it into his hand, to assure himself of its identity. "How this thing could have come into his possession exceeds my calculation: he surely cannot be guilty of an act so nearly resembling theft!" And, indeed, he remembered that, previous to the time of missing the watch, Justus had not been in the room. "Sambo is concerned in this. Here, Betty, put this thing where you found it;" and, administering a well-deserved reprimand to the servant, he rejoined his guest.

It was his intention to inform Justus of the new discovery, and at once dismiss the business; but on his return, he learned from the latter that Sambo had confessed the theft, and had promised to show the place of deposit. Curious to witness the denouement, he withheld his disclosure, and signified his willingness to join in the search.

Sambo had no difficulty in finding the place, and his surprise and alarm were apparent at the absence of the article he had there deposited.

Justus himself affected surprise, and inquiringly said,

"Are you certain, Sambo, that this is the place, or that no one saw you? Perhaps you were observed, and the watch stolen from its place of concealment."

McMinime had said nothing. His surprise exceeded even that of Sambo, though not from the same cause. He well knew the watch was not there, but was astonished at the manner of its leaving. Suddenly the negro exclaimed:

"I 'spect Mas' Justus, he foun' it; he say 'e seed me a *hiden* it."

"You must not talk so of Mr. Justus, Sambo. Had he found it, he would have informed me, knowing how deeply I am interested——"

The tone of irony changed, and the gentleman paused, as he reflected how nearly he himself occupied the position about to be charged to his guest, who, although in possession of the watch, might, at the proper time, make satisfactory explanation.

"I 'spec' he did doe, Mas' Tom," persisted the negro. "He tell me 'e know I hide it, an' give me dis to show it;" exhibiting, at the same time, a silver coin.

The hiring of Sambo to show the watch was the effect of a sudden impulse, to save him from the threatened punishment, without a thought to the inevitable result: no sooner had it been effected, than the after consideration, presenting itself, would have led him to cancel the bargain, but the return of the master at that moment left him no alternative.

Evidently confused, the other replied, "Yes; while walking yesterday, I observed some one, who seemed disposed to keep himself and operations concealed; and, as I approached nearer, he fled precipitately. Learning the watch was gone, I felt Sambo was the thief; and wishing to shield him from the punishment you threatened, I intimated my knowledge of his crime, and induced him to show where he had lodged the stolen article."

This speech established to McMinime's satisfaction the duplicity of the abolitionist. Previous to this moment there was some slight grounds for suspecting Sambo's agency in the finding of the watch among the baggage of the other, but his own admission, together with his carefully guarded language and embarrassed manner, too clearly indicated his guilt.

Smothering his anger and contempt, he determined to dispose of the matter at once, and forthwith dismiss the abolitionist, whose longer stay would evidently lead to trouble. Turning to the slave, he sharply asked.

"Did you receive that money from this gentleman for bringing us here?"

"Yes suh; Mas' Justus gib it to me to show 'im whah 'bouts I hid de watch."

"Hand it back to him instantly. I do not hire people about me to commit rascality."

Justus interposed, as the negro reluctantly extended the money:

"O, sir, never mind; I would prefer that he should be allowed to keep it."

"Never mind, *you:* I do not wish my servants hired to steal. Receive it from him; for he shall not retain it under any consideration. And now, sir," he continued, "after redeeming my promise, and paying for your lost watch, our connection will be at an end, and you can depart at your earliest convenience."

Justus was not really dishonest, and, though taunted by the words of the slave-owner, could not allow himself to accept his offer. Could he have indeed foreseen the termination of the affair, he would at first have disclosed his discovery of the watch; but, under the present phase of things, that was not to be thought of.

"No," he replied; "I will not take advantage of the generous offer, made after the bill of sale had left my possession. I will try and evince as much liberality as yourself."

"A very proper spirit," half sneeringly remarked the other; "but recollect that our truce has ended, and I wish no more of my hands corrupted."

CHAPTER XI.

AN UNEXPECTED MEETING.

"Et tu, Brute!"

AGAIN the abolitionist addressed himself to the task of carrying out, as he considered it, the harsh and unjust order received at the camp-meeting, to "leave the country." Since the failure of his late experiment, he had abandoned the thought of a return to Boston—his object being, to seek some other and more favorable location at which to conduct his observations. Whether or not this was in accordance with his inclination, it was now a necessary measure, as he had rashly exposed himself as a man possessed of principles dangerous to the interests of the community. To be able, then, to conduct his future work in safety, he must remove beyond the reach of those in whose vicinity this reprehensible part was enacted.

He had entirely recovered his enthusiasm; and the thought of abandoning his efforts in the cause of humanity—which, during his perplexity on Sambo's account, had more than once occurred—was now, if possible, at a farther remove than ever before. His views, however, during his brief sojourn in the South, had undergone a slight modification; and he did not now feel willing to impute to every one owning slaves all the crimes which he had ever been wont to associate with the names of those whom, in his ignorance, he had been accustomed to hear execrated, and to denounce himself, under the title of "*slaveholder.*"

As remodelled, his creed admitted that those owning slaves by inheritance, where the laws did not admit their liberation, might perhaps retain them in servitude, treating them kindly, without wrong; notwithstanding the thing *itself* was no less evil—the responsibility being merely shifted to another quarter. This being his opinion, it was still, with him, a righteous act to restore a slave to freedom by any means whatever.

It may be thought this change was a matter of small importance; but to Justus it assumed a very serious aspect, and bade fair to compromise him with his Massachusetts friends, with whose opinions in this respect he was in direct conflict. The result of his change, when communicated, was considered by them such a defection, that many

entirely discarded him; and an association, formed
by a number of young men anxious to contribute
their mite to the cause of philanthropy, by assisting
in preparing for the press, and publishing, a work
on the horrors of slavery, was at once broken up—
thus leaving Justus to depend on his own exertions.

With his change of views came also the percep-
tion of the necessity for an alteration in the plan of
his incipient work, or a material addition thereto.
He had previously thought a full exposure of
slavery was alone necessary to cause its hideousness
fully to appear, and the practice to be for ever abandoned; but finding in the system circumstances
that in some measure justified those concerned with
it, something more than a simple *exposure* was
needed for its suppression. In regard to the exact
nature of the change demanded, his ideas were
rather vague. However, to invent and discuss a
plan by which the difficulties in the way of emancipation might be removed, and the whole slave
population liberated, was the matter for consideration. To carry out this design would require a long
and close examination, not only of the system of
slavery, but of the whole workings of Southern
institutions. For this he resolved to labor—con-
fining himself to no one locality, but selecting tem-

porary residences wherever he might be able to effect any thing bearing on this great mission.

While engaged in this manner, marking out his future course of action, and fancifully depicting his success, he was wending his way, he knew not whither; but as the distance between him and McMinime's was rapidly lengthening, it gave him no concern. Having made up his mind to commit his movements for the present to chance, or Providence, and being on a public thoroughfare, which must needs conduct him to a shelter for the night, further anxiety on the subject was abandoned.

The day at length wore away; and as the sun was sinking from sight, the gratifying prospect of pleasant quarters, in the appearance of a very attractive residence, cheered the tired traveller. His request for accommodations met with a prompt response; but scarcely had his feet touched the ground, when a friendly hand was extended, and a familiar voice exclaimed: "Why, Justus! Bless my life! Where did you spring from?"

A warm grasp of the hand, and the answering response, "Well done, Sampson!" gave intimation that friends had met.

Mr. Sampson was one of Justus's Boston associates, but had been for some few years settled in

Texas. The joy of the latter was unbounded in thus meeting in a strange land a warm personal friend, whose education and former associations well qualified him to sympathize in his present object and misfortune.

"I am really glad to see you, Justus," said his host; "you have arrived very opportunely, too. My brother George, whom I have not seen since you and I parted, came also to-day: we will have a merry meeting."

"Nothing for many a day, I assure you, has given me so much pleasure as this circumstance," replied Justus, who mentally continued, "Nor will our pleasure be marred by the sight and presence of the poor oppressed slave."

"Jake!"

"Sah!"

"Come take this horse!"

"Yes, sah!"

This colloquy broke into the reflections of the abolitionist; and, as a stout, well-fed African made his appearance in obedience to the summons, he could not repress a sigh at human inconsistency established in the fact before him, of his friend's connection with the hated thing of slavery.

On entering the house, he met the mistress of the dwelling and the younger Sampson, both of whom he had known previously.   For a while the conversation was general; referring to former years and the scenes of early life, it was of a most interesting character.

"Have you become tired of a city life, Carolus, and resolved to make your home in our young State?" asked the elder brother, "or have you merely come, like George here, on a pleasure trip?"   Justus explained the design of his visit, which was received by the questioner with a quiet smile.   This was annoying to the abolitionist, who was anxious to read his friend a lecture on the subject, but was perplexed for a proper starting-point.   The younger brother asking something in regard to the wages of workmen, happily opened the way, and he accordingly inquired:

"John, how much by the month do you pay that negro man you have here?"

A still broader smile than before was the only answer, while the younger brother indignantly assumed the reply:

"Why, he gives him just what he can *eat*, and the few clothes he wears."

"It surely cannot be possible that he *owns* him! he who once so bitterly denounced slavery and slaveholders, and whom I have so often heard declare, in the language of Cowper:

'I had much rather be myself the slave,
      And wear the bonds, than fasten them on him.' "

"Yes, sir, not only possible, but actually *certain*. That thing he calls Jake, stuck in that cabin yonder, is his *slave*, as well as Mrs. Jake ——, whatever he may be pleased to call her; and some two or three little Jakes. And, to tell you the truth, though I have not seen him for years, I have been vexed and grieved with him ever since I first set foot in his yard. And, on this account, I really do not think I can afford to make my visit half so long as I had intended."

"Gentlemen, just allow me to inform you that you know nothing in regard to the matter of which you are talking. Remember I was once as full of such notions as yourselves, and equally honest in them. But a little observation has convinced me that, though such fine sentiments as those of mine just alluded to may sound very pretty in some localities, they are but little, if any, short of nonsense: they do not harmonize with the actualities of life, either in the past or present."

"I am really *ashamed*, John, no less than surprised at such language; and still more so at your actions. Indeed, I am really *horrified* at the thought."

"Well, my dear brother, can you inform me what it is that so strongly excites your horror ?"

"Simply the diabolical thing your laws recognize by the hateful word *slavery;* and more especially my brother's connection with it."

"Beg your pardon; you do not state the case exactly; it would be more proper to say the name denoting the thing, etc. For you can view with complacency what is no less horrific in reality, only bearing a different *name*—never mind that, though. But why, of all the multiplied ills of life, have you selected slavery as the object of your philanthropy, or, selecting this, by what means do you design to mitigate its evils?"

"Emancipation!" ejaculated the others in chorus. "Nothing can be plainer than that this would effectually remove the evils of this scourge to humanity."

"Perhaps this might be a summary process of dispensing with slavery in its present form, but it would inevitably originate evils of a deeper grade and more pernicious influence. To say nothing of the thousands of vicious beings, now properly restrained, with the worst passions of depraved human nature developed in their largest forms, turned loose upon society to swell the catalogue of crimes, and more deeply corrupt the world, the loss to the industrial resources of the country where slave-labor is so well rewarded would be only one of the many calamities, far more fatal in its effects than all the imaginary ills of the present system of slavery combined. Shut up the brothels at home, that entice to licentiousness and crime; close your gambling-hells and drinking-saloons, that lead to degradation and death in their most revolting forms, before you begin a crusade against the fancied ills afflicting the happy negro, existing only in the wild vagaries of fanatical folly."

"But ours is a free country," replied Justus; "and men have an undoubted right to spend their leisure time in such amusements or enjoyments as they think befitting; and the law throws around them its strong protection, if in their excesses they violate none of its obligations."

"If you justify a course of moral evil, because upheld and protected by civil law, shall we not plead the sanctions of the same law in vindication of our rights? Rights, too, nowhere in the canons of inspired truth denounced as moral evil. Our slaves are our property, purchased as such, and taxed as other property; and if personal rights and enjoyments are not by government to be infringed, our rights in this respect are as sacred and inviolable as the titles to our homesteads. But apart from all this, what good can you see accruing to the slave by his emancipation?"

"What? why, sir, tens of thousands of most miserable beings will be restored to freedom and happiness."

" Does your experience tell you that the condition of the free negro is sufficiently in advance of that of our servants to justify the experiment? The idle, dissolute, and wretched condition of the larger portion of this class of society, is a sad comment on the freedom and happiness you are so anxious they should enjoy; while the oft-repeated efforts for the liberation and elevation of the slave show an improper expenditure of false sympathy, that, benefiting no one, has conduced to untold evil to the unfortunate slave, who, formerly contented and happy in his lot, finds himself in a condition where his natural imbecility offers too weak a resistance against the force of temptation to indolence and degradation continually besetting him."

" Yes, but there are exceptions. Look at the men of note among the free negroes—Douglas, etc."

"But how few such men do you find among the many thousands of free negroes, compared to the vast crowd of the worthless vagabonds to be met with! That there are some intelligent men among the former class is no evidence that freedom develops their capacity or talents; for many an honest slave rises far above the standard of mediocrity among his own race.   There is my neighbor Smith's 'Uncle Abe,' who, though a slave, has learned to read very well; and if he cannot equal a Bascom in preaching powers, he is yet held in no mean estimation even by his white brethren.   Why, sir, if this man could be so far corrupted as to escape to the North—which has been more than once attempted—he would be lionized, not only by the rabble, but his name would figure, with laudatory commendations of his genius, in all the abolition prints of the country.   And there is Stout's 'Brother Ben,' not a whit behind him, besides others whom I could mention in my limited acquaintance."

"Well, I cannot say they are all persons of intelligence, nor yet that they are all outwardly in a condition to enjoy life to the best advantage.   But this is not confined to themselves alone—there is unhappiness the world over; but the chances for happiness among the blacks you must acknowledge to be in favor of the free negroes."

"I can acknowledge nothing of the kind; for freedom alone cannot supply the comforts of life. Good slaves are one of the happiest classes of people.   Their few wants are all supplied, and, content with their situation, they have but little to annoy them.   Now, there is that poor Jake you are so deeply pitying, as happy a man, I have no doubt, as can well be found. If you wish to see a picture of earthly bliss and contentment, you should, unobserved, mark him among his family, after the labors of the day. And, in the general, so far as my observations have enabled me to judge, I believe the condition of the free negroes at the North is infinitely worse than that of our slaves.

"But come; let us choose some other topic of conversation. This is but a waste of breath. You will never be able to effect the change you desire here, and I am more than willing for *you* to hold just such opinions as suit you."

"What does that mean?" asked Justus, as a voice engaged in earnest prayer rose on the still air, but too indistinctly heard to convey the import of the words.

"That," said the elder brother, "is the ' *thing* Jake,' at his evening devotions, and, if you have no objections, we will walk out and take a stand nearer, that we may hear what he has to say." They assented, and the two silently left the room.

The strangers to Jake were astonished at the fervency of his petitions, and the apparent gratefulness evinced for the mercies acknowledged. Among the objects of special supplication, the master and mistress were affectionately mentioned, together with the strangers sojourning for the night. The

fervor of an honest heart was expressed in the simple, touching pathos of his voice, while his language
betokened a degree of intelligence hardly to be expected in one of his condition.

At the close of the prayer, he began a hymn in a
rich, clear, melodious voice, in which the mellow,
sweet tones of his wife joined. As the singing
proceeded, the visitors stood spell-bound under the
influence of deep emotion. The interest deepened
as, with evident feeling, was warbled forth,

> "The things eternal I pursue—
> A happiness beyond the view
>   Of those that basely pant
> For things by nature felt and seen:
> Their honors, wealth, and pleasures mean
>   I neither have nor want.
>
> No foot of land do I possess,
> No cottage in this wilderness;
>   A poor wayfaring man,
> I lodge a while in tents below,
> Or gladly wander to and fro
>   Till I my Canaan gain."

The singing ended. At the suggestion of the
owner, they entered the cabin. Both Jake and
Hetty seemed surprised at the visit, but received
the gentlemen with frank politeness.

"Jake," said his master, "these gentlemen have
taken a notion that you are a miserably unhappy
being. Is it so?"

At this remark Hetty quietly laughed, and remarked, in an undertone, sufficiently loud to be heard,

"Mis'able, indeed! I'd like to know what put dat in dar heads."

Jake answered, "No, indeed, Mas' John; I b'leve I's as happy a person as lives. I jis hope they's no more mis'able than I is. Why they think so?"

"They seem to think you would be glad of a chance to leave me, and set up business on your own hook, or to be free."

"They's as much mistaken thar as before. I dunno what I might wish, Mas' John, if I did not know I ain't fit for nuf'n else than jis what I is; but I'm well satisfied with that. Contentment's better'n any thing else, an' this makes me happy."

After a few more words, the party withdrew, with a kind "Good-night."

The argument was not renewed, and from the serious and silent manners of the guests, it was evident they were busy with their own reflections. Conversation being thus at an end, the party soon separated and retired for the night.

After a few days spent agreeably, Justus took his leave, pleased at the result of his providential meeting, in which he had seen slavery in a new phase, and obtained some further insight into the arguments employed in its favor. As he rode slowly down the lane, he mentally exclaimed, "Who would have thought, five years ago, that this man, then so zealous in the cause of freedom, would at this time actually be a *slaveholder!*   But the weakness of some men is to be pitied. Their principles too easily give way under the influence of temptation or evil association."

CHAPTER XII.

PROFITABLE EMPLOYMENT.

"Delightful task! to rear the tender thought,
And teach the young idea how to shoot."

THE questions, "What shall I eat? what shall I drink? and wherewithal shall I be clothed?" are rather of an undignified character, having neither poetry nor romance connected with them; yet, under certain circumstances, will they be ever recurring. The condition of Mr. Justus at this time was such as to make these ideas rather prominent in his calculations; for, on taking an exact inventory of all his available means, he found the solution of these questions, beyond a very limited period, an extremely difficult problem.

His reduced state of finances was owing to a failure in receiving remittances; and as relief from this quarter was still uncertain, it became important to decide on some pursuit by which to supply present wants, at least, if not to provide for future operations. He had never marked out his sphere with the common herd, and was wholly unprepared to delve; yet, possessing great self-reliance, with considerable ability, he felt assured success in some calling awaited him.

Though at first quite repugnant to his feeling, the vocation of teacher was selected; and, as the least objectionable form of that employment, he decided on securing the post of private tutor in some respectable and wealthy family. This arrangement was happily effected, and he found himself pleasantly domiciliated in the family of Mr. Holmes, an intelligent planter, with a large number of slaves; affording him the opportunity, while at his legitimate business, to conduct his previously-prescribed course of observation.

The residence was in a beautiful and fertile section of country, rather sparsely populated—the cause of former failures to support a school. This, together with a preference of the gentleman for having his children taught at home, made Justus's application quite opportune.

His pupils were agreeable, and the task of instruction, which he feared would be irksome, turned out in reality to be a pleasant recreation. Rosalind, a sweet girl of fifteen, handsome and intelligent, was quite well advanced, yet requiring some future assistance, especially in music. Leonidas, some two years younger, rather neglected since leaving their Virginia home, had not made much proficiency; while Semiramis, Isabella, and Theodore were more youthful disciples, and yet in the rudiments.

Having been taught prudence by his former experience, the real character of the tutor was not suspected. Possessed of a handsome person and agreeable manners, he formed a welcome addition to the household, while the faithful performance of his allotted duties gave universal satisfaction. His charge were much the same as other young people, requiring the patience of their teacher to conquer the aversion of the younger portion to study, and break them of a fondness for sport and other irregularities, to which juveniles are so much inclined.

Justus met with marked success in his new pursuit. The facility with which he wrought his way into the affections of his pupils, and made himself acquainted with their natural inclination and peculiarities, was astonishing, even to himself; while their rapid advancement was matter of sincere gratulation, as insuring the extension of the good opinion his success had already created. Indeed, so strongly did these facts arrest his attention, that occasionally doubts would arise whether he had not mistaken his proper sphere of action; and if he would not be able to confer more benefit on his kind as instructor of youth, than by all the abolition efforts he could make. Yet these thoughts were but momentary; his settled purpose being, by all means in his power, to advance the great object of his life—the work which he fondly hoped was to strike the death-blow to slavery. He was, therefore, as far as a strict regard for prudence would permit, ever on the alert for whatever might further his undertaking.

His operations at the camp-meeting were of too notorious and exciting a character to be soon forgotten, or confined to the locality witnessing them. They found their way into the public journals, and he was subjected to more than one ordeal, in listening to the various current versions of the affair, and the invariably accompanying strictures. At one time, soon after becoming an inmate of Mr. Holmes's family, while seated in the parlor, that gentleman, after a sudden hearty laugh, handed to Justus a newspaper from which he had been reading, remarking: "Just read that, will you?"

His excitement prevented the discovery of Justus's confusion as he read:

"A GOOD ONE.—We learn from a late exchange

that a gentleman direct from the North was recently found at a camp-meeting, near one of our county towns, endeavoring to persuade slaves to abscond. It is said he had obtained the consent of one or two to accompany him to a free State; when he was taken in hand, and treated to a ride on a rail and a dip in the creek. We have no later advices from this worthy, but presume this mode of treatment has cooled his ardor, and put it into his head to return home. It may be, however, that he is trying his fortunes in some other portion of the State, and our readers would do well to look sharp."

Justus of course joined in the laugh, but the sound was its only reality; and in that, he was not far behind Holmes himself.

"It is really strange to me," said Holmes, "that these abolitionists will expose themselves to such risks in their madness. Some of them, too, with an energy worthy of a better cause."

"Perhaps," replied Justus, recovering his self-possession, "they may *think* their cause a good one. Otherwise their earnestness seems unaccountable."

"Perhaps they may; but this does not at all excuse them."

Quite on his guard, the abolitionist warily

replied: "I did not say, by any means, that it did."

Holmes was soon again absorbed in his paper, and the subject was allowed to rest.

CHAPTER XIII.

TOO CONSERVATIVE.

"How look I,
That I should seem to lack humanity
So much as this fact comes to?"

Justus considered his present engagement only
in the light of a short digression from his proper
course, which he would resume so soon as the
receipt of funds, shortly expected, should enable
him to do so. But his hopes were scattered by one
fell blow of fate. It has been stated that he had
informed his friends of some slight change in his
views in regard to Southern slavery; and that they,
considering it a matter of vast importance, had
abandoned him as one whose principles they could
not endorse, and by whose labors in the field of
abolitionism they could not hope to prosper. The
sad blow came from this quarter. Up to this time
he had received no official information as to the
manner of the reception of his communications;
yet he did not imagine there was any thing in them

objectionable, coming as they did from so staunch a friend to the slave as himself. For weary weeks he had been looking for the remittance and cheering words of comfort and encouragement. At length his hopes seemed about to be realized, and the long-expected letter came. With joyful eagerness he broke the seal—heart-chilling discovery! There was not the pecuniary aid he expected; there were no cordial salutations, but merely these cold words:

"A letter received from you in Texas needs no explanation. We can only say we were pained to receive such a communication ; for we *did* consider *you* an incorruptible philanthropist. Yet we cannot esteem any man who can be so suddenly changed, and to the extent your communication indicates, as longer worthy our confidence. Our advice would be, to return home before you become fully imbued with the principles you sought to combat, if it be not already too late to save yourself. For, when one of our party can make the admission that slaves can be *innocently* held in bondage, he is in a fair way himself to become a *slaveholder!*

"You will understand that the association formed to aid in publishing a work on the horrors of slavery no longer exists; and we would at no time be surprised to learn that your noble mission had been prostituted to a defence of said devilish system.

"Yours, etc."

For a while the mortified abolitionist felt overpowered with indignation; and hurriedly pacing the room, he tore the unconscious missive to ribbons.

"And has it come to this?" he said. "The taunt of that puff of a Southerner, who insinuated a probability of a change in my views, was hard enough to bear! but that my *friends* should impeach my consistency, is more than I can bear! *I* become a slaveholder! *I* write a work in *defence* of slavery! I! who, for love of the slave, have voluntarily exiled myself; who, in the very stronghold of the 'dark power,' have dared risk my life to show him what he is, and what he might be; and who can demonstrate that dangers have been braved, and the binding obligation of a solemn oath assumed, in the face of difficulties, for the purpose of freeing only one of this unfortunate class!

"But let them go. I can do without them, and they shall know it. They did me a kindness by assisting me in the outset; but that shall be repaid. Then, if I wish to become a slaveholder, they will share none of its responsibility. *A slaveholder!* Was I not a slaveholder when under oath to liberate the ungrateful Sambo? and have I not that now in my possession which still proves me to be one? But has this affected my consistency? Am I not as loyal to my principles as ever? Yes! and nothing could ever induce me to use my power but the opportunity of giving to that individual the liberty he seems so lightly to esteem."

A letter was speedily penned by the persecuted philanthropist, embodying the substance of the above reflections; containing, besides, an account of the prominent points in his transactions with McMinime and Sambo. He regretted his friends could not see things through the medium his position offered, and that he should be condemned for opinions to which he had been irresistibly driven, and which they themselves would embrace, with his opportunity of observation. His book was still to be forthcoming; and, so far from being a *defence* of slavery, it would expose more fully the other side of the question than originally contemplated. He concluded with the hope that their hasty decision would injure neither him nor his great work.

His long-cherished hopes of assistance being thus cut off, he found consolation in the thought that whatever honors might attach to the production of such a volume, would rest alone on himself. Yet he saw he had been too sanguine in his expectation of an early completion of the work; for, though in the midst of the field in which his materials were to be collected, his supply fell far short of his calculations; and he even found himself several times on the point of admitting that the system with which he warred might have some grounds for defence. But on such occasions he would reason that he had been permitted to see only the milder forms of its workings; but that in his further investigations its true character would certainly be developed.

While suffering under his wrongs, and laboring against his various disappointments, he had been led to hesitate, and even at one time contemplate the entire abandonment of the enterprise; yet his determination in his calmer moments was, that it must be carried on at all hazards.

As yet the work was in a chaotic state, but the plan was duly arranged, and the thrilling annals of untold sufferings to be forthcoming would tingle the ears of an outraged community.

In the quiet of his city home, Justus had never thought of such a thing as mirth or enjoyment among the poor overwrought slaves of the South.

It was more in consonance with his tenets to picture them groping their way to their wretched
hovels, and still more wretched beds, after being
driven from early morn till far towards the "noon
of night," by some grim overseer; having perhaps
been subjected, previously to being allowed this poor
luxury, to a most brutal castigation, to gratify the
gust for such sport of his inhuman master.   His astonishment may then be imagined, in witnessing the
scenes detailed in the following chapter.

CHAPTER XIV.

THE WEDDING.

"On with the dance!   Let mirth be unconfined."

THERE were preparations for some kind of merry-making going on at Mr. Holmes's, the nature of which Justus was at some loss to determine. Judging from the unusual bustle in the kitchen, observable in his passing about, it was no common matter. Under ordinary circumstances he would have felt no concern for any thing of the kind; but on the present occasion he had an anxiety to know the cause—one, too, which the coveted knowledge would at once have dissipated. One of his pupils was but a small portion of the usual time under his superintendence. This, together with the other signs visible, led him to fear that the young lady was about to be removed altogether from his charge—an event by no means delightful to contemplate. For in the midst of his arduous labors of giving instruction to his younger and more thoughtless pupils, the agreeable manners of Rosalind, and the force of her example on the others, made her an auxiliary in the work; to say nothing of the pleasure it afforded to have it in his power to communicate instruction to one so eager to receive, and so prompt to appreciate the efforts made for her benefit. He found himself far less than ordinarily satisfied with his position while surrounded by his now diminished class. To the communicativeness of little Isabella he owed it that he was not long suffered to remain in suspense as to the cause of his disquiet. Having learned the same herself, she could not be satisfied until her tutor was informed that "Sis. Rosalind" was helping to make Sue's wedding-dress. Little did she imagine the satisfaction her words gave. Justus was now at ease, so far as his former fears were concerned, and had only to regret the days yet to pass before his school-room would possess its wonted attraction.

"Sue," he knew as the "house-girl," whose sprightliness and perfect contentedness, together with the neatness of all her arrangements, had often attracted his attention. Yet so rejoiced was he at the information received, that it was some time ere he could recollect himself sufficiently to make the proper reflections on the singular interest manifested in a slave marriage.

Days wore on, and the one so anxiously prepared for was at length ushered in. As the evening drew near, Justus was surprised to see crowds of negroes, comprising, as he rightly estimated, all in the entire neighborhood, wending their way to the residence of Mr. Holmes. They came, some on foot, some on horseback, in merry groups, making the circumjacent woods ring with their pleasant jokes and hearty laughs, accompanied ever and anon by snatches of song, religious or otherwise, according to the taste of the singer. And from different groups, or from different persons in the same group, would arise at the same time, in tones of real melody, some devotional strain, such as,

"Alas! and did my Saviour bleed!"

and,

" Git out o' de way, ole Dan Tucker,"

or something kindred to it; each gallant, the meanwhile, most assiduous in attentions to his "fair" partner. Occasionally a colloquy, something on the following order, would engage the attention of and afford momentary amusement for the whole party:

"Hello, Bill, whah you recon Tony is now?"

"Ah! boy, dat mor'n dis chile know; but 'spec he's sneakin 'bout somewhah, laf'n' at de way he cut me out. But jis see 'f I don't fix 'im for it; I'll break 'is neck, or shoot 'um off at de knees. To go right by me, an' take Miss Susan 'way, for all he know'd I 'd a liked to a had her myself."

"So rock de cradle, Lucy,
And listen to my song,"

he sings.

"Yah, yah! Hurrah for Tony!"

Arrived near the premises, all noisy mirth ceased, and, entering the yard in perfect order, they disposed themselves according to their several tastes, to pass the time most pleasantly till the important moment should arrive.

Justus saw and heard the rabble, as he termed it, approaching in the height of their glee and noise; nor could he at first divine the meaning of this vast turnout, unless it might be that the poor, oppressed slave had at length resolved on a general rise for the purpose of vindicating his rights.

You may smile at his simplicity, plain matter-of-fact reader; yet such a thing actually possessed his mind until, bethinking himself of their pacific appearance, as well as of the gay visitors recently arrived in the persons of some of their masters and mistresses, who had preceded them in their carriages, he began to receive new light. He now recollected having heard something in regard to a wedding

that was to take place; and though not before
dreaming of such a parade over the affair, the conviction at length settled upon him that this in fact
was the cause of the present influx of sable faces.
Then he mused:

"What in the world does Holmes mean in collecting all this rout on his premises? A pretty time
there will be here to-night, truly! It will be surprising if the poor untaught wretches do not tear down
his house, or perform some other outrageous act."

But when they put on their grave demeanor upon
nearing the house, his astonishment took a different
turn, being surprised that they should so becomingly
conduct themselves. He then, too, first found leisure to observe their outfit, which in nowise diminished his surprise. For though not regulated
by any particular fashion, but of all styles and
colors, there was quite an imposing show of delaines,
merinoes, swiss, etc., among the females, while the
males, with equal pride and satisfaction, displayed
their cassimere, cassinet, and broadcloth.

"Can it be possible," thought he, "that there is
such a semblance of happiness among persons so
situated? As anxious to make a display in dress as
the gayest of their superiors! To see them, and
hear their merriment, one might fancy they had
never known care. Might not such scenes as this

lead to the conclusion that there is something in the very nature of the negro, pointing him out as capacitated only for the condition in society held by these persons?

"No, it cannot be. This happy seeming is only put on for show; it is all hollow; or, at least, the result of ignorance of the wrongs they endure, and of the rights of which they are deprived. Yet are not all the pleasures of this world, to a certain extent, hollow? And if a person can enjoy himself, even though having real cause for unhappiness, which yet he does not see, is it not the part of wisdom, of humanity, to allow him to remain undeceived? Ah! but the mind! Should not the immortal soul be thought of? Yet may not the state of these persons be as favorable for piety as it seems to be adapted to enjoyment?"

The scene was too unusual, presenting too many objects worthy of attention, to admit of longer time for reflection or moralizing; so, noting this down as a matter for future consideration, he addressed himself to the close observation of what was transpiring around him.

"Is Brother Burns come, Miss Rosy?" asked the expectant bride, of her young mistress, who, as the evening drew on, came to see that every thing was in proper order.

"No, Sue, he has not arrived yet, and I am afraid he will not be able to do so, on account of the recent heavy rains," answered she, quite seriously; but continuing, with a merry, light-hearted laugh, "You need not be concerned about that. Uncle Simon's here, and that amounts to the same thing, as he can perform the ceremony quite as well. I have seen him marry several couples, and he officiates with so much dignity and propriety, I have thought of calling his services into requisition when *my* time comes. O! I forgot; I am not going to marry at all, you know."

"I dunno any sich thing, Miss Rosy. If you ain't, that Mr. What's-'s-name is wastin' a heap o' time comin' here so much."

This sally of Susan's brought her a general burst of applause from the bridesmaids and others in attendance.

"Well done, Sue! He, he, he! Dat's a good un, shoah; an' its de truf, too, fur jis' see how Miss Rosy's plagued."

"O he just comes to visit father, and pass off the time. You know he seldom ever sees me, anyhow."

"He wasn't visitin' Mas' Joe last Sunday evenin', when you and him was walkin'——"

"Be done with your nonsense; you tell every

thing you know. But that just happened so at *that*
time. It is no sign of—a wedding."

It was now the unanimous decision of her sable
attendants that Sue was "hard to beat," and, furthermore, that there was something of truth in her
insinuations, as testified by Miss Rosy's blushes,
which did n't go for nothing. "And they would not
be one bit surprised if there should soon be some
big doin's at Mas' Holmes's for the white people;"
while the bride, quite elated by such a eulogy on
her sagacity, exclaimed triumphantly,

" O yes, Miss Rosy, you think Sue aint got no
eyes; but she can notice some things. An' you 'd
better mind, too, how you tell your little tales, or
I'll have to tell de preacher when he *does* come.
But, Miss Rosy, for my part, I 'd sooner wait a while
than not to have him here."

" O ! you 're foolish to talk that way, Sue; every
thing is now ready, and there is no such a thing to
be thought of. If it were *my* wedding, I would not
wait ten minutes for any minister in the world, if
Uncle Simon were only on hand."

" There it is again ! Don't you think it is wrong
to tell so many—what shall I call 'em ?"

" White lies, I reckon, if you will have it so. I
do not think it is altogether right, Sue, but I cannot well help it. I mean no harm in the world, but

am so full of mischief, and so fond of sport, I forget myself."

"De Laud bress your lively soul, Miss Rosy," exclaimed Aunt Hager, the mother of the groom; "if you never dus nuf'n wus'n dat, you needn't be 'fraid but what you're good 'nough. I don't b'leve dur's one bit o' harm in a little fun o' dat kin'. Eb'rybody knows what you means, an' 'taint no lie 't all."

Were it our place to moralize, we would say we did not exactly agree with Aunt Hager, for the two simple reasons following: A healthy degree of mirth may be enjoyed in connection with a strict regard for truth; if not, we do not know that the second reason is entitled to much weight—to wit, the habitual indulgence in a very slight evil renders the commission of a greater easier than it otherwise might be.

Yet pardon, kind reader, this digression, designed to neutralize what might be otherwise a pernicious sentiment.

The old woman's remarks excited quite a lively debate, which was interrupted by Rosalind with, "Come, come! Sue, are you fully arrayed? for I see, by the bustle, your Tony has arrived, or it may possibly be the parson. Though you must make the best of it, should you be disappointed. I will regret it myself for your sake, yet we cannot help it."

Uncle Simon was a negro noted throughout the country for the goodness of his heart and his sincere piety. He had, partly through his own industry, and partly by the indulgence of his master, purchased his freedom; though still living under the guardianship of his late owner. He employed his spare time in preaching and holding prayer-meetings, and was in great demand generally, whenever there was a marriage to be performed among his own people. The Methodist preacher on the circuit, Mr. Burns, had agreed to perform the ceremony on the present occasion, in accordance with the earnest wishes of both parties, who were members of his charge; but he having already delayed longer than was anticipated, Susan's apprehensions became seriously excited. And, indeed, it happened according to her fears; for after waiting until the last moment, they were fain to call on Uncle Simon to supply his place, which, in verification of the prediction of "Miss Rosy," he did with quite a grace.

This matter disposed of, that in which the majority of the guests were more nearly interested— the supper—was quickly in process of preparation.

The hall had been set apart for the accommodation of the sable guests; and it had been contemplated to leave to them the entire control of their own table, while the whites supped around Mr. Holmes's customary board. But against this all the leading negroes loudly protested, earnestly entreating that the "white folks" would take their places at the table, and be served, after which, as they said, "Dur'll be plenty foh us. An' we aint in no hurry; but 'ud heap ruther see our mastahs and mist'esses eat fust, and wait on 'em." This was agreed to, and in due time the "white folks" had eaten, and the tables were prepared for another supply.

Justus, by request, took his station as carver, and many were the amusing incidents coming under his observation. At one time, Rosalind, who was the most industrious waiter, being as near as might be in every part of the room at the same time, came laughingly bearing a plate, saying, "Here, Mr. Justus, Uncle Sam says he wants a big slice of that ham, or two of your little pieces. He thinks you are a 'nice hand to carve,' but that you have 'never waited on field hands.'"

"See how this will suit him, then," said he, smiling in return, as he served the plate rather bountifully.

"Uncle Sam says that supply of ham 'looks like

doin' sumf'n,' said the lady, on her next return. This showed to Justus, at least, that though many of the plates were left almost untouched, Uncle Sam, for his own especial part, did not intend to suffer *his* modesty to curtail his enjoyment of the feast.

The supper ended, the tables were removed, and such another scene of merriment Justus had never witnessed. The mirth and confusion were quite uproarious; and he almost began to fear his prediction of the evening would be verified. But, during this time, the leading characters were in conclave to consider what form the general sport for the occasion should assume, to educe order and harmony from this discord.

While the confusion was at its height, Uncle Simon arose to make a suggestion. Not being observed, he mounted a chair, and, exercising his lungs in a few stentorian calls, attracted the attention of those about him, when it was passed from one to another, that Uncle Simon had something to say to them. Soon order was restored, and the old man remarked: " My friends, it's been a long time since I seen you all before, an' it's more 'n likely I 'll never see you agin after to-night, as I 'm gwine away. I don't want to stop your sport; fur young folks will have amusement, and I reckon dey need it; but I jis' got up to say to those that takes more pleasure in servin' the Lord dan in any other kind of enjoyment, dat we're goin' to have a prayer-meetin' down at de gin-house. Dur's no cottin in now, and Mastah Holmes says we can have it to-night. I'd be glad to see all go who feels any way like it. I would also be obleeged to any of our mastahs dat will go an' help us carry on meetin'."

So saying, the good old man descended from his stand and left the room. The number that followed him quite surprised the Northerner. He would not have believed that so many of that gay crowd would leave the house of mirth for that of prayer. He was himself perplexed about his own proper course, having an anxiety to witness each performance; but as that could not be, he decided to remain.

After the secession, the residue quickly arranged for a dance; but it appeared, to the sincere regret of all concerned, that this was in a fair way to fail for want of some one to supply the music. "Ben," it was said, "had his fiddle wid him; but he says he's jis a larnin, an' can't begin to play for a dance." And before this matter was adjusted, there was another slight interruption: the reverend gentleman, whose absence had been so much deplored, now came to hand. His late arrival was caused by having missed his way. Nothing would now satisfy the groom and bride but the re-performance of the ceremony by the new-comer. They declared it was the hope of this very occurrence that had kept them from attending the prayer-meeting; and as their wishes were earnestly pressed, they were duly gratified.

Rosalind, who was as much excited at the prospect of the enjoyment of the negroes in their exhilarating sport as any one in the room, observed with deep regret the probability of its failure. Encouraging them by her assiduity and happy laugh, she assured them they need not be disappointed in their expected pleasure; yet, in spite of all her efforts, there seemed no advance towards the consummation of so desirable an object, and, approaching the focus of consultation, she heard sadly remarked by one of the most conspicuous of the group—

"Well, I reckon we 'll hab to gib dis up, an' try sumf'n else. Mighty sorry, dough, fur we 'd a had lots o' fun."

"Never mind, Pete," she exclaimed, as a new idea flashed across her mind. "Never fear; just wait a while, and you shall have a fiddler yet."

"Thanke, Miss Rosy. You 's berry kind to us; but you put yourself to a heap too much trouble."

But she was gone, having heard but the commencement of the reply. Pete looked after her, a tear glistening in his eye, and a "God bress de young lady!" flowing from his heart, and finding utterance from his lips.

Justus had observed the interruption in the merriment, but could not imagine the cause. He felt an inward regret at the apprehension that he had witnessed the end.

"What is the matter?" he asked, on being rejoined by his fair pupil. "Is the night's sport so soon over?"

"I hope not; scarcely begun. They are in want of some one to make music for them, however, which I have undertaken to secure; and as the last resource, I have come to beg of you to act in their behalf."

Justus pleaded, quite feebly, however, more than one excuse: "Would it be right for him to take such a part in sport of the kind? Could he do so with dignity?" But Rosalind's whole soul was enlisted; and, with a warmth quite unusual and surprising, she set aside his objections: "There could be no harm in a simple dance of the kind they desired. They needed some excitement at times; and she was very anxious to see them gratified at the present. It might not be altogether becoming under other circumstances; but it is well enough, once in a while, to lay aside our dignity, and forget for the time that we are masters and mistresses. A little familiarity on such an occasion is not likely to be presumed upon."

His scruples were entirely removed; and, this fact communicated to the assembly, the trouble was entirely at an end, and hilarity again became the order of the night.

Merrily did the violin pour out its melodious strains, and merrily did the feet of the dancers move in acknowledgment. The latter performance, it is true, would not have been considered exactly in the style of a Parisian or Fifth Avenue demonstration, yet it was by no means wanting in grace, and moved on to the perfect satisfaction of the participants. Those not disposed to join in the dance amused themselves by covert love-making, flirtations, and gossip generally; and many a pretentious belle and self-confident beau congratulated themselves on their triumphs of the evening.

The passage of time was altogether unheeded: hour after hour sped on. The graver portion of the guests—the worshippers—had long since ended their services and dispersed. Yet still the dancing progressed, and in that joyous crowd the most intensely pleased seemed to be Rosalind. She was entirely absorbed in the contemplation of the scene of mirth. Nor was the gratification experienced by Justus much less intense; but his emotions were mingled. Of course he was pleased to see "the poor oppressed slave" forget for a moment his "toils and wrongs;" he felt joyous likewise through sympathy; but he exulted, he was happy to witness the disinterested efforts of his pupil in behalf of her dependants. Another element in his joy was the fact that himself was in some degree the dispenser of the satisfaction enjoyed by the rest.

The clock noted the hour of twelve, and still the jollity continued: one, and yet no abatement, but the power of excitement was growing weaker: two came, and it was voted time to desist. The lively music ceased, the feet of the dancers rested. Then came the invocation of a thousand blessings on the heads of Mas Justus and Miss Rosy, the bustle of preparation, the departure, and the hall was left in quietness.

Such was the first negro-wedding our Bostonian had ever attended, his first party in the South. A comparison between it and the happiest efforts of the kind he could imagine among the poorest classes, even in his own free Boston, could not be avoided; and he felt convinced that, beside the scene just closed, the balance was largely in favor of the slave. Yet, not to decide hastily, this also must be noted for further consideration.

CHAPTER XV.

A DISCLOSURE.

"A change came o'er the spirit of my dream."

A VISION of the display he had witnessed haunted Justus for days following; he could not escape from it. He seemed constantly to hear the merry laugh of the negroes, and to see their smiling faces; and then a form of almost angelic brightness would pass among them with a radiant smile, and words of cheering and encouragement. Again he passed in review the various occurrences of that night, particularly the points on which his mind had been brought to doubt. But the matter was disposed of by a summary process. "Preposterous thought! that a portion of God's intelligent creatures are formed for slaves. It is true, by a course of reasoning from such a data lately presented to me, backed by inclination or interest, one might almost conclude such to be the case. Yet it is treason against the majesty of Heaven to *reason* on such a subject; we *know* it is not so, for all were born free and equal; and we must not set up our weak reason as a standard." This conclusion arrived at, the next very naturally was, "all the happy seeming of his sable friends was hypocritical, or otherwise a person may be very well contented in a sphere for which he was not designed, feeling at the same time that he is degraded; or, in other words, may be quite happy in a state of unhappiness."

How much it is to be regretted that he had not previously witnessed a thanksgiving supper in "*Paradise Square*," that precious den in a large free city, that he might have known precisely how far perfect wretchedness can simulate satisfaction and contentment!

But if the frolic, with its attendant incidents, had wrought no change in the gentleman in this respect, yet it was potent in another quarter: whether in bringing about a new state of things, in hastening what was before slowly but inevitably proceeding, or simply in revealing a condition already existing, yet unacknowledged and even unknown, we wot not. Yet from one of these circumstances there was a change.

Previous to this time, Justus had regarded Rosalind simply as his pupil—the favorite one of them, it is true; but had been aware of no feeling save such as a pleasant, respectful, and ready scholar might reasonably excite in the mind of a tutor; though he was wont to look upon his duties, so far as the lady was concerned, not as a care, but rather as a relaxation from trouble; yet for this there was sufficient reason. For at the same time that her eager desire for knowledge and rapid advancement in its acquisition were a source of gratification to him, the force of her gentle influence over the younger pupils was far more effective than that of his own authority. No one, at least no one acquainted with his pursuits, its troubles and perplexities, will at all wonder that Rosalind should be an especial favorite with her instructor, and her absence from her place in school a source of deep regret to him.

The young lady had been wont to regard her tutor as one very competent to give instruction, and, at the same time, to please by his agreeable manners. She felt grateful for the deep interest manifested for her improvement, and perhaps her regret when detained from her place at the regular hours was scarcely less than his own. Yet did she only think of him as her teacher.

But during this affair, each had observed and admired the other. It was cheering to the heart of the instructor to see his lovely scholar so anxious to secure the enjoyment of the "poor oppressed slaves," while she looked with equal delight on his self-sacrificing efforts to the same end. Justus knew not why he was so much more than usually happy in her presence, and why his thoughts were so constantly of her. The lady experienced much of the same feeling. But to be drawn into a connection with slavery by marriage was a thing he had never allowed himself to contemplate. If he had ever previously given a thought to the subject, he considered the strength of his resolution sufficient to counteract whatever dangerous influence there might be exerted by constant association with his fair charge.

Could it be possible he had overrated his strength? Ah! what else mean those flutterings of heart, and those other nameless attendants of love?

"Yes," was his mental ejaculation. "I have not been sufficiently on my guard. I have forgotten the preceptor in the admirer. How stupid! not to be aware that no one, unless by ceaseless vigilance, could suffer himself to dwell as I have on the personal and mental charms of that girl, without loving. And now I find I am awakened barely in time. Or shall I give myself up to the indulgence of this delightful passion?

"No, it must not be! Thou must not forget it, Carolus; for no beauty or grace can compensate for

the sacrifice of principle thou wouldst make.   Yet
it may not so easily be forgotten; for

> " He who stems the stream with sand,
> And fetters flames with flaxen band,
> Has yet a harder task to prove—
> By firm resolve to conquer love."

All efforts to banish the intruder were ineffectual,
and he was at length forced to the conclusion that
absence alone could enable him to overcome.   He
would tarry no longer in *reach* of temptation.   But
still his plans were not yet ripe for a departure.
" Could he not justify himself in the indulgence of
his love?" was his next reflection.   "Even if the
affair were to proceed to a final consummation,
would the number of slaves be greater, or their
condition worse?   Surely not; but there would be,
on the contrary, a greater probability that some at
present under the yoke would be advanced to a state
of freedom.   For there can be no doubt such a pure,
gentle being would at once see the propriety of doing
all in her power for those falling under her care;
and once having her attention drawn to the wrong
of retaining them in a state of slavery, it needs no
prophetic ken to foresee her course."

Thus he gained, fully gained his own consent to
woo and wed, on certain contingencies, a lady who
would inevitably be a slaveholder.   How great the

generosity, how sincere the love, which could thus risk the fearful doom of being ranked among "*man-buyers!*"

Having thus decided, he was not long in making known to the lady the peculiar state of his feelings. The lessons were finished, and as the children retired, Justus requested of Rosalind a favorite air on the piano. She complied at once. He drew his seat beside her, gazing intently on the keys of the instrument. But his thoughts were not on the performance; this he scarcely noticed. He was meditating some graceful manner of introducing the subject that so fully occupied his mind. On ordinary occasions he was not wanting in a ready command of language; but now was unable to form a sentence or even an idea to his wish.

The music was finished, but he did not seem to realize that the strain was ended, still continuing his steady gaze.

"My performance must be indifferent, to throw you into such a state of despondency," said the lady, smiling a little archly, as she saw the music itself was not likely to elicit any remark.

"I was rather drawn off from the present in meditations," he replied, with a great effort to preserve his self-possession. Then added, "Your improvement, Miss Rosalind, has been very rapid; indeed,

I consider you well-nigh perfect in the art and science of music. All you now require is practice."

"I am afraid you are too partial. I think I can discover many defects myself."

"Not at all. With strict regard to rigid rules of criticism, that must be the decision of any one."

Here an awkward pause ensued, the invention of the gentleman the meanwhile on the rack for some becoming mode of declaring himself. The lady arose as if with the intention of leaving the room. Then Justus spoke, but hesitatingly :

"Stay yet a few moments, Miss Rosalind; I would have some conversation with you; it is but seldom we are favored with an opportunity for—social enjoyment in this way."

She blushed slightly, and was not altogether able to express by her voice the entire unconcern she designed, as, resuming her seat, she replied: "I am always pleased to hear my tutor converse, and consider myself very much indebted to him for his kind efforts in my behalf."

Had Justus been himself less embarrassed, the confusion of the lady during the utterance of this sentence would not have escaped him. But he was too deeply engaged in trying to devise some gradual way of presenting the declaration about to be made. There was another embarrassing pause, which he at length broke, saying, with still increased agitation, and with but little relevancy to the point :

"It is a great source of pleasure to me, Miss Rosalind, to reflect on the fact that the cultivation and refinement of your mind is, at least in some small degree, the result of my humble endeavors. And I shall ever remember, with emotions of gratefulness, the tractableness and sweetness of disposition manifested by you. I am well aware that the restraining of the other pupils from errors, as well as their advancement in their various studies, has been as much through your example and gentle admonitions as my own exertions."

It was evident he was bewildered, and spoke, he did not very well know what, simply because he had begun to speak, and must say something. His auditor blushed deeply, as she answered :

"It is indeed true that I am indebted to your faithful instructions for that portion of my mental acquirements I most highly prize. And I trust there has been no act of mine calculated in any manner to give you pain. Still, I cannot flatter myself with having done more than was simply my duty; and if I have in any manner rendered you assistance in your labors, I am well pleased, and consider the fact alone an ample reward."

Justus's perplexity had now reached its extremity.

He concluded to defer his suit to some future time, and the conversation took a different turn. They talked of the late wedding, and other matters, and the lady became quite animated. He alluded to the gratification felt in witnessing her conduct on that occasion. She was silent—busy with her own thoughts, which she dare not speak. She, too, had there experienced emotions before unfelt. A deep blush mantled her cheek.

How intimately important interests are connected with trivial things! The crimson glow stealing over her face, adding a higher charm to her beautiful countenance, did not escape the notice of Justus, who, interpreting it as a favorable omen, dismissed at once all hesitancy, and thus continued:

"It was not such commonplace topics as these that inspired my wish for private converse, Miss Rosalind. I have that to say, the response to which will have a powerful influence on my future happiness—may I not hope your own also? But should my declaration not meet your approval, I still hope the purity of my motives will shield me from reprobation, and that my conduct will not be considered as influenced by unwarrantable presumption." He paused to observe the effect produced upon her by this venture; and he hardly doubted but that, in the downcast eyes and crimson face before him, he could

read his complete triumph. Then he continued:
"After what you have just heard, you will not be
surprised at the avowal I now make. Lady, your
charms have captivated my whole nature. And
now, how shall I express myself? Excuse my seeming rudeness, for my feelings are such that they cannot be dictated to by any of the rules or conventionalities of common life. But I here declare the
most consuming love, and offer to you my hand and
heart, entreating a reciprocation of the act."

He paused to breathe, and for a few minutes
gazed in silent admiration upon the lovely girl, who,
in a state of deep agitation, sat with her face concealed in her handkerchief. Emboldened, he took
her unresisting hand and pressed it fervently to his
lips. At length he asked:

"What reply am I to expect, dear lady? May I
construe your silence into a token of assent; or at
least may I not take it as an evidence that my suit
is not wholly rejected?"

As her agitation only increased, he added, "I shall
not press for an answer now; but O! can you not
give a slight ground of hope, or at least appoint
some early day when I may receive a decisive answer?" This being ineffectual to elicit a reply, he
continued: "I will for the present retire, dear lady,
and leave you to yourself; but I crave an inter-

view to-morrow, at which I may receive your response."

An affirmative inclination of the head was her only reply, and he retired.

We will simply say, by way of disposing of this matter in the present place, that in due course of time all Justus's doubts were removed, and his happiness secured, by an acceptance on the part of the lady. Her views in regard to the time of consummating their bliss did not, however, coincide with his own, as her extreme youth forbade the thought of marriage for some length of time to come. The happy day, then, was left to be determined by subsequent events.

CHAPTER XVI.

THE VISIT.

"In order to save all, it is sometimes necessary to risk all."

"Ah! yes, that well-remembered spot!
What scenes of sadness brings it to my mind!"

AN unexpected and momentous change of circumstances awaited Justus. On the very evening of the
interview described, he was informed by his employer of a contemplated visit to a brother-in-law
residing in a distant part of the State. The plan of
arrangement was as follows : The entire family, that
is, the white portion, was to compose the visiting
party, himself included, if agreeable, in the same
capacity in which he acted at home. It was likely
that Mr. and Mrs. Holmes, accompanied by Rosalind, would embrace the favorable opportunity
offered of extending their jaunt to Virginia, as he
felt confident that his overseer would conduct
affairs as well in his absence as though he himself

were present. In this latter event, Justus was to maintain his present relation to the other children, left in charge of their aunt.

Less pleasing information could scarcely have been communicated. The thought of continuing in his present vocation, and yet separated from Rosalind, he could not endure. Previous to his engagement with her, he had determined, so soon as his contract should expire—an event now near at hand—to remove to some other point of observation, and engage in a more becoming pursuit.

The only thing, then, that could induce a continuance in the employment, was the privilege of being near the object of his affections, with the hope of removing her objections to a speedy union. This the present phase of things bade fair to preclude; yet his fears were somewhat relieved by the assurance of the lady, that she did not intend, if able to avoid it, accompanying her parents to her native State. Yet there was another source of uneasiness, and scarcely less troublesome than the other. The visit was to lead to the very county in which he had figured as an abolitionist, and been publicly disgraced.

Had this announcement been made but a few days earlier, he would not for a moment have entertained a thought of being of the party; but *now* the peculiar circumstances in his connection with Rosalind rendered the prospect of a separation particularly unpleasant. Should he be thrown from her in his present state of uncertainty, who could foretell the consequences? How many causes might conspire to prevent their future meeting! He seemed to have a presentiment that, parted thus, they would never realize their fond hopes. And he did not fail to take into account the loss in this event to result to the cause of mercy, which could not be disregarded, especially when so closely connected with his own interest.

Nor was the other horn of the dilemma much more attractive: to return to the very county whence he had been ejected under circumstances so humiliating, and perhaps to the identical neighborhood! But it might not even require this last inevitably to secure his disgrace; for the probability would be very slight of failing to meet with any one conversant with the circumstances leading to his expulsion. The prospect was far from gratifying. Though, for the reasons named, rather inclined to be of the party, he felt a degree of hesitancy quite unnatural. A knowledge of the name of this brother-in-law might possibly aid him in coming to a decision; for should it chance to be either of those so officious in his case, he would not go. Sooner should all claim to the hand of Rosalind be resigned, if separation must needs be a resignation, than to be humbled before her, and have her respect for him destroyed by such a disclosure as in that case must be made. He would learn from Rosalind the name of the family. But it was not a familiar one, and she could not at the moment call it to mind. In imagination he almost heard the name of McMinime, or Blanton, as she hesitated: "O! it is——" and his head grew fairly dizzy, when, after a short pause, she concluded—"Clayton." Such a relief! His feelings for the moment were such as a convicted criminal may be supposed to experience, reprieved at the last hour.

Though so much rejoiced at the time, his pleasure was merely negative: he knew he was not going to visit the family of either of those regarded by him as particularly his enemies; yet how far he might be from their neighborhood, or at what unlucky moment he might meet them, he had no means of knowing, and there yet remained much cause for painful perplexity.

The sage aphorism on a choice of evils here kindly came to his relief, but the question still remained unsolved as to the magnitude of the ills evoked by either course. On one side was absence from his heart's love, with, according to his presentiment,

7

almost the certainty of a final separation; on the other, the probability of the same loss, after a disgraceful exposure of himself in her eyes. In mental agony, he cursed his folly in the first fatal departure from right. But for that, he might without shame or fear proudly have borne himself in any community. After a painful conflict, he decided on going at any hazard; and endeavoring to become calm in outward appearance, he succeeded admirably. But there was still an uneasiness not to be banished from his mind; and it was not altogether an open exhibition of feeling, that, when the journey began, he was as cheerful as any one. This disposition, however, was maintained almost to the end. The party highly enjoyed the travel, passing the time quite agreeably; but as they drew near their place of destination, gloomy thoughts again began to annoy Justus. No wonder! They passed the camp-ground where he had heard the announcement of preaching to the negroes: to him, hapless place! O that he could but recall that portion of his life; that this one scene were to be enacted over! How different would be his conduct! Such, doubtless, then were his views of the case: different indeed might his action have been with his present knowledge of the result. But, alas! rashness purchases experience that may never profit. Not then seeing the consequence of those acts, to-morrow a case may arise in which this will be no precedent: then learn less to trust to the direction of thy impulses.

He observed there were persons employed on the ground, fitting it up, he supposed, for another meeting.   He saw familiar faces there.   Among a group acting as supervisors of the work, he noticed his old friends Blanton and McMinime, and, with the negroes at labor, were his protégé "Sambo," and "Uncle Moses;" and "Darkie," too, figured in the crowd.

The cortége consisted of two carriages, the foremost of which was occupied by Justus and Rosalind, with two of the children.   There were no pleasant associations connected with the place to induce the abolitionist to tarry, and soon, to his relief, it was left behind.   He crossed the creek in which almost twelve months previous his persecutors had plunged him, and he could almost feel the cold water closing over him.   His feelings were too powerful to be resisted, and he involuntarily heaved a deep sigh.

His companion, who had scarcely ever thought there could be care weighing on the light heart of her cheerful teacher, was herself startled from rather a sad train of reflections.

"What mighty sorrow," she gayly exclaimed, "lays its burden on your mind? That sigh indicates a cause of sadness, as weighty as unusual."

Evading the question, he drew her attention to the condition of gloomy suspense in which he was placed by the indefiniteness and uncertainty of their agreement, heightened by the fears of her father's disapproval. This was spoken as though the real cause of his depression of spirit. It had the desired effect; and, checking her levity, both became meditative. A sudden thought seized the gentleman— a thought never before indulged—he would tell his history.

"Do you recollect, Miss Rosalind, reading, months ago, of a fellow being dipped in the creek for trying to persuade slaves to leave their masters?" he asked rather abruptly. More than once during the afternoon Rosalind had ineffectually attempted to engage her companion in conversation, and in despair had as often given it up. Pleased at length that her object was about being gained, she replied:

"I do not now remember reading the account, but, to me, occurrences of this kind do not yield the satisfaction others seem to receive from them, and therefore do not make so deep an impression on my mind. Yet do not suppose I have any sympathy for those who think our servants to be the suffering race their fancy portrays. The lot of the serving class in all countries imposes a burden, perhaps not pleasant to be borne, in which, of course, the slave has his part; but I do not believe that in the present order of things, taking into consideration the state of society, and, indeed, every thing bearing on the matter, his condition can be radically bettered. Still, when hearing of one whose imprudent zeal has led him into difficulty of this kind, while my judgment condemns his wrong as worthy of punishment, my heart is still disposed to commiserate his misfortune. This may be my weakness, yet sympathy for the unfortunate, you know, is the characteristic of our sex. Why do you ask, Mr. Justus?"

"This, I suspect, is the very creek in which that act was performed, as he was taken at a camp-meeting." The question bringing him so suddenly to the opening of the narrative, rather threw him off his guard, causing him to answer hesitatingly; yet, at the same time, increasing his love for the fair Southerner, whose views, with suitable instruction, would so well harmonize with his own.

Unwilling to suffer the former oppressive silence to be renewed, the lady playfully remarked, "Perhaps there is more than one camp-ground in the

State, with a creek conveniently situated for such a purpose."

"Miss Rosalind——." A voice from the carriage in the rear interrupted him:

"Ho, Justus! don't you suppose this is the creek in which they ducked that nigger-thief of whom we read?"

"Really!" laughed the lady, "this is a singular notion you have both taken."

"I was but just making the same remark to Rosalind. Yet why should we both take up such an opinion? Is it not rather strange?"

"Merely from the fact, I suppose, of finding a place so suitable, and so near a camp-ground." And the animated conversation of the gentlemen left no opportunity for Justus to proceed in the revelation he had even begun, until the recollection of the abrupt termination had ceased to harass the lady, and Justus had resolved to postpone the confession.

The sun had set, and they were nearing the residence of McMinime. "We had better spend the night here, Rosalind, had we not? We have had a long and tiresome journey to-day, and it is yet some distance to your uncle's; too far, I fear, to be performed by night."

Justus started, and regarded his companion with

an anxious look during the utterance of the foregoing words by her father. Without seeming to notice this movement, she replied:

"I would prefer to proceed now, but have no anxiety either way."

"What do you say, Justus? I am in the minority, and will be obliged to yield, having so promised, unless you will come to my relief."

"I suppose I must side with the ladies," he replied; "the more especially, as, if I do not, it will be a difficult matter to find one to act as umpire." This he spoke in a seemingly indifferent manner, happy that he was allowed a voice in the decision of the question.

They passed through the wood through which Justus had walked to allay his emotion on the occasion of his disagreement with Sambo's master.

He thought—how could he otherwise—of the watch and its strange history—the bill of sale—and he mentally exulted. "How I would like to know whether either of them have been satisfactorily accounted for," was his silent exclamation; "or has the paper I so fortunately obtained yet been missed?" And his cogitations turned: "Gave him a pleasant dipping in the creek, ha!" At that moment a dark thought flashed across his mind, and, as he reflected thereupon, his frame trembled sensibly.

"What affects you?" asked his companion, manifesting uneasiness. This question, also, was evaded by a reference to the difficulties and uncertainties in the way of the attainment of his hopes; at present, with much truth, though not exactly in the way he would be understood.

He soon became more composed, and could not forbear a smile as they traversed the lane through which the memorable chase of "George Washington" had led.

Night settled down upon them, hiding surrounding objects from view. Then he grew lively in conversation, and the time passed pleasantly enough.

The moon rose over the tops of the trees, discovering to them the fact that their journey was almost ended. Then a certain familiar appearance flashed the truth on Justus's mind, that he was not in his present locality for the first time.

Though late, the family had not yet retired, and the visitors were cordially received, and welcomed with a becoming degree of bustle and confusion.

A single glance at the interior of the house served to satisfy Justus as to his whereabouts. It was the identical place at which he had been treated to an account of his own performance at the camp-meeting. He felt unwell on the present occasion, his night's drive not agreeing with him;

and, therefore, took an early opportunity of retiring. But for weary hours his overture to the oblivious Somnus was in vain. He was separated from the company by a thin partition; and, though he could hear distinctly but little that was said, a constant hum of voices reached his ears, broken, ever and anon, by the same noisy mirth that had so harshly grated on his nerves on a previous occasion while occupying the same position.

His feelings cannot be described, as a burst of laughter of uncommon energy saluted him. Writhing in agony, he mentally exclaimed: "No doubt they are rehearsing the whole story. The same coarse laugh with which they regaled me before, which nothing else that is human can imitate! Yes! on my word, there it is again! Ah me! I am afraid I deliberated to poor purpose when I decided to make this trip. I have but little doubt it will yet bring me into serious trouble."

Notwithstanding the fears of Justus, the minds of the others were very little occupied about him. The brother and sister (Mr. Holmes and Mrs. Clayton) had been parted for many years; and had, as a matter of course, many matters of mutual interest to discuss. Their time, therefore, was not to be devoted to minor subjects.

It is true, her uncle, who had noticed the handsome stranger attending Rosalind, made her the special object of his pleasant jests; and from this cause, probably, arose the merriment which so much annoyed that worthy.

This was innocently begun by Mr. Clayton, merely for the sake of a little pleasant diversion, not thinking to what it might lead.

His niece had been but little used to such inquisitorial proceedings, and exhibited rather a tell-tale expression of face: indeed, her confusion was so plainly manifest as to betray to any one who observed her countenance that it was produced by no trivial consideration.

There was one in the room who read her emotions more minutely than any one else, and with far different feelings. His brow darkened, and vengeful thoughts arose in his heart, as he saw partially the state of affairs. He had never entertained the idea of an attachment between his daughter and Justus; and the sudden truth that such had actually taken place could not but affect him unpleasantly.

"You are too hard on her, Robert," he said, desirous of changing the subject: "you have so badly confused her she scarcely knows what she is saying or doing. She is young, and has never been used to jests of that nature; and as for this gentleman, of course she only thinks of him as her tutor."

Whatever opinion the other may have entertained in regard to this excuse for the confusion of his niece, he made no reply; and this mode of amusement was abandoned. Yet, however much her father might hope his explanation to be correct, he had his doubts—nay, he was satisfied that his daughter was more interested in her teacher than a due consideration of his being an unknown adventurer would justify. To what extent the affair had gone he could not divine, but duty demanded a prompt inquiry.

CHAPTER XVII.

THE DISCOVERY.

" Thought they their iron band of pride
Could break the knot that love had tied ?"

On the following morning, there was more than one troubled countenance among the late arrived, nor was that of Justus, as might have been expected, the most conspicuous of the number. Indeed, so well had he profited by his stern schooling, that he could now assume a degree of unconcern under any ordinary trouble. But Holmes was not so fortunate: he could by no means hide his uneasiness, and it was matter of no little wonder to those who observed, what could have occurred. He must surely be unwell. But all efforts to ascertain the cause of his concern met an evasive response, as he declared himself in usual health and spirits.

Nor was Rosalind altogether so cheerful as was her wont: perhaps her thoughts dwelt on the ordeal of the past night, or she may have been disturbed by her father's apparent distress. She had immured herself in her room, whence, upon opening the door, responsive to a gentle tap on the outside, the object of her solicitude himself entered.

His abstracted manner and constrained deportment told most plainly there was a burden on his mind, the character of which she could not guess, which she would yet gladly remove.

He sat in silence, though she could discern there was something he wished to communicate.

"You seem disturbed. What can be the matter, dear father?" she asked. "What can it be that gives you trouble?" alarmed by his moody silence.

The cause of the visit was a delicate matter, and he had been extremely perplexed to find suitable words with which to introduce it. This relieved him of his embarrassment, and he answered:

"I trust there is no serious cause for my apparent trouble; yet this hope may be fallacious. You are the person to remove the difficulty. My object in seeking an interview was to have my doubts settled: if there is nothing amiss with you, I have no ground for uneasiness."

"Your language is mysterious. If the state of my health excites your fears, I assure you they are groundless; and if, from any other cause, you have apprehensions on my account, I pray you dismiss them as needless."

This was uttered with an evident composure, in strange contrast with the excitement occasioned by her father's words. Too unused to life to concern herself with its cares, she yet saw something had affected her parent, and the vague allusion to herself in connection with it at once distressed and alarmed her.

"That you believe so, my daughter, I have no doubt; still, my opinion is different. The subject on which I would speak is one I scarcely know how to approach; yet it will perhaps aid you to arrive at my meaning, if I say, that what I observed on. last night has opened my eyes to a state of things I never before even so much as thought of."

A suspicion of her father's meaning came over her mind, and she blushed deeply. Speedily recovering her self-possession, however, she spoke with great earnestness:

"You alarm me, dear father! Of what great impropriety have I been guilty? Speak your meaning plainly, I entreat; for, although it can be no light matter, since it moves you, I can afford to hear it, and may be able therefrom to learn some useful lesson, at least to guard against a repetition of the same offence."

This answer, so different from what he had expected, quite disconcerted him: he felt, moreover, a slight degree of vexation, for he could not forbear the thought that his daughter had wilfully mistaken his meaning. With difficulty concealing his emotions, he continued :

"I did hope, Rosalind, you would understand me from a hint; for, indeed, it is a thing painful enough even to think of, and more so to speak about. But since I must declare myself plainly, if I have not been strangely deceived in the reading of your countenance, you have suffered your affections to become entangled most unwisely—have placed them on your *music-teacher*. I wish now to know whether or not I am correct. Answer to the point : is this so, or is it not ?"

Instead of a reply, she buried her face in her hands, and burst into tears.

For a few moments her father looked on in silence, in doubt as to what cause he should ascribe her emotion. Was it regret that the course she wished to take was displeasing to him ? Or might she not grieve to be charged with so flagrant an offence against common intelligence, as to "fall in love" with an unknown stranger?

She restrained her tears, and meekly replied :

"And if I have, dear father, is it a matter to which you would feel any violent opposition ?"

A shade of anger passed across the parent's brow, and he answered somewhat sternly:

"That question, my daughter, has entirely dissipated my half-formed hope. But I did not wish my question thus answered; so be pleased to return a positive reply. Yet that is *now* scarcely necessary."

Partaking of her father's spirit, with a tone of suppressed indignation, she replied: "Father, do you not think there is an inconsistency in your conduct? It seems that either your present proceeding is wholly uncalled for, or you have heretofore been very remiss. Had you waited, in due time you would have been properly acquainted with my feelings; and if, in setting my affections on him, there is so great a wrong committed as you appear to think, I certainly should have had a timely hint to that effect long since. But, as I must answer your question, father, I do love Mr. Justus, nor can I perceive the harm to grow out of it."

Unable longer to control his anger, her father rejoined with much bitterness: "No harm, indeed! Have you ever considered what may be the result of this idle passion?"

"Father," she replied, with great respect, yet in a tone of firmness, "it is no idle passion; or it is not, if I am capable of any thing else. But I will

frankly acknowledge the extent of my considerations as to the final result is limited—about the
same, I presume, as that of other young persons in
the same circumstances."

For a while he was silent and deeply troubled.
Then he asked : " Is your heart so fully taken up in
this affair, that if your father were to forbid all
further communication with this stranger, you would
not yield obedience to him ?"

"O ! do not put me to the test, father," she exclaimed eagerly, and with great energy.

"Answer me, daughter. Try deep in your heart
both sides of the question, and if your love is of so
rank a growth that you would rather take the most
important step of your whole life in violation of
your parent's commands than endeavor to overcome it, say so. Let me know on what I am to depend."

A look of mingled anger and grief was cast on
him by the fair girl, but she remained silent, trembling like an aspen.   The voice of her father aroused
her, and she replied :

" Father, I will endeavor to do any thing you
command, even were it this very thing. But do not
let any light matter induce you thus to restrain me.
I will not say it would destroy my peace, or any
thing of the kind: I might overcome, I might

again be cheerful and happy; yet, it would be a violent tearing loose of my heart's best affections, and would cause me many a bitter pang. Were I acquainted with any thing in him demanding such a proceeding, it might be attended with less pain."

"But consider, my dear daughter, you know nothing in regard to this man; he is but a stranger. He may be worthy, but we have no evidence of his respectability, save in his deportment before us; and as he has evidently been playing for a stake, he has had sufficient motives of interest to induce him to act with circumspection."

"This much I know in regard to him: he was received into my father's house, and that, too, into a responsible trust, and was at all times treated by my father as an equal. And, further, I know during my acquaintance with him, he has conducted himself most becomingly at all times."

He smothered down his ireful feelings so far as he was able, and replied, yet in no very amiable mood:

"Such language to your father very ill becomes you, child; but I suppose you mean by this to charge the blame of your imprudence on me; as though I could not employ a person to teach my children, but my daughter must take it for an equivalent to declaring him a suitable match for her. Whereas, his being engaged in the occupation of a strolling music-teacher should excite an abhorrence of the very idea."

"No, father, I do not censure you for any thing; nor am I yet able to see that any one is to be blamed. But I cannot do else than think, if it be so great a remove from propriety for me to allow my thoughts to run in this channel, a warning should have been sooner given. He is a handsome and intelligent young gentleman, possessed of agreeable and captivating manners. This you of course must have seen, and it was not to be expected that your daughter should be gifted with more discrimination than belongs to her sex and age. Nature is still the same; our hearts are susceptible of such influences; and being necessarily in his company—seeing him, hearing him, a natural consequence was to love him."

The gentleman answered not, but paced the room in deep and troubled meditation. His daughter, with forced calmness and composure, awaited the result. He paused near her, and spoke abruptly: "Yet you promise to take no further step in this matter without my permission."

"I have so promised," replied she, mournfully; " and should your decision be the death-blow of my hopes, I will still acquiesce; but consider it only a sacrifice to your will, for I never expect to love him the less, while I think him worthy; other than which I can at present scarcely imagine him to be."

Had she been in an observing mood, she might have noticed a tear start from her parent's eye as this answer was given. But he soon stifled his emotions, and said:

"Your answer, my child, both rejoices and grieves me. I am proud to know you possess so high, so noble a sense of duty; yet the reflection that your own well-being may demand such a sacrifice of you, pains me no little. I could not rest, Rosalind, after learning what I did last night, till I had heard from your own lips the state of your feelings in regard to this man. You are fully aware, I feel satisfied, that I would not unnecessarily pain you.

"Nothing but a solicitude for your own happiness has prompted my present action. I wish to sound a warning before it may be too late. Whatever else may be said of a connection between you, it would be running a fearful risk on your side. I do not know, neither do I seek to know, to what extent you may have proceeded in the matter; but for the present, let it remain just as it is. Examine well: you are young, and ought not to think of marriage for years.

"If he prove himself worthy, I will give my willing consent." There was no response, and the gentleman retired.

A few days after the arrival of the Holmes family, other visitors were received at Clayton's—Mr. McMinime and lady. Justus now looked upon his case as desperate; indeed, he felt certain an exposure of himself would at once take place. But, not less to his surprise than joy, he was not recognized; and, even when introduced, the name Justus did not seem to call up any recollection in the mind of the other. He now began to indulge the hope he might escape recognition entirely, and became lively and agreeable in conversation.

An unfortunate turn was given to their social amusement. Some one chanced to speak of the approaching camp-meeting, which suggested to Holmes the question, whether the ground he had passed was the one at which the abolitionist was taken last year.

A sudden feeling, as of a disposition to swoon, came over Justus, and objects in the room swam indistinctly before his eyes. It soon passed off, however, without having been observed; and the question not leading directly to a realization of his fears, he again breathed freely, and was almost ready to conclude that the Fates, though disposed to try him severely, had yet conspired in his favor. One question brought on another, but soon the climax came .

"Do you know what that fellow called himself?"

The name had passed out of McMinime's recollection, but, as he thoughtfully cast his eyes about the room, they rested on Justus.

"It seems to me," he said, "it is Justus. Yes, I now recollect distinctly, that is the name."

"Not my friend here, of course," said Holmes, "although he bears the same name; rather an unusual one, too."

"O, no! there is no danger of ever catching that chap here again: he thinks too much of himself for that," said the other, looking Justus steadily in the face. He paused for a moment, and then exclaimed:

"Yes! on my word, this is the same man, without a doubt!"

"Impossible!" exclaimed Holmes. "Mr. Justus, here, could surely never have assumed his present character, were he the same person you speak of."

The calmness of despair now settled on the abolitionist. He no longer had any room for hope;

his exposure and disgrace were inevitable. To McMinime's question, whether he had not, on a certain occasion, received from himself a bill of sale for a certain boy, named Sambo, he replied:

"Gentlemen, I have to acknowledge that I am the person, and yet not the same person either, I may say, having undergone so complete a change in my views. Do not weigh my former acts against me; but let circumstances speak in my excuse.

"Raised in Boston, it is not to be wondered at that I was an abolitionist; and feeling almost as the 'anointed of the Lord' for the extirpation of slavery, I could not have been expected to do otherwise than act rashly and imprudently. But that is past; I have seen the folly of my course, and, henceforth, you need feel no apprehensions for your property in consequence of my actions.

"You, sir," addressing Holmes, "may think you have serious cause of complaint for the deceit I have practiced upon you; but, I think, if you rightly consider, there is no real ground for censure. What could I do? My necessities drove me to choose the occupation I did, and not the desire to interfere with any of your property arrangements. You have no reason to believe I have acted in bad faith, and I assure you I have not done so. And now, if you do not question my word, will you grant me the particular favor not to revive this old matter, which, at the best, can do no good, and will only have a tendency to injure me?"

"I do not know, indeed," replied McMinime, "that I have any reason to credit you; yet in this I will; and promise both not to cause you any interruption, and to forgive your former errors."

"The former promise I will also make," said Holmes; "but do not know that I can forgive *all* that has passed. However, let it drop for the present."

The abolitionist soon left the room; and McMinime entertained the other guests with an account of his adventures at the camp-meeting, as they had come under his own observation.

"A complete change!" mused Justus. "Well, in one sense, that is entirely correct. But it is only that I see the utter hopelessness, nay, the madness of my former course; and not that my views in regard to slavery, or liberation, where it can be carried into effect, are in the least changed. I am afraid my visit to the South, so far as my book is concerned, will prove a failure. Yet, if my plans succeed, my labor shall not be entirely in vain; I will be the means of liberating some slaves, though not by means of stealing, as it is denominated.

"But I must go and make my communication

to Rosalind before she hears of this affair; and endeavor to counteract whatever prejudice against me may be aroused."

CHAPTER XVIII.

A CRISIS.

"The course of true love never did run smooth."

He gave her an epitome of his history, relating the cause of his visit South, his adventures and sufferings; ending with the recent painful scene.

"I made up my mind," he said, "at the time we crossed the creek, to give you this account, but have delayed it for want of opportunity.

"And now what shall I say in regard to my conduct? It is true I have practiced a slight deception—though, I think, justifiable under the circumstances; for, although my views in regard to the rectitude of the thing are the same, having seen the folly of my former course, owing to the impracticability of carrying out my plans, and, determined to interfere no more with the relation of master and servant, I was aware my presence simply could be an injury to no one. And yet, I knew, to declare the principles I had held would exert an influence against me. Do not understand me to say I consider the views influencing my course formerly to be correct; yet I as much as ever consider slavery an evil, if there were any means of doing it away. But may I not hope, Rosalind, that the recollections of my past errors will not be allowed to prejudice your mind against me?"

"I shall not allow a corrected mistake, and one the result of education, to weigh against you, especially as your motives were supposed philanthropy."

This was very cheering to Justus, yet it did not by any means place him at ease. There was yet another cause of trouble, scarcely less potent than the one just disposed of, and which, indeed, rendered of no avail the advantage he possessed in the continued confidence of Rosalind. He scarcely entertained the shadow of a hope that her father would now consent to their marriage; and he desired to know whether, in that case, the lady could be induced to take such a step against his will. It was a delicate matter, and might give gross offence; yet, by dexterous management, without betraying his design, he elicited the desired information. But, knowing her promise to her father, the reader need not be told that this was not in accordance with his wishes.

Thus enlightened, he determined without delay to apply to Mr. Holmes, and learn at once his doom; for if the Fates were to declare against him, it would be well to understand it immediately, and to endeavor, by a separation from the object of his affections, to forget his love and its griefs. This is here stated quite coldly and in a commonplace manner, but it must not be supposed the lover's cogitations were thus conducted. Yet, however impetuous his passion, the time for action had come. If his suit should be denied by the father, his hope would be entirely destroyed: then, to be near each other, would only render their mutual lot harder to bear; and delay in ascertaining this fact would not soften one pang.

Induced by such reflections, amplified and extended with many a bitter sigh, he formed the before-stated determination.

Despair lent him unusual courage, and he boldly and unhesitatingly opened the business, stating his feelings and his wishes.

"Young man, you astonish me!" with a look of the utmost surprise, was the only reply returned.

"I am very well aware, Mr. Holmes," he said, "that circumstances lately transpired are not such as would most likely influence you to a favorable reception of my application; yet I hope to regain,

by my future conduct, whatever I may have forfeited of your good opinion. If you have no
insuperable objections on other grounds, though
you may not feel disposed to give your consent to
the measure at present, allow me to enjoy the hope
that the future may be more propitious. Do not
consign me to utter despair by entirely rejecting
my plea; and this I ask as much for your daughter's
sake as my own."

"Do you perceive no considerations of prudence
which, independently of the circumstances you
speak of, might lead me, in the view of securing
my daughter's happiness, to refuse listening to
your proposal?"

Justus comprehended but too distinctly the
meaning of this question, for it was but approaching the point which had so much troubled him
from the inception of his passion—the inferior
position he himself occupied in society. Though
he did not rate his own worth below that of the
other, in consequence of their relative circumstances outwardly, yet he ever reflected with painful emotion on the scorn which he feared an application from one in his position for the hand of
Rosalind would provoke. Yet, restraining the
display of feeling excited by this allusion, he
answered with dignity, and in affected surprise:

"I really am not aware of any such considerations, and may perhaps be able to remove your scruples in regard to them, after they shall have been stated."

"In the first place, you are a comparative stranger to my daughter, as also to myself, and even this, alone, calls for circumspection, in a matter thus important."

"This difficulty, however, my plan would obviate. Appoint me a reasonable time for probation, and in the meanwhile make such observations as you may deem fit. If, at the end of that time, you are satisfied of my rectitude in every respect, as a citizen and a man, let your decision be in accordance. But if otherwise, I can *then* only receive and acquiesce in your determination, as the result of a calm and well-weighed conviction of duty, which at this time I might very reasonably consider the result of sudden passion; or, at least, that it was not duly deliberated in all its bearings."

Holmes felt a strong inclination to inform him that he was at perfect liberty to consider what he chose, and, more particularly, to go his way and trouble him no more; but a thought of his daughter restrained him: he wished to conquer her attachment, which he did not doubt accomplishing, if he had not mistaken his man; but, not wishing to employ harsh measures in the agency, he replied mildly:

"You seem to forget that this is not the only reason I might have for withholding my approval; but there is one of scarcely less importance. I do not wish to wound your feelings, but the subject demands plain dealing.

"Rosalind has been brought up in affluence, and were I assured your position in life fitted you for equality, still your resources are not such as to warrant the hope that you can maintain the style of living to which she has been accustomed. You surely cannot wish to become the instrument in bringing her to a reverse, which, from her previous life, will be the more keenly felt?"

For a time Justus was silenced: the unwholesom truth flushed his cheek with shame, and for a moment he felt doubtful how to act. Should he take this as an explicit denial, or only look upon it as a trial, and demand a decisive answer? After musing a while, he said:

"Let this also be a part of my trial. Say what amount of property I must accumulate—of what kind, and all this will I accomplish."

A feeling of admiration took possession of Holmes, and for the first moment he felt a doubt in regard to the course he ought to pursue.

"If I only had reason to be satisfied that this is not all affected on his part, and that he has no ulterior design to accomplish, it would certainly show him in a far more favorable light than I ever before viewed him. But if he is not swayed by pure affection, what can be his motives?"

He could not divine, yet he had his suspicions. And though they might seem somewhat unreasonable, he could only think of the dishonest attempts the same person had once made, and conclude that no intentions a sane man could impute to such antecedents would be absurd. Suddenly, a new idea entered his mind, and he had a plot laid by which to assure himself whether he were influenced entirely by love. Addressing Justus, he continued:

"I have objections on my part, sir, that I do not think can be removed; but if, after a full consideration of the case, the dangers and uncertainties in the way, Rosalind is still of her present mind, you shall have my consent."

If Justus had inclination, he had not opportunity to express his gratitude, for at that moment McMinime made his appearance to take leave of his new friend.

"I see, Mr. Justus, you have replaced your lost watch," said he, withdrawing his hand from the contact with that gentleman, and with a significant expression of countenance which the other did not exactly know how to interpret. He did not, however, concern himself about his meaning, and simply answered:

"O, yes!"

Although he felt a strong inclination to ask if the missing bill-of-sale had yet turned up, he prudently restrained himself.

That part of the story related by Justus, in which his former conduct had been exposed, was repeated to Rosalind by her father, closing with the question:

"Do you not think you now have made the discovery which you yourself proposed should free you from your obligation to him? I mean, the discovery that this man is unworthy of your love or regard."

"I must confess, I cannot see wherein he has so proven himself, father."

"I am sure, then, I can scarcely imagine what could render him unworthy in your eyes. What is he doing here, or for what purpose did he come? Simply, to steal our property, should a favorable opportunity present; and, at best, to devise the most practicable ways and means for those of his party to carry out their thievish designs."

"Not stealing, father; not thievish; at least so far as *their* view of the matter is concerned."

8

"Not stealing! Why, would they not deprive us of our own, without any kind of an equivalent?"

"Most true; yet they view the thing in a different light. They think their actions justifiable, nay virtuous. And though I am far from approving their conduct, I think their faith in their opinions should clear them at least of part of their guilt."

"The admission of such a principle would destroy all protection to society and property. Wicked and misguided men can always justify themselves in any wrong. The principles they assume would teach the vicious and profligate the justice of depredating upon the stores accumulated by the patient industry of the virtuous; and even the sacrifice of the life of a good citizen would be viewed as a virtuous act, when revenge or interest prompted the deed. No, my child; their 'faith in their opinions' cannot clear them from guilt; but to my mind, their arrogance enhances it. Why should those who know nothing in reality of our slavery, except the name, have their holy horror so much excited on its account? Why set up their mere opinion above the calm conclusions of able and candid men, who have given their earnest attention to the subject, and anathematize a whole community for a supposed sin, warranted and countenanced by God's word! Forgetful of more real

suffering at home, they put themselves to much inconvenience to inflict an injury both on us and the
objects of their pity. I say injury to the slave himself, for, not to mention the sad condition of many
they steal, where one is thus liberated, the state of
hundreds is often made worse in the necessary pre-
caution to prevent them sharing the same fate. At
least, such is the natural tendency."

"Admitting all this, even, it will not apply at present to this person, who, having seen his wrong in
the course he was pursuing, has wisely abandoned
it."

"That *may* be, but I doubt it very much; yet
hear my conclusion: You are at full liberty to use
your own pleasure in this matter; but, as I think it
unsafe to put any part of my property in this man's
hands, look for no assistance from me. Would you
marry him under these circumstances?"

"What kind of an opinion do you entertain of
me, father, that——. But nothing of this kind can
influence me; your consent is all I ask; though,
to me, it seems you are disposed to hasten the affair
to a crisis; yet, perhaps, it is as well."

He did not seem to hear the latter part of the
reply, and said:

"You will of course take the earliest opportunity
to acquaint him with this decision: for be assured

there will be a vast difference in his feelings when he finds the prospect is to connect himself with poverty, instead of comparative wealth."

"With *some* this might be true, but not with *him;* and, indeed, you think too meanly of my suitor. Perhaps you may one day see it, and regret the course you have taken. Do not think, however, I repine at your decision, though I might consider it cruel, for this can have no influence on me, and I have no doubt it will be the same to Mr. Justus."

"Perhaps so, but that remains to be seen."

It was not difficult for the lady to observe the evident uneasiness of her father; but being in a mood to impute his proceedings to unnecessary harshness, she little knew the real cause of his distress. But could she have read his heart, as he retired, she would have found something equivalent to the following meditation :

"It is a source of real grief to me, thus to inflict pain upon her, and I am not altogether pleased with the deception I am practicing, yet I think it is allowable. I believe this change in affairs will work a far greater one in that fellow's mind ; and Rosalind, being a girl of sense, will learn to overcome her unwise attachment, seeing how unworthy he is. But if the effect anticipated is not produced, I shall be forced slightly to alter my opinion of him ; and, my promise being out, I can object no longer, and must of course do all I can for them."

The reception Justus had met from Holmes was not calculated to inspire him with very lively hopes; but, as the matter, after all, was to be decided by Rosalind, he felt a feverish anxiety to hear what effect the representations of her father had produced in her mind. Almost infinitely to his relief, he learned there would be no opposition to their wishes; the conclusion of the sentence conveying the information, however, was productive of a vast change in his feelings; indeed, it threw a complete extinguisher over his joy.

"They would be cut off, and left dependent on themselves."

For a time his surprise was too great for utterance. Obtaining command of language, he remarked, in a tone intended to be one of pleasantry:

"You jest, Miss Rosalind; it is only your intention to try me."

To say the lady was surprised, would but poorly describe her sensations. A sickly pang of disappointment blended with the doubts that took painful possession of her; yet it was more the manner of the speaking, than the words uttered, that affected her; and, as she observed the successive changes of his countenance, she could not repress the thoughts of her father's words regarding the change to be produced in her lover by this very announcement. She was pained to witness his emotion, the cause of which the most stupid blindness could not fail to see; yet, as it was the first and only thing yet observed calculated to weaken her faith in the love she had hitherto believed as pure as her own, a lingering hope remained. Sudden joy and surprise at the consent so happily obtained, might have produced undue excitement, which strangely reflected his true state of mind.

Still, her doubts were exceedingly oppressive, to remove which her course of action was speedily taken.

"No," she replied; "not jesting, not trying you, Mr. Justus; but, as our engagement was entered into at a time when I occupied a different position, justice would forbid the thought that you are still bound by the promise then given, if in the least in conflict with your present feelings. And I now release you from your obligation."

It required no slight effort on the lady's part to give utterance to this declaration; yet, considering it as an act of duty, she suffered nothing in her manner to give the lie to her words. That in the warmth of her heart's first love she entertained a secret hope of her lover's reässeverating his attachment, there is strong ground to suppose.

Justus was a philosopher. In no important act, since assuming his present character—"a friend of the slave"—had he lost sight of the great business of his life. He had even refused to give indulgence to his regard for the prospectively wealthy Rosalind Holmes until his reason had become convinced that, in this way, as much, perhaps, as any other, he might advance the object of his mission; and now, to consummate the matter by cutting off all hopes of accomplishing any thing in his proper line, not to speak of the want of personal advantage, was a thought not to be entertained. Had he been fully aware that the determination of her father, as represented by the lady, was final and irrevocable, his course would have been distinctly pointed out. "But might not he temporize until some favorable change should occur?" Yet, to return a favorable response, and avoid committing himself on either hand, was a delicate point.

His hesitation and embarrassment were rightly interpreted by Rosalind, whose crushed heart now saw that her reverse of fortune was more potent than his love. Her sensations they only can imagine who have had the painful truth forced upon them, that a really beloved object is unworthy their regard. Did we possess the ability, we would not attempt to analyze that heart.

His deep thoughtfulness seeming unlikely to result in a decision of any kind, the lady at length broke the silence, remarking, in a tone of attempted calmness, yet slightly broken by emotion:

"I am, then, to construe your silence into an approval of my suggestion, and to consider you free from any promise you have made to me? It now only remains that we mutually endeavor to forget."

Before he could recover himself sufficiently to speak, she was gone. Whether to her apartment, to lament and bewail her fate, and mourn over the heartlessness of man, or to seek strength to bear up under, or subdue her grief, we know not; but, from her disposition and subsequent life, we presume the latter, and that she was successful.

All that we can certainly state is, that, as she chanced to pass by "Aunt Rachel," that ancient domestic exclaimed, in much surprise:

"La, Miss Rosy! what de mattah? Cryin' like a chile!" she continued, as "Miss Rosy" hurried on, without so much as a passing notice.

This was pushing matters to an extremity the abolitionist had not anticipated; yet, feeling that, for the present, the stake for which he had been so long playing was lost, he determined at once to withdraw from her company. Still trusting, however, that fortune in the future might favor their union on favorable terms, he sought to leave open the way to that event by the following note, written on the eve of his departure:

DEAR ROSALIND:—Language cannot express the pain I feel at the thought that you might suppose my love for you changed by the information communicated in our last interview. As my present fortune would hardly justify me in asking you to share it, the hope of its improvement now tears me from you. Little know you the strength of my affection, could you suppose I desire a release from our engagement. Think not of this, but let us look to the happy day when we may be one.

Your ever faithful
CAROLUS.

The wounded heart of Rosalind was not thus to be healed. With true womanly instinct, she had read the secret of her calculating lover; and though at the cost of a painfully protracted struggle, she determined to banish him for ever from her mind.

CHAPTER XIX.

A REVIEW—A NEW FIELD.

" What has been done, no good result portends:
A change, perhaps, success may yet insure."

"Allured by prospects bright, my hopes I've built
On a frail base, that sinks beneath its load."

THE only tie that could have bound Justus to his occupation of private tutor, was now severed; and he was left at liberty to carry out the design formerly experienced, of seeking a new and more favorable point for observation. But he now felt some slight misgivings as to the success of his enterprise. Before proceeding further, it seemed necessary to review his past course, to determine, from the success already attained, his subsequent movements.

"What has been my aim in this Southern tour?" he first proposed for consideration.

"In the first place, I wished personally to watch the operations of slavery, and, from these observations, to write such an exposure of its iniquity as would convince the world of its wickedness."

Further reflection raised a doubt as to the eligibility of the latitude in which he had fallen for his particular purpose; and the fact was before him, that his conduct on every occasion had not strictly harmonized with the rule of right. Yet, by an easy application of his principles, his conscience stood acquitted; and in their connection his errors assumed the form of commendable virtues.

"But have I accomplished any thing commensurate with my vast design, the difficulties and dangers to which I have been exposed, or even the suffering actually endured?"

He could call to mind no pointed success, but would glance over his manuscript. It had grown quite bulky, but it failed to give pleasure: he had none of the rare incidents there recorded which he had expected to find. Reflecting on what he had himself seen, he even indulged the thought—could his Northern friends ever forgive it—that such cases as those of "Old Prue," and "Uncle Tom," were merely the creation of the novelist; or, otherwise, but one of those exhibitions of human barbarity that *will* occasionally be witnessed, and that not only where there is "wholly irresponsible power," but even in the face of law and authority. He was fully aware, at the worst, such things were never common, if he had not been very unfortunate in his notings, or else they belonged to a bygone age.

"A bygone age," he repeated; "but if slavery has ever produced such results, can it not do so again? Admit it is no part of the system; still, ought any thing to be tolerated that is so susceptible of abuse? But what is there so noble or good that it cannot be turned to bad account? Alas, nothing; and I have lived long enough to learn that the abuse of a thing argues nothing against it."

After all this, however, he was not fully prepared to admit that slavery was any thing but an *abuse*, at its best estate: he simply doubted its being responsible for all charged to it by its opponents.

On a cursory examination of his manuscript, he was disappointed at having collected so little to his purpose; and this feeling was deepened to a degree of shame as his attention was arrested by the surmises he had stated as indubitable facts, but which he had since learned were wholly unfounded.

"I will burn it," said he, turning to the fire for that purpose. "I will burn it, and direct attention to some other quarter for usefulness and fame."
But ere he had performed that rash deed, a better determination arose.

"Stop!" he said; "it may be put to some worthier

use, though of no service to me.   All has been said on the subject that can be said; but to this I will append a brief account of my adventures, and place it in the hands of a friend, whose genius and fancy can easily supply what my facts have failed to discover.   I would not be surprised if it should turn out a splendid affair, and my portion of the profits yet prove no inconsiderable amount."

Alas for the uncertainty of human calculation! This brilliant scheme was unhappily frustrated by the unfortunate loss of the precious documents, a calamity that occurred before he reached Massachusetts—a source of grief to the individual sufferer, and an irreparable loss to the philanthropic world.

Having thus disposed of the great work that had hitherto been the prime object of his life, his mind lingered for a time on past scenes and transactions of minor consideration.   They reverted to the camp-meeting, and his dealings with McMinime, his recognition by the same person; and as the temptation presented to him during the night's ride again returned, he muttered half audibly, while his frame again trembled under the strength of his emotion:

"Yes! he is the occasion of it all.   He must have recognized me as I passed; and that is undoubtedly the reason of his visit here—merely to expose me!   Holmes would never have thus acted

but for this. Well, he has defeated me again; but
he may make the most of it. He knows not the
advantage I hold over him, though it may be learned
at some future time, when circumstances are favorable to my wish. If it were only Henry, he would
feel it more sensibly. But all this hereafter."

The revenge meditated is already apparent to the
reader. The abolitionist having been frustrated in
his design by McMinime, could easily reconcile it
with his views to retaliate in any way that might
further his interest. Feeling he had him in his
power, he reserved the right to use it, until circumstances should develop a suitable opportunity.

Having thus disposed of these important subjects, his next care was for himself personally. In
his heart he felt a yearning for the scenes and
friends of his childhood's home; but from other
considerations, the South had more charms for him,
and here he resolved to fix his home. But how
should he employ himself? On this he did not long
debate; he had of late noticed an advertisement in
the papers for a competent person to take charge of
a certain academy, and for this place he resolved
to apply.

We pass over the parting with his late friends.
To Rosalind, despite her previous resolution, it was
painful in the extreme; while to Holmes it was a

matter of profound satisfaction to be thus rid of the unpromising aspirant to a family connection. In his joy, he freely gave a recommendation to the late tutor for the position he sought, who soon found himself installed the principal of a flourishing high-school.

Prosperity now dawned upon him. His salary was liberal, and he set to work in earnest, providing himself a home, with all its comforts. Soon a graceful mansion arose on a lovely site, selected and purchased for the purpose; and a portion of the cir-cumjacent prairie was converted into a fruitful farm. This was the establishment of the president, the sounding title by which the new teacher was called.

Justus now began casting about for that first, last grace of a home; that without which the most splendid residence is unworthy of the name—a suitable wife. And on more than one occasion had his thoughts strayed away to the beautiful, the ac-complished Rosalind Holmes; but this was for-bidden ground, and they were speedily recalled. We may inform the reader, in this place, that, sub-sequent to his departure from Mr. Clayton's, he had received a billet from the lady, breaking off uncon-ditionally all connection between them, and for-bidding in an equally decided manner all attempts

to renew it. But for this, his conduct might have
been diff'erent.

In his prosperity, Justus could have been excused
for the thought,

> ——"full surely
> My greatness is ripening."

But, in the very height of his success, a cloud was
gathering over his head—a most portentous cloud!
To be brief, it burst upon him, and removed him
from his place of profit and honor. His reverse
was brought about by his latent propensity for reform.

The phonetic system of instruction had been but
a few years in use in our country. Chancing to
come in contact with it, he considered it the very
improvement needed—a great desideratum ; and it
was at once introduced into his seminary. Soon he
thought Noah Webster, with his antiquated spell-
ing-book—which may yet have suited his day very
well—would be forgotten, or only remembered to
add brilliancy, by its contrast, to the late discovery.
Not only did he receive the new system under his
patronage, but took every occasion to decry the
"dull and stupid Roman." Believing his protégé
to require only an introduction to general notice, to
supersede entirely the old method of communi-

cating on paper, he left no means untried for that purpose.

He even went so far as to hold the other mode, with its great apostle, the said "Noah," up to ridicule in a little ditty, picked up, or invented for the occasion, which he sometimes sang in school.

For his own part, he would never write another sentence in the "tiresome, cumbrous" style now in common use; and that all might be convinced he *did* possess the wonderful art—at least, to such a motive it was generally attributed—each Sunday would find him, much to the disturbance of some, and greatly to the honor of others, duly prepared with note-book and pencil, to take down the sermon.

A little common sense might have led any one to see the folly of this course. But Justus was a reformer, and, in spite of his intelligence, his theories led him into wide extremes. As an abolitionist, he saw only in slavery a wrong not to be tolerated. As a teacher, the time had now come when, at his decision, a long-established system must be abolished for an untried novelty.

He did not reflect that, even should he establish the superiority of his plan, it would be a matter of some difficulty to induce those who had grown hoary in the use of something different, to concur.

Those in advance of the age cannot expect the sympathy of their contemporaries. As their common fate is, to be unappreciated, it is not marvellous that our reformer had soon raised a storm of opposition.

The "reverend graybeards" looked upon the whole measure as perfect nonsense. "The old plan had always worked well: the new could do no better."

Justus had hitherto been universally esteemed; but the charm was now broken. Some one had been found to assail his favorite system, and *now* his faults began to multiply.

Some discovered he was "no teacher anyhow," and, since he had taken this "idle whim into his head," he was "doing no good at all." "His pupils," they said, "were afflicted with a complete mania on the subject of phonographic writing. Their other studies were, in a manner, neglected in consequence of the demand upon their time of regular stenographic correspondence with schools of a similar kind." And they did not "believe the authors would themselves be able to decipher the letters a week afterwards, without diligently comparing them with their 'alphabets.' And, not to speak of the time wasted in acquiring it, each one was wont, at stated periods, to spend as much labor in penning a few lines as would suffice any youth of moderate ability in acquiring a knowledge of that time-honored puzzle, the 'Double Rule of Three.'"

This is only a specimen of the complaints urged on this one point; the charges and specifications were almost innumerable. We do not pretend to "take sides" in the quarrel; yet, we will say it seems evident that his opponents were unwilling to grant him a fair trial, and charged on his system what was, in reality, due to a want of time and experience. As to who was in the wrong, or whether there was any wrong, the reader himself must determine.

It was in vain, at this stage of the proceedings, that the president made concessions: he would even lay aside the new method of teaching entirely; but it was now too late for this to avail. His patrons had become dissatisfied, and nothing but his removal could atone for his fault. As the only alternative, he was forced to resign his position.

Thus left without occupation, he was at liberty to carry out his long-meditated design of revisiting Boston, and no time was lost in making his arrangements for this end.

CHAPTER XX.

THE LIBERATORS.

"They touch our country, and their shackles fall."

THE plan of Justus's travel was, to take the boat at Shreveport, and descend to New Orleans, thence to his destination.

It was night when he reached the hotel in the former place, and, while registering his name, he cast his eye above, where he read—

"T. McMinime, and servant;" destination, "New Orleans."

"So, we meet once more, do we?" he mentally exclaimed. "Well, I presume he can do me no further injury." Yet he could not help feeling a strange kind of excitement.

We find nothing worthy of attention in the trip to the Cresent City. It was accomplished without accident or delay.

McMinime and Justus met much as other travellers thrown together under similar circumstances would have done. They beguiled the time with social intercourse and lively chat; and one would have thought Justus had forgotten all his animosity.

Arrived at this place, the Texas planter learned that, on account of circumstances he had not foreseen, it would be necessary to continue his journey to New York. This was a source of no little regret, for he was attended by his most valuable servant, and he knew the risk of having him forcibly taken from him. He might, indeed, leave him behind, but that would interfere with his plan of return. He decided on retaining him in his own company, trusting, as his business would detain him but a day or two, to be able to keep his presence a secret to the New Yorkers, having the promise of the captain's assistance, who was to have him in charge, as a hand on the vessel.

They who have the leisure and tact, may descant on the *beauty and propriety of this state of things, under which the citizen of a great nation is forced to skulk and hide his property when visiting another portion of his own land!* We have only time to call attention to it, knowing not how sufficiently to admire the moral heroism of those who, forgetful of their own *little* imperfections, would entirely disregard the rights of others, and subvert their country's laws to extricate their neighbors from a state of imaginary guilt, sanctioned by God, as the sacred records show, and practiced by His acknowledged servants.

In due time they were under way for the Empire City, Justus taking passage in the same vessel.

During the voyage, the abolitionist expressed some solicitude lest the Southerner should lose his servant; and he even asked Henry, in the presence of his master, what he would do if the abolitionists of New York should lay hands on him.

"I reckin, mastah, dey wont take me 'way when I tell *um* I don't want to go.   Will dey?"

"Don't trust too much to that; they will scarcely pay attention to any thing you can say, should they make the effort. So, your only chance for safety will be to keep concealed, and thus escape observation."

"If they can get Henry off with his own consent, they are welcome to go with him," remarked his master. "All I fear is, that they will force him away without listening to his remonstrances."

The interest Justus seemed to take in the safe-keeping of the servant was a cause of no little wonder to McMinime; yet it was a something he could not doubt, proceed from what source it might. "And why did he have such fears of an attempt at liberation? Was there any possible way in which he could have received intimation of such a purpose, or was it alone from his knowledge of the character of the persons among whom they went? It surely could not be the former."

At any rate there seemed to be a presentiment in his mind that an attempt would be made to liberate Henry. Before the voyage had ended, he sought opportunity to warn the negro, in case he should be taken, and not be pleased with his lot, to have himself placed under the guardianship of his present adviser, who might, perhaps, find means to reconduct him to Texas.

The steamer was in a state of preparation to depart for Galveston. Every thing had, so far, answered to the wishes of the Texan planter. To Henry the time had passed heavily. His reflections had been of home, of his loved wife, and sweet child. "Ah! should he ever see them again?"

Often had he wished that "Mas Tom had 'nt neber fetched him away from Cindy and Charley." However, his troubles have in a great measure ceased. He shall soon be on his way home. One would hardly feel disposed to chide the negro for his manifestation of delight as he felt that *now* all danger is over; for surely, at this late hour, as the fire is beginning to glow in the engine-room, the most fearful heart could anticipate no evil.

Yet, at this very time, the vessel was boarded by

some twenty or thirty rude looking men, many of them under the influence of liquor. The person who seemed to be the leader, approached the captain, abruptly remarking:

" We have been told there is a slave on board this vessel; is it so ?"

The captain saw the case was hopeless, and was for a moment undecided. It was, however, but for a moment. Whispering a word to one of his men who chanced to be near, he turned on his assailants:

"And if there is, sir, I presume he does not belong to you; and as you are intruding on my rights, I warn you to retire at once, or abide the consequences."

McMinime, on hearing the question, felt for his pistol; for though the odds were immense, he was determined to resist to the last extremity; and he was not sure but the sight of a " six-shooter" in the hands of one well skilled in its use, might scare the rabble off. He had, however, left it in the cabin. To descend for it was but the work of a moment. On regaining the deck, he heard the former speaker exclaim in a loud and angry tone :

" You have him stowed away in the cabin, but it will not avail, sir; we will take the privilege of searching, and will have him in spite of all your efforts to the contrary."

As this was uttered, the captain took his stand beside the owner of the negro, at the head of the stairs. At the same time, they were joined by all the crew who could be spared, armed with such implements of defence as could hastily be gathered.

The boarding party, now reinforced by as many more, also pressed on valiantly.

"I will kill the first man that advances another step," said McMinime, laying a peculiar emphasis on the word kill.

"Then you will kill a good many of us."

The closing part of the sentence was drowned in the report of the pistol, which had been deliberately aimed at the head of the foremost man. To the surprise of each one of the defenders, he kept his feet, merely clapping his hand over his eye, and taking a position back in the crowd.

The pistol was immediately discharged again, with a like result, varied slightly by a cry of rage and pain from the recipient of its contents, as he hastily followed his fellow. Yet, still they pressed on, and shooting was no longer practicable. Then, raised high in air, the heavy cylinder, descending with wrathful force, laid one of the assailants heavily on the deck. At the same moment the captain's fist performed a like office for a second;

and the crew joining in, the mêlée for a time became general.

But it could not avail. The very number of the assailants soon left no room for further struggle. The crew were overpowered, but the bruises of the enemy bore evidence of a dearly purchased triumph.

Henry was found amusing himself by whittling on a stick, with a formidable looking dirk-knife.

"Are you not kept here against your will, my friend?" abruptly asked the spokesman of the crowd.

"No!" was the laconic reply. "Heah's jis wah I *wants* to be."

"At any rate, my dear sir, we have come to liberate you, to take you from the hands of a cruel master, and make you a *free* man; and you must prepare to accompany us without delay."

"I don't want to go wid you ge'men; so jis le' me be."

"O! you need not fear your master now; his power over you is gone, and we will protect you. Then come along, without more ado: we have no time to lose."

"No, mastah's, I'd ruther stay heah."

"We well know it is only dread of your master that leads you to talk and act thus, but you need not regard him as any obstacle in the way of your freedom. But if you continue to hold out in this way, we will be compelled to take you by force. Think better of the matter, and consent to go with your best friends."

"I won't go, ge'men; and it mout be as well fur you not to lay hands on me," replied he, dropping the stick he had hitherto held, and clutching the knife with a desperate grip.

At this stage of the proceeding, the guard left on deck passed word to their comrades below, that it would be as well to hasten operations, or they might take a trip oceanward.

When he first became aware of the presence of his visitors, the captain had given orders to use all possible expedition in getting under way. He was fearful he should not be able to contend successfully with the mob, but hoped that they would be so disconcerted at finding themselves afloat, and cut off from assistance, it would be no difficult matter to make terms; or, having the advantage of weapons, the crew might be able to overpower them when cut off from succor on shore. In the latter case, the freebooters would learn a valuable lesson, when left in Galveston, to return home at leisure.

The arrival of the reinforcements cut off this

hope, especially when he saw the crowd boldly and with impunity defy the pistol; but, having gone into the measure, he resolved to see the end of the experiment.

This new danger left no longer time for debate with the negro, and it was at once decided to seize him and *forcibly carry him to freedom.* But, in performing this act, the foremost received a dangerous, if not a fatal wound. Further resistance was impossible, and his new-found friends now bore off Henry in triumph, together with his profusely bleeding and shamefully misused friend.

Arrived on deck, the prospect was truly exciting. The boarding party had formed, and maintained a communication between the steamer and wharf; but the vessel, beginning to feel the force of the stream, was slowly receding from its place. There was not a moment to be lost, and the rush for the shore was most precipitate. The first motion only had been communicated to the vessel; still the distance between her and the shore gradually increased, as, yielding to the propelling power, the movement became sensible. It cannot be another moment until she will speed away, cutting off the communication at once. All knew this, and acted accordingly. The greater part had reached the shore, with the plank still crowded, when the fearful momentum came, and all who were in mid-passage were precipitated into the water.

But two of the invaders remained on board.

"Now go to the bottom for me!" exclaimed Captain Gilbert, looking complacently on the struggling rabble. But there was no fear of that: help in abundance was at hand. Then addressing those on shore, he cried:

"Those comrades of yours here shall take that boy's place."

"All right!" was the exulting response.

Night had fairly set in; yet, by the light of the moon, the movements of the party on shore could be distinctly seen from the deck, as, under a head of steam, the vessel pressed out of the harbor.

Some were vociferous in praise of their late achievement, and in demonstrations of joy thereat; while others vainly strove to reconcile the afflicted Henry. The wounded man was at once conveyed to his home.

Though fully under way, it would not do to depart without an attempt by the planter to test the power of the law for the restoration of his property. Thus the plans and calculations of all on board were thwarted, and a much regretted delay incurred.

The captives are taken into custody; and, while

assisting in this duty, McMinime interrogated them.

"This, sirs, is a pretty business you have been at; what think you now of yourselves?"

"Think! Why, sir, that we have assisted in the performance of a praiseworthy act."

"And what do you think will be the consequence to yourselves of this noble deed?"

"As you have us in hand, you may perhaps take our lives; and it is presumable, under the circumstances, that you can do so with impunity. But it is the fortune of war, and we can only submit."

"You misapprehend me, sir. It is our intention to give you up to the authorities here."

"Very good! Well, in that case, we will go through the form of a trial, then be set at liberty to receive the commendation and applause of all true philanthropists. I say *perhaps* this is the course matters will take; but it is difficult to see what charge you can bring against us, as we have done nothing that any man in New York will consider a crime. As it is wrong for you to enslave your fellows, it is right for us, by any means, to free the unfortunate."

"I certainly do not entertain so poor an opinion of the sense of justice of your fellow-citizens, as this."

"What charge can we bring against you? If nothing more, you have broken the peace, and committed a riot, though this is not all. But as you regard the matter so lightly, I presume you will have no objection to give me the names of your accomplices."

"None in the world, if it will be any gratification to you; and I have no doubt they will be ready to answer all your demands." The other took down the names, then said:

"We will see what can be done in the morning."

"You will certainly find your labor in vain; and I am really surprised at the folly of any one who can expect the laws of this free State seriously to interfere with its citizens for any thing growing out of an effort to liberate the suffering and unfortunate."

"We will see more about this hereafter;" and they were left to their own reflections and communion.

It is, perhaps, scarcely necessary to add that the application to the authorities for aid or redress was altogether fruitless. This was not all; but unmistakable evidences of a brewing storm induced Captain Gilbert to hasten his departure from the city of New York. Nor was the movement by any means premature: for by so doing, he barely escaped the serving of warrants on himself, as well as his unfortunate passenger, on various charges, among which was assault, and probable murder.

The result of the pistol-shots on the crowd was matter of astonishment to the two gentlemen engaged in the defence; the mystery was explained, however, or perhaps it would be better to say, rendered more mysterious, when an examination of the barrels yet undischarged revealed the fact that they were without balls.

"What a stupid mistake! Who before ever heard of such an egregious blunder! to put in a charge all around, and not one bullet!" were the vexatious exclamations of McMinimo, on making the discovery.

How much he had admired the heroism of his enemies in so unwaveringly advancing almost to the very muzzle of the death-dealing instrument! Yet, how little occasion was there in reality for fear, had they known how matters stood! Yet in their ignorance, they were undoubtedly heroes.

When Henry found himself on land, so much against his wishes, and the vessel in which he had hoped to be conveyed to his home, fast separating from him, he was almost frantic. It was to no purpose that his liberators strove to soothe him by a glowing description of the happiness in store for him.

"O, mastah! le' me go home! I don't care nuf'n 'bout all dese tings; I jis wants to git back home."

"Why, here is your home: here alone you can enjoy freedom, without which no place can be called home."

"I don't want no freedom, I tell you again; I jis wants to git back home onst more."

"You have no home but here. So, just reflect, sir, on the advantages you will hereafter enjoy, and do not be so unreasonable as to desire your former state of galling bondage——"

"Yes, I has, *dough*," answered he, paying no regard to the latter part of the sentence, and not caring to hear the conclusion of the speech; "yes, I *has* got a home, an' a good one, too, an' a wife an' chile *dar* besides. O! don't sep'rate us dis way; le' me go back home wid Mas Tom."

"If we did not separate you, your master would soon do so; for, no doubt, you have lived together pretty nearly as long as they ever permit. It might be, that——"

"'T is no sich a thing. You 'as neber dah, an' *dunno* nuf'n 'bout it," again interrupted the negro, irritated, and rather disposed to make use of the liberty accorded him by his new friends.

9

"No, I have never been there; but I have *heard* and *read* enough to satisfy me in regard to the thing."

"All great lies, dough," answered the boy, yet somewhat hesitatingly, as apprehensive he had gone too far, even with those who seemed to think so much of him.

"Well, well, we will not quarrel about that. You must, at least, acknowledge there is a probability of your being separated from your wife, were you to return. Therefore——"

"You's afeard somebody'll commit a sin; an' to save him from *sumf'n* dat *mout be,* you'll take de 'sponsibility on *youselves, shoah!* But I don't 'knowledge no sich *ting.* I'd neber be parted from her 'thout one of us 'as to die, or sumf'n oncommon happen; and *you,* even, may be parted from *your* wife, as much as me."

"As for the responsibility, we are more than willing to assume it; in regard to the other matter, you are very much in error; yet, we can lose no more time in the effort to convince you. Come, we must be off. In the meantime, do not doubt but that you will soon have reason to forget all about your old home, and even your wife; as you will be able to select one better suited to your condition in life. Why, man, you need entertain no fears if you desire such a thing, of being able, with your fine form and intelligent face, to secure the affections of a lady as fair as any you have ever called 'mistress.' What is there to prevent?"

"Well, ef you will take me 'way, I'd like to see Mas Justus, dat come in de boat wid us."

"Yes, we will conduct you to him, and he will take you under his own charge till you become acquainted with your new mode of life. But *do* quit that ' *Mas* Justus.' "

Finding further resistance idle, Henry accompanied them without more words, hoping, through the kind assistance of Justus, he might be enabled to see his home again

Two of the liberators, lingering behind their comrades, thus gave expression to their feelings:

"For my part, George, I do not find myself so well satisfied with this evening's proceedings as I had expected."

"You don't! Why, what is the matter? I was never better pleased in all my life."

"The thought has more than once before to-day crossed my mind, that perhaps we did not fully understand what we were doing in our deadly opposition to slavery; but *now* I am more than half *convinced* of it. Here is this poor fellow, whom, I have no doubt, we found a happier person than he ever will be again. What, suppose you, are his sensations, and what will be those of his poor expectant wife when informed of his fate? And on the other hand, what have we gained in the way of a citizen? How much better qualified is he to benefit the world, or himself, here, than on his master's plantation?"

"As for his qualifications, he will learn very readily in the school of experience. But you surely do not believe he was happier as a slave than here as a free man? I must confess I do pity his wife; still, the probability is, we have only hastened what would sooner or later have taken place. It is true, his appearance shows he has an indulgent master; but how suddenly and how fearfully do their circumstances change! For a ready illustration, just think of the case of poor 'Uncle Tom!' From this you see how uncertain is their condition, even at the best."

"I consider this 'case' as a very highly wrought picture of what might *possibly* occur; but I must confess I really feel a degree of shame to hear one who pretends to be candid, advancing as an argument against slavery, what may with equal propriety be urged against almost *every thing*."

"I cannot say that I altogether comprehend you."

"You do not? I will endeavor to enlighten you.

You, as well as myself—and thousands besides—are a poor mechanic, barely able to support, in decency and competency, your fond wife and dear children. Now, sir, you well know you are liable to be disabled by sickness or casualties, or even to be removed by death; and in such an event, what would be their fate?"

"Well, you certainly are a——. I was on the point, Tom, of making use of a rough expression; but, to say the least, there is not the shadow of analogy between the two cases; and it is sheer nonsense for you to talk in this manner. My wife and children would not be sold under the hammer to the highest bidder, and thus become for ever separated from each other."

"There is a closer analogy than you seem to be aware of; for it would almost be a necessity of the established order of things, that they should be separated in one way or another, and that, too, perhaps, under circumstances far more painful than in the case of the slave. For I am satisfied that, in the latter case, there are always circumstances calculated to moderate the sorrow of the breaking up. And though the servant may be called upon to part with those who are dear, it is, in all probability, to follow one scarcely less dear—one who has been to him almost as a child, or with whom he has been raised as a brother. My brother, you know, lives in a slave State, and is himself the owner of slaves; it is from him I learn these things, and he assures me he has known the case of an old servant choosing rather to follow her mistress than remain with her children. He says it may be the case, at times, that some are separated under other circumstances, but not often; and I say, were the probabilities of such a thing universal, it is nothing more than may happen to our own families.

"In the contingency under consideration, it is true, your wife and children run no risk of being sold; yet, might it not be much better for them to find themselves thus in the hands of a kind protector? Divest the thing of its name, and what better fate can a poor widow or helpless orphan desire, than to have some one to whom they can look up for support in any extremity."

"They can desire to be *free*—free from the domination of any one—free to labor for their own support!"

"Free, indeed, to labor!—to labor beyond the power of endurance for a pittance to support a cheerless, joyless existence: to spend the overtasked powers of their youthful days, in toiling for one whose only object is to make the most use of the poor apprentice, and then cast him out on the world, without having acquired one useful lesson for direction in life, save what his bitter experience must of necessity bring.

"Or, better still, they can be free to go to the street—to filth and to degradation.

"Do you observe those objects on the opposite side of the street?"

"To be sure I do."

"Will you be so kind as to inform me what they are?"

"What ails you this evening, man? Can you not see they are children? or are you merely trying me?"

"How do you know they are children, George?"

"Do you suppose I have no eyes, Tom? I see they are."

"But what I mean is this: were you going to prove those objects before us to belong to the human race, to what distinctive feature in them marking the *genus*, would you refer?"

"I do not know how to answer such a question, except by saying, I *know* they belong to *that* class: *every thing shows it.*"

"If you answer, *Every* thing shows them to be human beings, you have surely never observed them closely. Let us cross over and make an inspection."

"No, thank you! I do not wish to do so. I have seen many such sights, and *enough* of them, too. Yet, I am very well satisfied with my answer."

"Still, let me give you a better. It is form and speech alone, at least, so far as the eye and ear can aid us in determining. The rags with which they are covered, the filth and vermin with which they abound, the wretched abodes to which they are returning after a day, perhaps, of beggary and crime, and, above all, the marks of hardened guilt stamped on their young brows, might proclaim them as belonging to another race. And yet, these may once have been as yours—possibly yours may yet be like these."

"I know strange revolutions *do* sometimes take place, and it is within the range of *possibility* that even *this* you speak of may happen, but which may God forbid! Yet, I cannot clearly see the point to which your argument tends."

"You mistake entirely, my dear sir; I am not arguing, but simply trying to give you another specimen of your own logic. Indeed, I do not know to what conclusion a man could not bring himself, by such reasoning as you have just employed, and as others use. If applied to the common affairs of life, the practical result on the state of the world, if universally followed, might not be easily imagined."

"I begin to see what you are aiming at; but you are only in a dull mood, and wish to show your skill in argument, by taking the part of slavery."

"Not I; instead of taking the *part* of slavery, I was only contending that we should leave it to those who have the management of it, while we look after our own affairs."

"Well, I thank my Maker I have public spirit enough to attend to my *own* affairs, and yet give a passing thought to the wrongs of *others*, or to *act* in their behalf if necessary."

"It seems you are determined not to take my meaning rightly. If the master of this negro inherited, and could not consistently with the laws of the State, or the benefit of his social and moral position, liberate him, did he commit sin by retaining and treating him kindly?"

"Perhaps not; at least I will not assert he did."

"Had he failed, or died, and the family of his servants been scattered, would any one have been to blame? If so, on whom should censure rest?"

"The man—no—the system."

"Were you to die, leaving your wife and children unprovided for, or become so reduced that the latter should become like those we have just passed, and the former like we may suppose *their* mothers are, where would the blame rest—on the man, or the system?"

The other, turning short around, looked him full in the face for a moment without speaking; then said:

"Tom! for what in the name of Heaven did you ever marry? Entertaining such notions as these, I would no sooner have done it than I would own slaves."

"Nor I either! I should think myself the worst of men, if, condemning slavery on *this* ground, I had entered into the other relation. For I consider the two institutions in *that* respect similar. And in a slighter degree, as the consequences involved are not so vast, the same objection may be made against every pursuit in life."

"One thing, my dear friend, you seem to forget: marriage is an institution of the Almighty, and in regard to *it* we are under Divine command."

"You remind me now to make an explanation I had before forgotten. If slavery be, as its advocates claim, an institution of Heaven—I say nothing on *that* point—those practicing it are no more responsible for any evil growing out of it, than are we for the evils sometimes resulting from marriage, and other institutions of Divine appointment. And

to say that evil may, or even *docs* grow out of a system, is no disproof of its rectitude; otherwise, all
parents whose children are thus left to suffer, are
highly reprehensible for the connection in life that
gave them being."

"Come, come, let us hurry on; our comrades
have already left us out of sight; and I fear we will
yet lose the sport."

"I believe, George, I will turn down the street
here, and go home. I have seen *sport* enough for
one night. Hark, how they shout!"

Taking leave of his friends, he thoughtfully turned
himself homewards, and was soon by his own quiet
fireside.

CHAPTER XXI.

THE NEWLY-MADE FREEMAN.

"Woe unto you, Scribes and Pharisees, hypocrites! for ye compass sea and land to make one proselyte; and when he is made, ye make him twofold more the child of hell than yourselves."

DURING the late transaction, Justus was quietly employed at his lodgings, in preparations for an immediate departure. His arrangements were completed, and, hastily pacing the floor of his apartment, he manifested a spirit of uncontrollable impatience.

He heard the exulting shout of a crowd approaching, and was quickly on the pavement.

To these visitors, in part, the reader has been already introduced on board the steamer; but the number had been augmented during the passage through the streets; and now, a small army, they moved on vociferously, with Henry borne in triumph at their head. The occasional potations freely indulged in by the way, enlivened the wits of the abolitionists, and heightened the grandeur of the imposing scene they so cheerfully enacted.

Enthusiastic cheers, self-laudations, bacchanalian efforts at wit, and most boisterous merriment, generally, were strangely commingled.

"How I do wish I could get my hands on that fellow who is so ready to use his pop-gun of a pistol on all occasions; would 'nt I give him ——; he liked to have powder-burnt the side of my face off, the slave-holding wretch! He would have been glad to send a few of us out of the world anyhow. But was 'nt that beautifully done? Ah! we 're the boys that know how to do *such things!*"

What more this particular member of the assembly might have uttered, cannot be told; his voice was drowned in the sound of loud and prolonged cheers for liberty, New York, etc., together with denunciations of slavery and the South; and he vociferously joined in the chorus.

Another, who had imbibed rather more freely than the former speaker, as evidenced by his frequent hiccoughing, took up the strain :

"Hang me—*hic*—if I know *now*, what I am making such a fuss over that black scoundrel for! Wonder—*hic*—if he did 'nt knock me down! What a lick—*hic*—he did hit! Got a great mind to go and —*hic*—stamp him under the face of the earth for it, now. But we taught 'em—*hic*—a thing or two. Hurrah for our side! Down with the—*hic*—slave-holders!"

In a manner of which the foregoing is but a faint likeness, the crowd proceeded to Justus's hotel, where Henry was in due form committed to the guardianship of that worthy, till such time as he should be properly able to defend and provide for himself.

The abolitionist and his negro companion at once left the city, and, while the sleeping master was dreaming, perhaps, of the recovery of his stolen property, and the punishment of the abductors, by the aid of law, that servant was reluctantly putting distance between himself and owner, as fast as relays of horses could accomplish that end.

Justus was once more among the associates of his earlier years, and was welcomed by his friends with a heartiness he had not expected. But the fame of recent events, together with the part now performed toward the lately liberated slave, had removed from their minds the unfavorable impressions formed by his correspondence from Texas.

The dignified composure and silent gravity with which he received their adulations as well as apologies, were interpreted by them as a noble and self-satisfied assurance of the rectitude of his past

course, and a gratification at the result—too deep
to find expression in any· shallow demonstration.
Whereas, Justus was, in reality, conscious of a
change of views more material than that for which
he had been discarded by them; and though it did
not suit his present purpose to proclaim this, he was
equally averse to make any display of feeling on the
opposite side.

He now found himself an undoubted lion—a
bright star in the zenith of a Boston firmament,
though his light was somewhat paled by that of the
negro, who shone with successful rivalry in the
same orbit.

But it was not deemed sufficient for him to receive the private greetings of his friends alone; a
public meeting must be called, both as a compli-
ment to the man who had achieved so much in the
cause of humanity, and to collect a fund for the
present relief of the now *happified*, but still needy
object of his benevolent labors.

Old Faneuil was crowded: complimentary speeches
were made and applauded; a great many witty things,
or those, at least, designed for such, were uttered
and cheered, the blessings of freedom proclaimed
and extolled, and the evils of slavery denounced;
all with so much spirit and energy, that the genii
of that sacred locality might well have wondered

what new commotion had excited the citizens;
whether another "stamp-act" were about to be en-
forced, or a fleet of tea-ships to discharge their ob-
noxious freight at the peaceful wharves.

The assembly was called on to contribute to the
necessities of their friend, who having, until quite
recently, been under the control of a hard-hearted
master, and thus kept from acquiring that character of education needed for supplying himself in
his new condition, must be aided by others until
subsequent experience might enable him to overcome the disqualification. As the result of this
measure, Henry found himself in possession of more
ready cash, probably, than he had ever before
owned at any one time; obtained, too, in a manner
less calculated to teach him its true value, than any
of his former acquisitions. Indeed, so far as his *interest* was concerned, the money had better been
thrown away, though, should the reader doubt the
correctness of our judgment, we leave him to the
peaceful enjoyment of his own opinion.

Justus was then called out; whereupon he gave
a detailed account of his experience and observation in the South, which was received with hearty
applause. When the greeting subsided, it was
asked—a little hesitatingly, it must be acknowledged, as if the querist himself felt the absurdity

of the call—if Mr. Clay had not something to say for their entertainment; and the welkin rung with,

"Mr. Clay! Mr. Clay!"

Lest the reader should be in doubt as to the identity of Mr. Clay, it may be stated, he is neither more nor less than our *Henry*, formerly of Friend McMinime's cotton-farm, to whose previous name his late associates had appended that of the illustrious statesman.

Mr. Clay had been made aware that such, in future, was to be his style of address, and was at no slight loss to know why his name was so often pronounced, or, in his own language,

"What dey *hollerin'* at me so 'bout?"

"Your friends wish you to speak to them," whispered Justus.

"What I *gwine* to say to 'um?"

"Tell them you are unprepared; that you have not been used to public speaking; but thank them for their kindness."

Thus urged, and thinking himself competent to this slight task, he arose with much gravity, as another call for Mr. Clay resounded through the hall. But, as he looked over the vast assembly, his head grew dizzy, and not one word of what had been said to him could he call to mind. For a moment he stood trembling and stammering; but he could support himself no longer; and, rather gasping out than speaking plainly:

"I's forgot, mastahs," sunk into his seat.

After a brief consultation with his ward, Justus made to the auditory the explanations deemed requisite, trusting they would receive them as coming directly from his friend, by whose authority he spoke, and whose extreme modesty had prevented his making them in person.

This eclaircissement seemed to give general satisfaction, and to be withal highly edifying. And then, more deeply in love with themselves and the world in general—save the slaveholders of their own country—the meeting adjourned.

The circumstances of Henry's situation, so different from any thing he had ever known previously, soon wrought a corresponding change in his conduct and disposition, verifying, truthfully, the spirit of the adage, "Put a beggar on horseback," etc. While simple Henry, on his master's plantation, he knew his place, and acted well in it; but having been forced into a sphere above his own, and for which he had received no prior fitting, this good report was no longer his due. Being treated as a peer by those whom he had been wont to consider his superiors, and having a deference shown to his opinions, it is not to be wondered at that his arrogance was a source of annoyance even to his Boston friends. There was a very rational cause for this disposition, manifesting itself at an early day; and, but for this, he might, in all probability, have conducted himself differently. He had no respect for those who were so officious in his behalf, and would have been glad at any time to have returned to his former state.

The negro had, very early in life, acquired a decided partiality for intoxicating drinks, and in his primal condition, in Texas, used to say:

"De only thing Mas Tom eber got mad wid me 'bout, was gittin' drunk. But I could'nt *help* it. Jis 'peared like I *had* to do it, when I got sich a good chance. Dough ole mastah don't gib me many sich chances *since* dat time."

As Mr. Clay, in the midst of temptation, it is not surprising that he still indulged the old propensity.

It was but a few days after the meeting already spoken of, that Mr. Clay, attended by a few choice spirits, found himself in one of the establishments where his favorite beverage was dealt out. A few libations made them quite merry, and Mr. Clay's liberality was duly extolled, and his treat heartily enjoyed.

The revel held its high round, amid a boisterous flow of jollity, but the negro's powers of endurance soon gave way, and he early sank into obliviousness.

When Mr. Clay recovered from his debauch, he was a bankrupt. Of the donation of his kind friends he possesed not one cent. How it had gone, whether consumed in the jollification, or abstracted by some of his boon companions, his confused recollection could not tell.

As a natural consequence, the negro was ashamed of the part he had acted in thus abusing the confidence of his friends. In his reflections on their expected comments upon the affair, he could not avoid associating therewith the reproofs bestowed by his master for a like offence; and the most important consideration was to prevent the fact being known that he had lost all his money in a *drunken frolic.* The only course open to his mind, to secure this end, was to accuse one of his party of theft. As their mutual friends sided with the negro, nothing but the absence of testimony prevented an appeal to legal redress. Thus encouraged, he grew more insolent than before, and was quite loud in complaint of his wrongs.

The object of his accusation was now systematically persecuted by the negro, till, pressed beyond endurance, hostilities were regularly proclaimed. For a time, Henry avoided him, save when in the com-

pany of friends; but at last they met in an unfrequented alley, both the worse for liquor.

"I've got you *now*, you villainous blackamoor,"
was the courteous salutation of Mr. Clay's anta-
gonist.

"And I'se got *you*, too, you infernal white trash,"
said the negro, whose vocabulary had been consider-
ably extended by his new associations. "You wants
to steal more money, dus ye?"

A blow from a heavy bludgeon ended the alter-
cation, and brought the negro to the ground. This
coup d'e-tat was followed up by a succession of well-
directed strokes, despite the piteous supplication of
the prostrate and now-subdued Henry.

"I'll teach you to lie, you vile slave! I'll break
every bone in your —— body, and pummel your
carcass to a jelly."

"For de Laud o' massy sakes, please stop, mastah; don't kill me! I won't tell no more lies!"

"You've lived too long already, you drunken
vagabond! Die, and make room for a better man!"

The vengeful tone and furious manner accompanying this sentence, now fully disclosed to Henry
his assailant's murderous intention. Still clinging
to life, he felt the instinct of self-preservation rising
superior to fear, and though almost disabled and

insensible, he made one fierce effort at defence, then swooned away.

They were found, the negro half dead, and still insensible, the other, a corpse. Deeply buried in the dead body, was a knife usually worn in Henry's belt, which in the ferocity of despair had been plunged to the heart of his foe.

As there were no witnesses, nothing could be gathered in regard to the rencounter, save what the condition of the parties showed. The presence of the club, however, and the battered and insensible state of the African, seemed to indicate that the fearful act had been committed in self-defence.

The coroner's verdict was, that "George Thompson came to his death from a stab with a knife, in the hand of Henry Clay, a colored man.'

Painful weeks passed before the victim of benevolence was fully restored to soundness; but, by the management of his friends, he was subjected to no further inconvenience. His condition, however, was truly pitiable. An alien from home and all he loved, forced to provide for himself by means to which he had never been accustomed; and daily sinking into a state of degradation from dissipation, and the want of knowledge and capacity to fill the false position assigned him; and, more than all this, remorse for the fatal circumstances leading to the deed of death, continually preyed upon him.

In the belief that it would have a tendency to relieve his mind, at least in a degree, a return to Texas was more than ever desired; and yet for the accomplishment of this end all his efforts were ineffectual. But, in this exigence, Justus came to the rescue. The latter was himself preparing to return to his adopted State, and had been meditating, as he informed Henry, how he might be able to restore him to his friends.

"O! Mas Justus, ef you jes do *dat*, I 'll lub you long 's I libs in dis *worl'*; an' I know Mas Tom 'll pay you mighty well, besides. An' O! how *Cindy* 'll bress you!"

It was at once determined that both should make arrangements for a speedy departure; and to keep down suspicion, and prevent interference with the plan, Baltimore was selected as the point of departure. Thither Henry repaired, furnished with ample means by Justus, who soon rejoined him, when, as servant and master, they found themselves on the passage back to the land of their hopes and wishes.

CHAPTER XXII.

AN EPISODE.

"See yonder poor, o'erlabored wight,
  So abject, mean, and vile,
  Who begs a brother of the earth
  To give him leave to toil!
  And see his lordly *fellow-worm*
  The poor petition spurn,
  Unmindful though a weeping wife
  And helpless offspring mourn."

WHILE in Boston, Justus spent much of his time with a distant relative, who had been brought up at the South; but, from some cause or other, had chosen his residence in the North. This choice his friends had attributed to a spell thrown upon him during a college vacation, spent there at the solicitation of a chum. Nor was this opinion at all weakened when, shortly after having graduated M. D., he led to the altar one of the fair daughters of that city.

Although living in the North, the Doctor still retained his Southern predilections, and had suffered no little annoyance from Justus's attempts to show him his wrong principles on the subject of slavery, and convert him from the errors of his way. But since the visit of the latter to Texas, he was less inclined than formerly to engage in argument on this topic, and was often rallied by his cousin on having become a slaveholder.

"No," he would reply, "I am not a slaveholder, nor do I ever expect to be; but I have *seen* something for *myself*, and have learned that it is useless to make an outcry where no *good* can result."

"Not quite so bad a thing as you thought, after all, ha?"

"I have not said that yet."

"You will not believe, then, there are worse things, even in this city, and more to be deplored than Southern slavery?"

"No; and indeed I never before heard an opinion so wild and extravagant."

"Would you *believe* it, then, if I, on my veracity, were to tell you it *is* even the case?"

"I would presume not. What *can* compete with slavery, in this respect, not to say surpass?"

"Poverty, wretchedness, *licensed vice, slavery in a worse form.*"

"Yes, *slavery in a worse form*, if such a thing were

possible. But I perceive you are not serious, for there is nothing akin to that here."

"What does it take to constitute slavery?"

"To belong to another; to be compelled to do as he may direct."

"But the case, I presume, is made materially better, where to all this is added, as a pleasant alternative, the liberty of starving or doing worse."

"You don't mean that such is ever the case in the free States?"

"I wish I had no cause to mean it."

"Let us have an instance, then, of any such deplorable condition."

"How many mechanics, of the various orders in this city, would be thrown out of employment, were all the labor divided among such a number only as it would sustain in affluence, or even in competence? And yet, all these persons must subsist by their labor. In such a state of affairs, can there be any independence? No! They must have work. The employers have the advantage; hands are plentiful, and readily obtained. And while the circumstance of sickness or scant days' labor does not effect the interest of the slave, the free hired laborer suffers a reduction or loss of wages, should bad health, or other causes, prevent his continual toiling. What

indignities and insults, too, are they often compelled
to endure from a purse-proud employer, on false
or trivial provocations! And, though free to abandon the service of the selfish and unjust, it is, as in
the other case, too apt to involve the loss of employment, and consequent suffering of the family.
Hence, as an inevitable choice, thousands in the
bonds of a heartless servitude are compelled to

> '——beg a brother of the earth
> To give them leave to toil.'

"Yet we will admit this is not the case you demanded. You may call these free, independent,
happy, as they certainly are, in comparison with the
lower classes. What though they are compelled
through necessity, to sell their sons! I say *sell*, for
it can scarcely be regarded in any other light. Sent
away from home, at the very time they most need
parental oversight to foster the good principles that
we will suppose already implanted, into the hands
of one who, oftener than any other way, may have
no further regard for them than to get the most he
can for the food given them—to say nothing of the
kind, or manner of serving it—for the five, seven,
or nine years they are to belong to him. This, it is
true, is slavery only for a limited time; but still, it
is a despotism—not the endearing relation of father

and child. The parents have sold all the right they ever had to his services, to be clear of the expense of supporting him. There is, indeed, another ostensible object—the acquisition of a useful trade. But, were it not for the slavery of inexorable circumstances, more oppressive and unrelenting than that over which hangs the 'dark shadow of law,' what father would not select other means of teaching his son a suitable occupation? And, even with all the sacrifices made for this end, how often does the *'prentice* find himself turned out on the world, at man's estate, with scarcely any knowledge of his business?

"What phase of Southern slavery can be more harrowing to the feelings than the condition of a Christian mother, forcibly, I might say, deprived of the society of her son, doomed to mourn over his estrangement from his own fireside, performing the drudgery of life for others, learning vicious habits, and exposed to the hardening influence of wickedness, unrestrained by a mother's gentle influence. Or, perchance, to be compelled to listen to complaints from her poor delicate child of abuses which it is out of her power to correct or prevent, which *must* be endured, and which she yet sees are wearing him to his grave."

"You are entirely carried away with your theme,

and forget that every evil you have portrayed can be found in the South as well as in the North."

"There are, I know, ills that belong to society in any division of the world. But do you not find objectionable features in this system that negro slavery in a great measure obviates? But it is a matter of indifference to me whether or not there be as much suffering among the free, where slavery exists, as where it is unknown. The indisputable fact that we have, in the latter places, a large class who cannot boast of surpassing in real enjoyment the slave population, should teach us the stupidity of making an outcry against slavery, especially when it is so plain that nature, by their inferior capacity and cheerful submission to their lot, has so well fitted them for this position.

"I set out to show you one of this class, but have already spent too much time. I will only direct attention to the sewing order—needle-women, and those having no settled calling. I have a visit to make this afternoon; ride with me; perhaps before returning, our views may yet harmonize."

As they set out, Justus remarked, "You will admit, Doctor, that negro slavery is dishonorable and degrading to the female. To what excess of bestial indulgence and sacrifice of virtue, does it tend!"

"I am aware," returned his companion, "much has been said and written on this point, and a false sympathy in this direction has overlooked vice and abandonment of a deeper hue, and nearer home.

"Do you observe that female just passing the sidewalk?"

"I do."

"She is a beautiful woman, is she not?"

"Very, indeed!"

"And that is not all; she is intelligent, educated, and well-bred; yet, with all this, she is an abandoned, ruined woman. Consorting with the lost and vile, she inhabits a den of infamy, and leads a life of sin.

"Once in good circumstances, her father's reverses reduced her to the condition of a servant-girl.

"Her story, though a long one, is full of interest, a mere outline of which will suffice.

"Her personal appearance and pleasant manner excited the bitter jealousy of her first mistress, who, after a series of shameful abuse, gratified her hateful passion by dismissing the girl, and blasting her character by base and unfounded reports.

"I need not depict the mental agony of the unfortunate woman, thus spurned from her only home; nor the mortification and shame attending her frequent application for a place. The mistress' story had done the work, and effectually barred the door to her employment.

"How long and painful the struggle before she fell, none can tell. But, neglected and cast out by the virtuous, and assailed by insidious temptation, she found, in the end, some justification for wrong in a plea of necessity. She is now the depraved being you see, lost to society, and an outcast from virtue.

"As low as she may have fallen, she is but the type of a large class, who, through inclination, temptation, or necessity, are thus degraded, and, like festering sores, lend their influence to blast and destroy others; when, by their capacity and talents properly directed, the world in them might have been blessed.

"The condition of the female negro slave finds no parallel to this; for, how much soever in this prospect she might be degraded, her social and mental *status* would neutralize its influence for evil; while the ample provision made for her comfort and support, creates an absence of necessity often so fatally misleading others."

By this time they had reached their destination, and in silence entered the house. Though every thing denoted poverty, Justus was struck with the neat and orderly arrangement of the interior, among which several children, whose scanty apparel, joined to their scrupulous neatness, was not the least-noticeable feature. A frail-looking woman, evidently worn with watching and fatigue, welcomed them. Want, and consequent anxiety, had left their traces on her pale face, which, still pleasant, expressed more than ordinary intelligence.

The husband was the doctor's patient, whom he found much improved. Being an excellent mechanic, he was able, when in good health, to support a comfortable style of living; but having for a length of time been in a feeble state, his situation at present was really distressing. Indeed, knowing that such must inevitably be the result of sickness in his case, he had, at length, by struggling in his weakness against it, found himself entirely prostrated.

It was the story of the mother, however, elicited by the doctor, that chiefly attracted the attention of Justus, and excited his sympathy.

She had but recently buried a son, twelve years of age; a promising child, modest and retiring in his disposition, her hope and pride, and the idol of his young sisters. Unable to give the statement with the same mournful effect produced by the the weeping mother, we shall only transfer to this page the substance of the sad narrative.

Little Felix was a good boy; he was an intellectual child, but very timid, and of a delicate constitution. At the end of his tenth year, urged by necessity, his father determined to bind him to a tailor, that he might thus lessen the burden of family support, and learn useful employment.

"I need not say," remarked the lady, "that this to me was excessively painful. I could see he was unhappy, and at every visit from him my heart was made to ache; he would have so much to tell me of his little troubles. There was no one at his new home to confide in, for none there cared for him; he was made the butt of his fellow-apprentices, and his master's children treated him as an inferior being. Yet he was not complaining, but, in his simplicity, detailed the daily events of his young life, with patient submission, as though inevitable; yet by which, nevertheless, I could see, he at times became quite dejected."

It was in vain that his mother, on such occasions, endeavored to comfort him by picturing a brighter future. How could she hope to inspire him with the enthusiasm she herself felt not.

"No, mother!" he would reply, "I am only a poor boy; there is nothing else for *me*. I have none that can help me, and I sometimes think it

10

would be better to die at once. But for you and the children, O, how dark my life would be!"

"Poor child!" sobbed the mother, "he little knew how near he was to such an end!"

But one week before his death, he innocently incurred the displeasure of his master, and this, too, in a very trivial matter. It was his task to do the errands both of the shop and the house, and, on one of these occasions, he chanced to lose his thimble. The "boss" was angry, and threatened a prompt and severe punishment, unless the article were speedily found. Knowing from experience this was no idle threat, and wishing above all things to escape the cruel castigation in store, on his morning errand•to the baker's, he obtained bread of an inferior quality, and was able to invest the difference of price in a new thimble.

"Felix, have you found that thimble?" sternly demanded the master, on his return.

"Here is a thimble, sir," he stammered out, at the same time drawing it from his pocket.

"*Is that the one you lost, sir?*"

The child could not lie, and there was no response; but his lips quivered, and tears gathered in his eyes.

"*Answer me, sir! Have you found your own thimble?*"

"No, sir!" sobbed the boy.

"Where did you get *this*, then? I suppose, though, your foolish mother has given it to you, in hopes of cheating me, and saving you a whipping. But it will not do; I shall encourage no such carelessness."

"I bought it," was all the child could reply, for his tears.

"And where did you get the money, sir? you are not accustomed to having change of your own!"

No attempt at concealment was made, and the whole story was told.

"You stupid little blockhead! Did you think to play that kind of a game on me without discovery? You have only made the matter worse with yourself; for now, instead of one whipping, you are entitled to two."

Finding entreaties vain, the child attempted to escape by running. His master observing the motion too quickly, and his orders to stop not being heeded, he threw a billet of wood with such force, that, striking him on the head, it prostrated him. The whipping was then most savagely inflicted. At this point the mother's emotion completely overcame her. Recovering herself, she said:

"Yes, Doctor, you told me Felix died of a fever, but I thought then, and ever shall think that he was killed—murdered by inhuman treatment, and that this last punishment was the immediate cause of his death!"

It would have been intrusion to offer consolation to such grief, and the gentlemen withdrew.

CHAPTER XXIII.

CINDY.

"My friends! do they now and then send
A wish or a thought after me?"

THE connection of Henry with the subject of our story having rendered it necessary to say thus much in regard to him, it may not be uninteresting to return to the residence of McMinime, to note the effect of that gentleman's arrival without his servant.

It is needless to speak of the surprise and vexation of the white members of the family—the various *blessings*, or the particular form in which they were invoked on the head of all abolitionists in general, and Justus in particular. But let the reader just imagine one of the "little niggers" stopping his play, and rushing into the kitchen, bawling with the very utmost power of his lungs:

"Aunt Cindy! Aunt Cindy! Ole *Mastah's come back!*"

On the instant down dropped the tray, from which she had been putting her dough into the receptacle for baking, and Aunt Cindy, jumping up and capering with sudden delight, knocked little Charlie, who was just beginning to "toddle," sprawling on the floor. Not even taking time to quiet the squalling urchin, but simply standing him on his feet, and satisfying herself he was not seriously hurt, away she darted to the yard-gate to greet her husband, not entertaining the remotest doubt of his having accompanied his master home.

But—no!—does she see aright? There is a horse, and but a single one, and instead of Henry, Peter is silently conducting him to the stable. But one horse! what can it mean? A fearful suspicion crossed her mind, and, bowing her head upon the fence, she trembled with ill-suppressed emotion.

For a few moments she thus gave way to excess of feeling, and then, terribly calm, as if some fearful determination had been formed, she muttered between her clenched teeth :

"If he has, I 'll do it, if there 's ——;" then suddenly checking herself, "No! Mas Tom neva do it. He 'd jis as soon do any thing else. When we was married, he tol' me he would 'nt neva part us, and I know he would 'nt; sumf'n 's *happened!* I 'spect he 's dead."

Then bursting into tears, she returned to the kitchen, not possessing sufficient courage to learn by application to her master the true state of the case. Entering her cabin, she threw herself on the bed, not observing that the bread-tray, to the great danger of her dwelling, was about taking fire from the coals on which it had fallen, and gave way to a long and uncontrollable fit of grief.

In the meantime, the question was debated in the house as to how the mournful tidings should be conveyed to Cindy, and who should undertake the task; for it was well known she was devotedly attached to her husband, and inclined, on his account, too easily to yield to sorrow.

"I will tell her, ma," said little Fanny, the tears streaming from her eyes.

"O, no, daughter," said her father; "you have not the tact for such an office. You will be apt to afflict her more than need be. Mary, you have prudence, and can more quietly break to her the sad intelligence."

"No, no, pa! I believe Fanny is really better fitted for such a duty than I am, and will perform it more feelingly than I possibly could."

It was decided that Fanny should be the bearer of the unwelcome news, and with a full heart she went on her sorrowful mission.

"Aunt Cindy!" again bawled the little darkey; "Aunt Cindy! here comes Miss Fanny."

This announcement caused a fresh burst of grief, and, burying her head in the bedclothes, the poor negro awaited the confirmation of her worst fears.

"O Laudy!" she sobbed; "its done; he's sold, or dead, and they've sent Miss Fanny to tell me."

"O Cindy!" said a soft voice, tremulous and almost choked with emotion. A long-drawn, heavy sigh was the only response.

"Cindy!" repeated the same voice, and the gentle creature was removing the covering from her head.

"O Miss ——" But further utterance was prevented by sobs.

"What is the matter, Cindy?" and the kind-hearted child had taken her seat on the bed, and, with her poor dependant's head resting upon her lap, freely mingled her tears with those of the sorrowing servant.

After a few moments spent thus, the afflicted wife found strength to ask that which she wished to know, yet feared to learn.

"Where's Henry, Miss Fanny?"

A more copious shedding of tears, and a sorrowful bending over her troubled domestic, was the only reply of the little comforter.

"O Laudy! is he dead, Miss Fanny?   Laud 'ave mercy on me!"

"No, Cindy! he's not dead, or *was* not when pa *left* him."

"Left him!" fairly screamed the negro; but instantly becoming more calm, she said:

"Mas Tom has 'nt sold him, now, has he, Miss Fanny?"

"Why, how you talk, Cin! you *know* he would 'nt do such a thing."

These words inspired a ray of hope in the listener, and she eagerly exclaimed:

"Where is he, then, Miss Fanny?   Is he comin'? Will he soon be here?"   Then, with renewed weeping, the child told the tale, the recital of which crushed the joy excited by the former words, and overwhelmed with a burden of fresh despair the disconsolate wife.

"Could 'nt Mas Tom keep 'um from a takin' him?" were the first words after the sad narrative.

"No, indeed!   They took him by force off the boat, and a serious time they had of it, too."

Here she gave the particulars of the rescue.

"The mean wretches!" ejaculated Cindy.   "How I wish he had a killed 'um!   But ain't it strange, Miss Fanny, that he should miss both times, and so close, too, with his pistol?"

"There is something more yet: you remember the abolitionist that raised such a disturbance at the camp-meeting some years ago. He was the man that started away with 'Gin'r'l Washington,'" she continued, to aid the memory of her listener, which seemed to be rather slow.

"O, yes! I remember, now."

"He was on the steamer as pa went over from New Orleans; and ma says, she 's satisfied he arranged the whole plan, and took the bullets out of the pistols before he left the vessel, and I just expect he did."

Cindy vented her imprecations on the head of the scheming abolitionist, wishing most vehemently they had "*drownded* the low-lived scamp in the creek, when they gave him that duckin'. She did not believe, for her part, that such folks was any sort o' use in the world, no how."

For a time anger seemed to have gotten the better of her sorrow.

> "But faded soon the borrowed force;
> Grief claimed its right, and tears their course."

Again she grew calm enough to ask, "But don't you think he 'll come back, Miss Fannie?"

"Well, Cindy," she replied, with some hesitation, "pa told me to say nothing to excite hope where there was no ground for it, and he says there is no earthly chance of his ever returning. But still, I cannot avoid thinking that, some day, I may yet see my good Henry again."

Fanny's efforts to stay the grief of poor Cindy were of but little avail; yet, if she could not comfort, she could at least weep with her. Leaving them thus engaged, we proceed with our narrative.

What character of sorrow can wholly resist the soothing influence of time? Cindy, having long refused to believe that her husband could not come to her again, had at length resigned herself to the sad fate of widowhood; and though by no means forgetful of the past, found her grief gradually assuaged, and life again wearing its usual gay smile.

At length it came to be a subject of remark among the negroes of the plantation, that "Jim has got to have a heap o' business at Cindy's house." "Jim" was one of the hands on a neighboring farm, and his "business," at least during many visits, one would have supposed to be simply to sport with little Charlie, for this was the only inmate whose notice he seemed capable of enlisting. But in this, at any rate, he had no difficulty, for, having his pockets always filled with something to please the palate or eye of that most important youngster, he soon found himself a great favorite with him; and thus, by degrees, wrought his way to the good-will of the mother, whose reserve gradually wore away, till at length Charlie was not the only one to anticipate his coming with pleasure.

In due course of time, Jim, with all the gravity the importance of the case demanded, waited on McMinime, praying his sanction to the union of himself and Cindy, a measure in which he assured him their mutual happiness was intimately concerned.

"Why, how now, Jim? Don't you know she has a husband already?"

"I know she *had* one Mas' Tom; but he's jis de same's dead to her now: she wont see him no more."

"This is an awkward affair, Jim. You know Henry and she were married, and she is still his wife; though, as you say, there is no such a thing as their ever meeting again ; and I see no particular reason to object, if such is her will. But I did not think Cindy would entertain such a thought so soon."

They were married. Another year rolled away, and Charlie, who had grown to be quite a boy, had been duly installed in the office of nurse to his little sister. Still no word from Henry had been heard to mar the quiet of that pleasant negro cabin fireside, for Jim, at his own earnest request, had been purchased by the master of his wife. But a cloud was gathering over the peaceful scene.

" Just read that, Mary," said McMinime, one day, upon returning from the post-office, and tossing, as he spoke, a letter into her lap. The lady had noticed that her husband's countenance indicated trouble; but, asking no questions, she took the missive. It read :

" DEAR MASTER :

"I am in Texas again, in Titus county. I got with Mr. Justus in New York, and have been with him ever since.   If it had not been for him, I should never have got back to Texas.   He says he is going to take me home so soon as he can arrange his business to leave; but so many things have happened to keep him from going, that I thought you might be able to come for me before he gets ready: so I got a gentleman to write for me.   Tell Cindy and Charlie I hope to see them before long; and give my love to all the folks.

" From your faithful servant,

" HENRY.

" P. S.—I have written just what Henry told me, and as he told it, with the exception of the language; but do not believe Justus ever intends to return him home.

"A FRIEND."

"Say nothing about it, Mary," remarked her husband, as the lady abstractedly folded the letter; "or be careful to say nothing that Cindy can hear. And now, what do you think about this affair?"

"We are likely to have a gloomy time here, should Henry return. But could you not contrive to let him remain where he is?"

"I have been perplexed no little since receiving this letter; and one plan that suggests itself to my mind is the very thing you propose. I wish most sincerely, as matters have thus turned out, that he had remained in New York. But wishing never did any good, especially in a case of this kind. As it is, if he were only with some good man, he might retain him for his own use. But I cannot bear the thought of his staying much longer with that Justus. I shall start after him to-morrow. And now the question is, Shall I bring him back, or sell him?"

"I assure you my perplexity equals your own, and your judgment must decide the point. I cannot suffer my mind to rest on either horn of the dilemma, without a sensation akin to horror. To have him here, under the circumstances, will not do; and yet, how hard the opposite will be to him! To crush at once, and for ever, the pleasant hopes with which he has, no doubt, been solacing himself during his long and cheerless captivity! Either way, the case is too sad to contemplate. But if you are going after him, let me ask it as a favor, that you will not treat Justus harshly. It may be possible we have wronged him by our suspicions, and perhaps you owe it to him that the boy is not yet in New York."

"I had made up my mind to deal pretty harshly with him, should we meet again. But I will try and remember what you have said, and not be hasty."

"I hope you will do nothing rashly, as it might expose you to the pain of lasting regret, should subsequent events prove his innocence of the base conduct indicated by circumstances, and show him, instead, to be your true friend."

"I am not apt to act rashly; and in regard to the other, the discovery you anticipate is not very probable; yet I will be as mild with him as the nature of the case admits."

CHAPTER XXIV.

BLASTED HOPES.

" Then fancy her magical pinions spread wide,
   And bade the young dreamer in estasy rise."

"Ah! woe to thy dream of delight!
   In darkness dissolves the gay frost-work of bliss."

WE parted with the abolitionist, in charge of Henry, on the voyage from Baltimore to Galveston. The trip was speedily accomplished, and in due season he found himself once more in his Texian home.

Justus was a man of taste, and had erected his mansion, and laid off his grounds with the view of making them the seat of comfort, and the ornament of the neighborhood. And it was with no little pain he saw the changes that one short year had wrought. The place had been let out, and its whole appearance plainly told the absence of an owner's oversight. He had extended to Henry a promise to convey him home, so soon as circumstances would permit, but, until his affairs were restored to their former state, it was out of the question to attend to aught else. In the meantime the negro was put to work.

At times Henry indulged the thought of trying to make his own way home without longer waiting on Justus; but the difficulties to be overcome, with his ignorance of the geography of the country, were too numerous, even for his anxiety; especially as he still relied on the integrity of his guardian, whom, notwithstanding, he could not but consider rather tardy.

Justus had now realized his most ardent wishes, and was a married man. This event occurred shortly after his return to Texas; but the change had no apparent tendency to shorten the period of Henry's detention. As month after month passed away, and, according to his mode of computation, he had seen the seed put in the ground, and the harvest gathered in, a suspicion began stealing over him that it was not intended he should see home again. With this thought came an earnest desire to defeat the design.

He was on intimate terms with a person of his own rank, whose young master had taken a singular interest in him, and this youth he determined to make his confidant, entreating him to write to his master in his behalf.

The plan succeeded, and as Justus was to remain in ignorance of the transaction, the letter was written under a strict promise of secrecy.

"Why, that Justus is a scoundrel!" said the young gentleman, after Henry had finished his story. "If he has so much desire to restore you to your master, he should have taken you home at once. I know he would have been amply rewarded for his trouble and expense. It is quite sensible in you, Henry, to wish to write, which I will do for you with pleasure."

The reader has already been informed of the result of this effort, which leaves us no further explanations to make on this point.

It chanced that Henry's plan was not kept so profoundly secret as he wished. He was overheard by some of the negroes, while talking to his young friend, and by some means it reached Justus; not, however, till the lapse of some two or three weeks from the occurrence. The information evidently excited him; and, hastily summoning the negro, he reproved him for his ingratitude and want of confidence; then ordered him to prepare at once for his return home.

The preparation was speedily accomplished, and the same day found them on the road. Henry, for the first time in many months, felt really happy, and his exuberant joy vented itself in snatches of song, among which—

"Dar's no place like home," etc.,

rang out most frequently, and quite melodiously.

"You's tuck de wrong road, aint you, Mas Justus?" asked the negro on the morning of the second day, as he spurred his lagging horse alongside of his conductor. "Aint dis de wrong road?" he repeated, after gaining that position.

"No, I guess not, Henry. If I am not very much at fault, our instructions were to take the left-hand road; though, if you think otherwise, it is not a great way back to the house, and you can return and ask."

"'Pears to me now, dat is it, too; and I reckon you's right."

As they continued on, Henry became quite animated in conversation. He talked freely, recounting the anxiety he had formerly experienced, and indulged in pleasant anticipations on the prospect before him. Then, referring to his escape from the North, he remarked:

"Mas Tom 'll be mighty glad to see me git back from dem fools wat wanted to make me a free man, anyhow."

An unintelligible smile passed over Justus's face, and he observed:

" Pretty well done, Henry, indeed !"

The day had well-nigh passed, and the negro very strangely felt a revival of his suspicions that they were not on the right road; and the impression deepened, as he remembered that the way-marks did not agree with those described on their proper route.   Again he accosted his conductor:

"Mas' Justus, 't seems t' me *yet* we must've missed our road, somehow."

" Why so, Henry ?"

" Why, you know the gen'l'man said we'd pass a big field whar de road'd fork agin."

" I seem to have a faint recollection of something of the kind; but I presume it is on ahead, as he really did tell us to take the *left* road."

" I know he did say de *left;* but mebbe dat wus de second time.   An' I jis b'leve now, dat wus it, an' we's done made a mistake, an' bin all day goin' wrong."

" I would have you know, Henry, that I can understand enough of English to be able to follow directions; and I do not wish to be interrupted again in this way."

This, if it did not satisfy, effectually silenced the slave.   But the more he reflected, the stronger did his suspicions become that they were not travelling towards his home.   He resolved to inquire of the first one he might meet. Fortune soon threw in his way one of his own color, when, to his astonishment, he privately found he was at no great distance from Shreveport. He remembered having been at this place with his master, on his journey North, and knew it was not in Texas. "What could Mas' Justus mean, then? Did he not know he had been travelling on the wrong road? He surely could not help seeing it. But, if so, why had he gone so carelessly? What could it mean?"

Then first his suspicions began to take tangible form. "Mas' Justus was goin' to do sumf'n wrong. What should he do?" It was not a case to admit of much deliberation. He would relate his story, and throw himself on the protection of the first person he might meet.

The time to act seemed to be approaching, as they were on the point of meeting some teamsters on the road. Henry began to con over the speech in which he was to make his situation known; but his cogitations were interrupted by the sound of horses' feet, approaching at no leisurely pace. Both turned to look; but a small eminence intervening hid the comers from view. They were not long, however, in presenting themselves, and—most unlooked-for, and, to the negro, joyful sight—it was McMinimc, accompanied by one of neighbors.

McMinime seemed prepared for war, as he held in his hand a pistol ready cocked. This, however, he soon returned to its case, remarking, "I had very little doubt, sir, this weapon would be called into requisition this afternoon; but as you have disappointed me in not attempting an escape, justice has kindly delayed its punishment of your continual villainies; though I suppose I owe it to good fortune and hard riding that this boy is not for sale to-morrow in Louisiana. The abolitionist has descended very low indeed."

"You are very opportunely met," said Justus, with forced calmness, "and I now deliver your servant into your own hands, and remove a load of care on his account that has long burdened my mind. But it seems to me, a different salutation might have been extended, indebted so largely as you are to my kind offices for his recovery and restoration; and I would fain ask, Why this rudeness?"

"I wish to be trifled with no longer, Mr. Justus. You have really a mean opinion of my sagacity, if you suppose me entirely ignorant of your dealings. But, as a reply to your question, I presume you consider yourself on the direct route from Mount Pleasant to Fayette county, and have no knowledge of the fact that you are almost beyond the limits of Texas. Rudeness, indeed! How could I, or why should I treat in any other manner one who, beginning a dishonest course by tampering with my negroes, develops, in the end, the character of a thief?"

"If an honest attempt to return your servant constitutes theft, then am I guilty. In regard to my going astray, it is by no means impossible to receive directions that may lead one wrong. He is a fortunate man, indeed, whose journeyings have all been in the right direction."

"With so many opportunities for correct information at hand, the wrong direction of your present journeying cannot but be wilful; and your base effrontery is an insult to the little intelligence I claim to possess. My good or evil fortune has brought me in contact with too many unprincipled men to be deceived by hypocritical cant. While I supposed Henry still in New York, you dishonestly assume his ownership and the profits of his labor; but when your conduct becomes known to me, his sale presented an easy means of extrication from coming trouble, and a pecuniary speculation too tempting to be resisted."

The countenance of Justus fell under the steady gaze of McMinime; yet, struggling to hide the indications of conscious guilt, he haughtily replied:

"You are entitled to the privilege of your own

belief, and I shall not condescend so low as to attempt a defence, even by a simple denial. Perhaps your present opinion is based on experience acquired by some such previous dealing of your own."

McMinime involuntarily clenched his fist, and, with an effort, restrained himself from dealing the speaker a blow, at the latter part of this insolent sentence. Checking his temper, however, he calmly replied:

"Suffer me to inform you, sir, that you stand on a very precarious footing, and the fewer such remarks the better. But I have no time thus to waste. Harvey, keep the gentleman engaged in conversation until I return. I wish to have a little private conversation with the boy, when, possibly, we may have other business to transact."

"I have no conversation for him," said the person addressed, "and would much rather keep him engaged with a good horsewhip."

A troubled expression of countenance was Justus's only reply.

"Suppose I were going to sell you, Henry," said his master, "would you like Mr. Justus to be the purchaser?"

A wild stare, expressive of great surprise and alarm, was at first the only answer; but, on being pressed, he replied, "No, Mas' Tom; not *him*; 'e's good 'nuf, ef 'e wa n't so hard. But 'e dunno wat a nigger's able to do, an' dur aint no sich a thing as pleasin' on 'im. But, Mas' Tom, you *aint gwine* to sell me? I's neva dun nuf'n mean!"

"Never mind that, Henry. But, that this hope may exert no influence over your choice, I am compelled to sell you. Then, if this man is a master whom you would rather serve than risk some one unknown, say so."

"Not *him*, any way," said the slave mournfully. Ef you's *got* to sell me, I'd ruther t'would be to somebody else."

" There is another thing I would be glad to know, Henry. Do you think Justus went astray by accident or design?"

The negro related the circumstances in connection with the day's journey, leaving his master to draw his own conclusions. "At any rate," mused the latter, " he could have been set right, had he desired it. He is, undoubtedly, a bad man, and should receive punishment, which I feel strongly inclined to inflict myself, rather than trust to the uncertain contingencies of law. But, as he may claim payment for his expenses in your behalf, I will at once settle with him."

In regard to this matter, Justus claimed a return of money expended, allowing the labor of Henry as compensation for time and trouble. The money was paid, when McMinime remarked:

"For obvious reasons, I am far from looking upon this as a just debt; but there is a righteous demand which should at once be paid; and you cannot object if, after such scrupulous exactness on my part toward you, I urge a fulfillment of the strict claims of justice in my favor."

"I didn't think you would wish your money back after such a show of fair dealing," replied the abolitionist.

" O, no! keep the money, sir ! and consider yourself rewarded for drawing the loads from my pistol; while, for the act of stealing my negro, a different guerdon should be given."

"Which will be to cut off his ears," said his companion.

"No, no, Harvey! though properly deserved, the act on our part might savor of cruelty and revenge; yet, as even the convicted hog-thief goes to the whipping-post, a few lashes well laid on might mend this fellow's manners for the future, and teach him proper respect for his neighbor's property. But I don't care to degrade myself by doing the hangman's work, and, for this time, he may go scot-free. Though, should he cross my path again, I'll not promise him so much mercy.

"So, now, Mr. Justus, as our present transaction is ended, I bid you farewell. You are not the first abolitionist whose pity for the poor slave has changed to a covetous and unjust abuse of him. And, while common honesty may have marked the course of others, the total absence of that virtue in the present case, has superadded to your other sins and hypocrisies, a vile felony, the absence of the proper punishment for which you owe alone to my mercy. The wrong done myself, I can easily forgive; but what atonement can wipe out your crime against humanity, and the peace of this poor negro, for ever destroyed by his forced and cruel separation from family and home. Could the 'man-stealer' on African soil, whose atrocities have so often excited your horror, be more ruthless! He thinks he is soon to see his wife and child, and enjoy again his former peaceful home, but your barbarity has separated them for ever, and left him but the wreck of that happiness once all he desired. Go, sir! and let this be our final interview."

As Justus obeyed, he muttered, "Not the final interview: we have one more meeting, then let him triumph who wins."

The day was drawing to a close, as McMinime and his party slowly began their return. The tired horses gave evidence of a hard pursuit, and nightfall finding them remote from a habitation, preparations were made for a bivouac in the woods.

Poor Henry! But one short night previously, he would have thought himself happy in his present situation; and such now would he have considered his lot, but for the sad intelligence communicated by his master. This preyed on his mind, foreboding the destruction of his long-cherished hope—the only solace in his painful exile.

The cheerful blaze of the camp-fire illuminated the gloom of the surrounding forest, giving a picturesque air of comfort to the lonely spot occupied by the travellers. The bustle of preparing and disposing of the evening repast had ended, and a quiet stillness settled on the little company, when the negro, with an anxious countenance, approached McMinime. His habitual respect for his master caused a hesitation in opening his mission. That master's word had never before been called in question, but he felt, in the present instance, that a matter of such vast concern to him as that now pending, might justify him in seeking an explanation.

'You ain't *raily* gwine to *sell* me, is you, Mas' Tom, from Cindy and Charley?" he began, in a tone of sadness, yet great respect. "You know I used to be de bes' hand on de place, an' I ain't forgot nuf'n since I's bin gone."

The evident distress of the servant disturbed the gentleman no little; he was perplexed the more from his inability to give relief.

"Yes, Henry," he replied, "I think it necessary, notwithstanding the requirements of the case render it no less painful to me. I have never yet been called on to perform a like act, nor should it *now* be done, were it not imperative. And, Henry, it is alone on Cindy's account and your own, that I *must* dispose of you."

A suspicion seemed to steal over the negro, yet he pleaded: "But, Mas' Tom, we's been married; can't you do no way 't all 'thout sep'ratin' us?"

"Henry, I had as well tell you all!"

And he related the circumstances transpiring at home during his absence, in which he was concerned; of Cindy's prolonged grief, and subsequent marriage. "For these reasons, I think it unwise for you to return. Try and forget your old home, and make the best of your fate. Yours is a distressing lot, but I do not believe you would wish to involve others in its misery, especially as they acted in good faith, believing it impossible for you ever to return. There is but one thing I can now do for you, Henry; that is, to secure you a good master. This I will endeavor to do; and I can only hope that, forgetting the past, you will commence your life anew, and still live to be happy!"

Henry did not reply; perfectly stupefied, he stood for a few moments gazing vacantly into the fire, as if trying to realize his master's words. No emotion was visible, and with a slow and sullen manner he retired to himself. On the following day he seemed rather dull, but was otherwise much the same as usual.

We simply state the fact that the sale was duly effected; the owner, in carrying out his promise, having transferred him to one who, according to the universal award of his neighbors, was a humane and Christian master. As for Henry himself, he seemed to be in no way affected by the change, receiving it with apparent indifference.

CHAPTER XXV.

JUSTUS A SLAVE-HOLDER.

"Is thy servant a dog that he should do this great thing?"

THE threat uttered by Justus on leaving Mc-Minime had a deep meaning couched in it. Determined to remain in the South, it had seemed a necessity to fall into the customs of the people, and adopt their style and manner of living. To do this, servants were necessary, and no plan seemed so reasonable as to have them of his own. Besides, being necessary to personal comfort, they added to one's respectability, while the proceeds of their labor was no mean source of profit. These motives were not without their proper influence on a man who, like Justus, though misled by the delusion of youthful enthusiasm, had still respect sufficient for his early training to remember that success in life, at last, depends upon the acquisition of gold. A desire for this formed no small part of the original motive drawing him South, and finding, after wise examination, his ostensible object unpromising pecuniarily, he prudently ignored his previous views, and became in fact a Southern man.

Having thus selfishly surrendered his principles, it is not surprising if, under the promptings of interest, similar sacrifices of his *remaining* honesty should at any time be made. This led to the results detailed in the preceding chapter.

The timely interposition of McMinime having prevented the sale of Henry, and his plain language exasperating the feelings of the abolitionist, hastened the development of a long-contemplated scheme. This was to obtain possession of "Sambo," for whom McMinime had given a bill of sale, for the purpose, as faithfully promised by Justus, of liberating him in a free State.

The failure of this plan, and the surreptitious possession of the bill of sale, made in his own name, gave the abolitionist an advantage he now determined to use.

On a pleasant morning in early spring, some few months after the events just narrated, two gentlemen were seen approaching each other on a public thoroughfare near the residence of Mr. McMinime. They met, and saluted with the cordial familiarity of old friends.

"Good morning, Mac; how go the times with you now?"

"Why, how do you do, squire? Well, you are the last man I was looking for to-day; though none the less glad to see you on that account."

After a further interchange, the first remarked:

"Your neighbor, Smith, has just informed me of the loss of your boy 'Sambo,' the negro you were so foolish as to give a bill of sale for to that abolitionist the boys put in the creek. You may remember I advised against it, feeling certain no good could come from trusting a man of his character. But, how is it? I thought the thing had ended by the boy's running away, and the return of the bill of sale."

"Yes, the boy came back, and we cancelled our bargain; and I supposed the bill of sale safe in my possession, until my friend, Shields, the lawyer, informed me Justus had placed it in his hands, to bring suit for the recovery of the negro. It was, and still is a mystery how he ever obtained it; yet finding he had the advantage in law, and was likely to make me pay hire, in addition to his loss, and having an abhorrence for an unpleasant litigation, I just turned him over to Mr. Abolitionist; and if Sambo don't cure him of his false notions of

11

slavery, I'll confess I am not good at forming conclusions."

"*Cure* him! why it looks to me like he was pretty well cured already; for I understand he like to have sold Henry for his own benefit, and he has actually as good as stolen Sambo. My word for it, there will be more need for curing him of useless severity to his niggers, now, than any thing else."

"Perhaps so; but Sambo is gone, and I am not sorry this turncoat abolitionist has such a hard case to learn to act the master upon. From *my* experience in *his* case, I suppose Justus will soon pity unfortunate owners of such fellows more than he formerly did the 'suffering slave' himself."

Forced, throug hmotives of policy, to change his views and actions on a subject, to which, more than all others, he had felt the strongest attachment, Justus thought it necessary to prove his sincerity by harshness towards his man-servant, whom he regarded as the nucleus of a large plantation force, soon to toil for his benefit. One would have supposed his previous education would have well fitted him for a humane master, and that, finding the destiny of a slave committed to his charge, nothing that kindness and sympathy could offer, would be lacking to lighten his hitherto heavy burden, and make his lot pleasant.   Such, however, was not the case; and if at any time his better feelings prevailed, and conscience chid him for severity, he found it easy to shift the burden on Sambo, whose insolent idleness continually provoked his ire.   Nor was the complaint confined to one side.   While Justus was annoyed at his servant's numerous shortcomings, that worthy felt no less harrassed by what he considered his new master's most unjust exactions. The ignorance and improper management of the master totally estranged the negro, naturally inclined to be respectful and obedient, while the harsh and ill-judged line of policy employed to restore him, excited only anger and contempt.

Matters grew worse and worse, and the crisis of an open rupture was daily drawing near.   At length it came.   No remedy was left but a severe castigation, which was inflicted in the most approved manner.

As he ceased to ply the lash, and drew himself into an erect posture, his ears were saluted by a voice indignantly pronouncing the words:

> "And, worst of all, and most to be deplored,
>   As human nature's broadest, foulest blot;
>   Chains him, and tasks him, and exacts his sweat,
>   With stripes that mercy, with a bleeding heart,
>   Weeps when she sees inflicted on a beast."

Justus turned to observe the intruder, and beheld

a genteelly dressed stranger, who, in the same indignant tone continued :

"O, shame to man ! and will the heavens behold, and not blast? Will the earth witness, and not open her jaws to engulf the perpetrator of so foul a deed ?"

"Quite sentimental, indeed! And, I suppose, you are ready to exclaim, 'I have found it!' But suffer me to ask, What horrible thing is it that calls for such an exclamation? What deed of darkness have you discovered, that so shocks your humanity, and calls for such summary vengeance?"

"Is it possible *you* can ask! The infamous act you have just been committing alone called forth my indignation. To think man should so oppress his fellow!"

"I presume you are now touching upon matters of which you are entirely ignorant; else you could not be so much concerned at the simple act of punishing a refractory slave. Knowing something of the inexperience which gives existence to, and sustains your intense feeling, I can excuse and overlook its present exhibition, having been, at one period of my life, no better informed than yourself; but in other localities, suffer me to inform you, it will not be so readily pardoned. If you desire your sojourn among us, whether long or short, to be a pleasant one, you would do well neither to see nor hear many things passing around you; for, if you cannot better govern your impulses, it may bring you into trouble. And no greater a matter than your remarks just now might, in some other place, lead to your unceremonious ejection from society, if nothing more serious."

"What! tell me a man is not entitled to the right of uttering his sentiments on any subject he pleases, without regard to time or place?"

"By no means! The fact is, persons holding such views as you express—which I am free to acknowledge were once *mine* also—have, by their conduct, rendered this quite an exciting subject; and those who are connected with slavery can ill bear such comments."

"Yes, I am well aware that men will become excited by any thing that threatens to cut off their gains, unjust though they may be. But who that is a philanthropist would desist from crying out against such an evil, because of man's displeasure?"

"Do you know what it is you are 'crying out against?' Have you ever devoted five minutes to a consideration of the system of slavery for any other purpose than to vituperate it? Or are you not rather one—there are many such—that, without examination, has formed an opinion that 'fire could not burn out of you,' but which a few weeks proper observation would entirely do away ?"

"Bah! Don't talk to me of examining, where the case is so palpable. What but wilfulness can thus blind any to the flagrant outrages committed in this slavery business!"

"My patience could not endure such remarks, did not the recollection of my own former state of feeling enable me to appreciate the spirit actuating you. Yet you seem more rabid than is common. But if your enthusiasm is not an idle emotion, and your sympathy entirely misplaced under the delusion of a name, why is it that you do not present some reasons for your opinion?'

"Reasons! Why, is not the very name '*slave*' as strong a reason as could be given? And yet there are other things; but time will not now admit of a discussion. It is drawing towards evening, and I must proceed on my way."

"Accept, sir, of my hospitality for the night; and, I doubt not, you will learn to view things in a different light. It is to be regretted that, in consequence of false views, you should expose yourself to the risk both of doing and receiving harm, when a fair statement of the question is all that is needed to correct the error."

"I thankfully accept your kind offer, hoping, at

the same time, to be able to call to your mind matters entirely forgotten, or not sufficiently dwelt upon. And you may possibly be brought to see the flagrant injustice of your present iniquitous course."

CHAPTER XXVI.

THE DISCUSSION.

"I also will show mine opinion."

JUSTUS found his guest an agreeable and entertaining companion; and, during the early part of the evening, their conversation took an animated and extensive range. After a somewhat longer pause than usual, the stranger rather abruptly remarked:

"I presume you have not read 'Uncle Tom's Cabin,' Mr. Justus?"

"O yes! I have not been so unfortunate as to miss that treat. On what did you found the opinion?"

"I had thought that no one seeing the evils of slavery as there portrayed, would ever thereafter have connection with it. But do you not think the author has faithfully painted the thing, and fully exposed its horrors?"

"I once entertained such an opinion; but investigating for myself, and seeing with my own eyes, have dissipated the fallacy, and led me to the just conclusion that it was the mere expression of the author's own peculiar views, very artfully performed, instead of a correct delineation of the subject. Slavery, as conceived by the novelist, is well pictured; but the arguments against it, as it is developed in the plan of the work, can, with equal force, be urged against other things, the propriety of which is by no one doubted."

"I did not expect to sustain my position by this book; yet it contains sufficient to satisfy and convince any reasonable mind. Has it never occurred to you that slavery, alone in the matter of locking up from use such a mass of intellect, is of incalculable injury to the world?"

"If such be the character of your boasted arguments, I trust a laugh on my part will not be misconstrued into intentional disrespect; for this ludicrous idea would relax the muscles and provoke a smile from Diogenes himself. 'Mass of intellect,' indeed! No, sir! but it *has* struck me, and that quite forcibly, that it keeps a great mass of wretchedness out of the world, by giving employment to the hands, and direction to the minds of so many, who, were it otherwise, would, by their idleness and thriftlessness, work nothing but mischief to themselves and others.   You need not let the dread of consequences from the deprivations of which you speak, in the least annoy you.

"Your author, George Harris, may, perhaps, possess the inventive genius of a Fulton, but, where there is one of this class, *if ever found*, how many thousands are almost infinitely below the standard of the most common capacity! So that, however desirable it might be to give the few the position their abilities would enable them to fill, the benefit derived would bear no sensible comparison to the greater evil resulting from assigning to the vast rabble the equality you demand for them.

"But allow *me* a question.   Has it never occurred to *you*, that as an abolitionist, your profession and practice are at direct variance? You preach the requirements of God's law, but constantly forget, in regard to this very matter, both the precept and example of Paul, its great expounder."

"How, now! Paul taught Christianity, and I never before heard that he had any thing to say in regard to this subject. So I am at a loss to know from what source you derive a knowledge of his teachings in this regard; and as to his practice, it is preposterous to speak of the apostle's experience in slavery. For he tells us he was 'free born;' and he surely never owned a slave himself."

"Perhaps you are too fast. He *does* notice the subject, and gives directions for the conduct both of masters and slaves, although he did not himself own a servant. Where *he* says, 'Slaves, *obey* in ALL THINGS your masters,' *you* say, '*Run away*' on all occasions; and more—to the extent of your ability, you *aid* them in so doing."

"You surely do not hope to blind any thinking person by such a quotation as that! I am free to grant that one who *hires* himself as a servant, should render faithful service. But do not flatter yourself that the apostle, any further than this, sanctions *your slavery*."

"You seem to forget, or possibly never knew, that the word here rendered 'servant,' properly means 'slave,' and, strictly speaking, one *born* so. Yet let this pass. We are taught in the words of the apostle, respect and obedience to established rule. But how different is this from abolition prate! He does not say, Ah! my dear friends, you are grievously wronged and oppressed beyond measure. Elope! Go to a free State! or, failing in this, sell your lives as dearly as possible. While boldly denouncing the evils of his day, many of them sanctioned by established usage and long observance, is slavery included? Are those in bondage even remotely notified that they are a wronged and abused race? No, indeed! But, substantially, he says to this particular class, 'It is not the design of Christianity to effect a change in your civil or political relations, but to give you also the benefits of the gospel. I therefore exhort to obedience, you whom God's providence has made slaves; and this not only to those whose treatment is kind, but also to the arbitrary and exacting. The ills connected with your lot exist under different forms in every department of life, and, while fidelity to God requires from each an honest performance of the duties of his station, obedience to your masters, from you who are in bondage, is specially enjoined.'

"To the masters he does not preach abolitionism, but, admitting the propriety of slavery, demands, on Divine authority, in behalf of the slave and as his right, humane and generous treatment.

"Another apostle, treating on the same subject, in his address to slaves, takes special care to guard them against a bad state of feeling, even when cruelly and wrongfully punished."

"You are certainly skilful thus to mingle matters; but what has all this to do with our dispute in regard to slavery?"

"It has this to do. I consider the Scriptures a very safe and certain guide for all moral actions, and as its teachings on this subject emphatically say, '*Slaves, obey in all things* your masters,' it is an inevitable conclusion, that the institution and obligation of slavery are thus recognized and sanctioned by the highest authority. But, as you seem not to understand the drift of my argument—it may be owing to my want of clearness—I will illustrate. It chanced that St. Paul, once in his travels, 'took up' a runaway slave. What was his conduct on this occasion? Did he say, 'My dear, abused brother, make off by the underground railroad: shove for Canada?' O, no! Remembering that slavery was an institution of Divine appointment, he despatched the fugitive to his master with a letter, in which he did not inform his friend Philemon, 'You have no right, sir, to call this man your property! he was created by his God as free as yourself, and is as much deserving of freedom. Therefore, if you have any hope or even desire to escape the curse of Heaven in this life, and endless torments hereafter, liberate him at once, and extend such further aid as he may justly claim for the service you have tyrannously exacted of him!' Far different was the tenor of the epistle. Something on this wise:

"'I send back your slave Onesimus. He has acted badly; but having reformed, and, moreover, being a convert to Christianity, through my ministry, affection for him induces me to plead that, for

my sake, you will forget the past, and receive him
with gentleness. I had a desire to retain him, that,
in your behalf, he might render me service; but
knowing him to be yours, I could not do so without
permission.'

"In imagination I can hear the venerable man of
God remark, as the runaway stands entreating not
to be sent back to his incensed master:

"'Yea, my son! duty requires you to go; I have
no right to retain you. Brother Philemon has paid
his money for you, and is entitled to your service.
It is true, you have not behaved well, and he may
be angry; yet return: I will write to him in your
behalf, and am satisfied he will listen to me.'"

"What reason have you for supposing Onesimus
to be any thing more than a hired servant?"

"Simply the evidence contained in the statement.
Had he been such, he could have left when he
chose; but the manner of his departure showing
that his will was not consulted, proves his bondage."

For a moment, the stranger seemed at a loss for a
reply; then he said: "Well, grant all that, and
what will it prove, further than that there were serious wrongs practiced then, as now; and that St.
Paul was not a true philanthropist? But must *we*
regard injustice with impunity, because *he*, through

an undue deference to custom and bad laws, and in ignorance of that nobler principle, 'the higher law,' counselled submission to the former?"

"But who is authorized to pronounce that wrong, which inspiration, by prescribing proper regulations for, has fully sanctioned?"

"Any one is competent to judge when a departure from a course of rectitude is made; and in so manifest a case of oppression as the one referred to, the knowledge is *forced* upon us. Then, as lovers of justice and humanity, how could we do less than endeavor to bring about a change?"

"Were this the only, or indeed, the worst form of oppression existing, there might be some reason in your attempt to wipe out the evil. But why not first experiment in a field nearer home, and where your sympathy and exertions are more needed?"

"You would insinuate there are evils in the North demanding redress. Such, sir, there may be; but were they even so deplorable as slavery, true philanthropists repudiate the doctrine that 'charity begins at home,' and are ready to assist all who need, including even those who will not see their wants, and who revile us for our good intention."

"Yet it might be better, perhaps, were you a little more selfish. We in the South, as a general thing, have a perverse way of thinking ourselves competent to manage our own affairs, without the intermeddling of others, who seem so much disturbed at that in which their own well-being is in no wise concerned. If we choose to own slaves, we have neither the power nor the inclination to compel others to possess them. Giving to them the liberty of choice, we demand for ourselves the same privilege."

"Yet, as you appeal to holy writ, allow me to refer you to one of its precepts, which you perhaps have overlooked:

"'All things whatsoever ye would that men should do to you, do ye even so to them.'

"Now, if you are not willing to exchange places with him you hold as your slave, try just for one moment to lay aside all bias in your own favor, and calmly examine if you are not living in the practice of a gross *wrong*—violating a positive command of the King of kings?"

"I see no necessity for a violation of this rule, even in owning slaves. If I treat him as I would be treated in his condition, the law is fulfilled."

"And this you can only do by liberating him; for nothing short of this would satisfy you."

"Were I the originator of the dispensation under which he is placed, or were even master of the means of changing the present order of things, your interpretation *might* be correct. But the very nature of this case, as well as of many others, shows the propriety of my construction of the 'golden rule,' and, that in its application, attendant circumstances are to have their due weight; otherwise, the regulations of society, that control the masses, by assigning each his proper position, would be entirely destroyed."

"This is an amendment we cannot allow; you might thus change the force of any command. A divine precept must be received without abatement or addition."

"Follow out the exact letter, without consulting reason or the fitness of things?"

"Most assuredly! When required to perform a certain act, that is the thing to be done, and in the very manner ordered, else no command were positive."

"Not at all! I do not plead for the discretion that would change or abrogate Divine law; but can you imagine no evils that might result from so literal an application as you propose?"

"Ah, sir! we have nothing to do with reasoning or propriety in a case of this kind; all that is left for us is, to decide how we would be dealt with, and act towards others accordingly."

"I have a little narrative that will exactly illustrate my position, and at the same time expose the absurdity you teach. If you have the patience to listen, I will relate it, as well to entertain as to convince you."

"O, yes; I shall be glad to hear it, and may, perhaps, by another, be able to show your inconsistency."

CHAPTER XXVII.

JUSTUS'S STORY.

"All things whatsoever ye would that men should do unto you, do ye even so to them."

"MR. APPLEWHITE, a gentleman residing in one of the States south of Mason and Dixon's line, was a wealthy farmer, owning quite a number of negroes, and was in the words of my authority, 'one of the hard cases.' He did not keep his servants for amusement, his prime object in life being the accumulation of property; and no one better understood the means of securing to himself the avails of their best performances. And yet he was not a cruel man, but 'action' being his word, his own feelings were made the standard of his demands from others. He thought his duty towards them performed in allowing a sufficiency of all the necessaries of life, suitable time for rest, and refreshment included. If a 'nigger' would do his duty, all was well; but woe-betide the wretch who thought to shrink his labor, or play off on his master. In short, he was a keen hand at driving a bargain in almost any line.

'It chanced upon a certain occasion that this gentleman attended a meeting for religious purposes, where a powerful revival was going on, and, during its progress, he was numbered with the converts.

"As he had been in other things, so was he in his new calling. Entering into it with his whole heart, as a natural consequence, the change in his outward actions was quite visible and marked.

"From the very incipiency of his resolution to reform, the text you quote made a deep impression upon him. Like you, he received it in a strictly literal sense, and, in this connection, thought of what he now considered his former injustice to his slaves."

"You seem to misapprehend me. I would not be understood as so far weakening the force of this scripture as your words might imply. *I* accept the precept as strictly literal."

"I comprehend; it was not a misconception, but an unguarded manner of expression. Allow me, too, an explanation, which should have been earlier made. *Every command* must be received with discrimination; for there are certain fundamental laws underlying all else, and to which every, all such injunctions must be subservient.

"Otherwise, the king, led by views such as yours, must lay aside his crown, to exchange place with some aspirant for that honor; the wealthy man impoverish himself, and take the position of those less fortunate or less industrious; while officers of the law would be required to connive at the escape of all classes of offenders. But to my story:

"So far as his slaves were concerned, Mr. Applewhite had been all his life disregarding this precept. Placing himself, with his fitness to grapple with the world, and the enlightenment to direct in the pursuits of life, in the position of a slave, without either of these elements of success, and considering only that, if in this state, he would wish freedom, he rashly determined to liberate them, forgetting that their difference in mental organism, capacity, education, and relation to society, presented no proper basis of sympathy for such ill-judged mercy.

"Their freedom alone was not sufficient; but they must be provided with the means of starting in business, as nothing less could he wish in his own case.

"It was to no purpose that 'old Uncle Abe' and 'Joshua' remonstrated against this plan, and wondered 'what in de name o' goodness we's gwine to do wid ourselves?' He was not to be turned from his purpose.   All were disposed of, with the exception of 'Aunt Isbel,' who, having been the nurse of Mrs. A. in youthful days, declared she 'would neber lebe Miss Sally in dis worl', nohow.'

"The result of this plan left Mr. Applewhite a poor man.   It is true his plantation and lands in part remained; but the means of deriving his usual income were gone.   He was not a man to be satisfied with this phase of circumstances; and, as the most feasible plan of bettering his fortune, resolved to seek a home in the inviting prairies of Texas, where his slender means invested in stock promised a return of former prosperity.

"Aunt Isbel had been well satisfied while near her children; and, to avoid the pain of a final separation, joined her request with theirs, that they also might be of the migrating party; but as free negroes were by law excluded from the new republic, the gentleman sternly refused to assume again the ownership of his former servants, the only means whereby their wishes could be accommodated. Earnest and faithful were the efforts of the negress to change her master's mind towards her children; but, inexorable, he assured her his conscience could not consent, though assured that, in their present condition, they were fast becoming worthless and dissolute.

"'A plague upon all such charity as you have shown!' spoke Mrs. Applewhite, with unusual warmth. 'I believe your religion is simply madness, for I never before heard of it depriving any one so completely of reason. Your anxiety to conform to this perpetually quoted rule might have led you to bestow a thought on the welfare of those who are entirely dependent upon you; and yet, so far as your own family is concerned, you seem totally indifferent. You have reduced us almost to absolute want. And what is now to become of our daughters, who scarcely know the meaning of toil or exertion, Heaven only knows!

"'And yet, I could endure the reverse, were it the result of necessity, or even of any useful measure. But what is the end and aim of so great a sacrifice? Merely to cast on the world a set of vagabonds, with the likelihood of their peopling the penitentiary or feeding the gibbet; for you *must* know that, of all to whom you have given freedom, there is but one or two who are not in a fourfold worse condition than when under a master.

"'And now, when a poor old mother entreats for the companionship of her children, and they are not the less anxious for the measure, to whine out a precept of Scripture! The father of all hypocrisics take such religion! It is no better than infidelity.'

"'Dat's jis my 'pinion, too,' muttered Aunt Isbell; 'fur I's hearn 'em read in de Bible dat he what do n't pr'vide for his own household's worser dan a infidel; an' I b'leve it too.'

"'Ah, my dear,' answered her husband, 'do not thus look on the dark side of the picture. Let the slight sacrifice of personal comfort we are now making, be considered as some atonement for the wrong we have so long practiced. Could you wish less done for you, had you been in their condition?'

"'Atonement, indeed! What wrong has any one suffered by controlling and keeping in useful employment those who, otherwise, would have only been a pest and nuisance in society? And as to being in their condition myself, what right have I to aspire to the station of position and wealth occupied by others above me? Does not the same Scripture about which you preach also teach, "In whatever state" we are, "therewith to be content?"'

"As all remonstrance was thrown away, Aunt Isbel was given to understand she could only enjoy her children's society by remaining with them. As she preferred accompanying her mistress, they were, accordingly, separated. As for her offspring left behind, the prediction of their mistress was fully verified. Those of them who did not fall into the possession of other masters, soon sank to shiftless poverty and worthlessness."

"This was because they were not properly educated," interrupted the stranger; "they should have been prepared for their new position by previous training."

"Education could not have changed their cast or capacity," replied Justus. "The error consisted in marring the harmony of a well-regulated system, in which the negro was made to subserve the true design of nature.

"Settled in Texas, Mr. Applewhite soon began to realize his expectations. As yet, however, his wealth was rather prospective; but time and the increase of population would soon develop the value of his possessions.

"The advantages of stock-raising in the country were so numerous, as to make it a matter of prime importance for each new settler to engage in this occupation; but as in many cases this class of persons had expended their means in travelling, it was found extremely difficult to obtain a start in that line of business. Mr. Applewhite having extensive herds, and being known as an accommodating and kind-hearted man, received many applications in emergencies of this kind. Governed by his lately adopted principles, he soon found himself in a fair way to lose, not only the profits of his business, but the greater part of his capital; for, though his debtors 'promised to pay,' his well-known leniency made him, too often, the dupe of the designing and dishonest.

"In this crisis, the fears of his more prudent wife again became excited, and her earnest remonstrance aroused the concern of the gentleman himself, who now determined on a change of policy.

"It was not long after this resolve, that Mr. Applewhite was again called on by an immigrant, who desired to procure, on a long credit, a considerable supply of stock. He was given to understand that, in consequence of losses by bad debts, and the large sales already effected, he had no more cattle to dispose of. The stranger having his cue in some previous knowledge of the other's character, feeling indisposed to be thus put off, continued:

"'Suppose we could change places—you a stranger without friends, in a new country, reduced by the dishonesty of others to poverty, yet with a fair prospect of retrieving your losses, could you obtain the means of beginning the stock business; I, comfortably living at home, with the means of assisting you without detriment to myself: would not a refusal indicate a want of sympathy for my fellow-man, and a total disregard of the command, "Do as you would be done by?"'

"I need not," continued Justus, "tell you the result; the misguided man again found himself the victim of guile, and the stranger departed, well pleased with his success.

"As time wore on, Mr. Applewhite saw his neighbor gradually increasing in prosperity, while he himself, from his manner of doing business, was still comparatively at the bottom of the ladder. The collection of his outstanding debts would have changed affairs, and released him from pecuniary embarrassment that was pressing him sore. Yet every intimation of a forced settlement was met with the 'golden rule,' which effectually staved off the application of legal force, so necessary sometimes in the maintenance of one's rights. Harrassed with heavy liabilities hanging over him; harrassed with accumulating cares, with the prospect of final ruin in view, life proved a burden from which he would have gladly escaped.

"About this time he was elected sheriff of his county, and hoped the profits of the office might improve his finances; but the prospect, at first so flattering, led only to deeper trouble.

"Among his various charges was that of a man

condemned to death for aggravated murder. Knowing the character of his keeper, the criminal conceived the idea of turning it to his own account.
As a preliminary step, he feigned penitence, as a
proper manner of exciting sympathy. Finding
this display, together with certain wily hints thrown
out, entirely disregarded, he came at once to the
point. The time for his execution was near at
hand, and he had just listened to a more than
usually fervent exhortation from the sheriff, who,
with good hopes of the prisoner's spiritual condition, was departing. As he reached the door, the
criminal said:

"'I trust, Mr. Applewhite, you are not going to
abandon your principles at this late day!'

"'I am not aware of any such intention,' replied
the gentleman, 'neither can I understand your allusion.'

"'It is simply this: you have made it a rule of
life to do to others as you would they should do to
you. Do you intend to keep me ironed down here,
to be hung like a dog, when *you* would be glad to
escape such a fate?'

"For a moment the sheriff was quite bewildered,
but, speedily recovering himself, replied:

"'Such language is idle and silly; I cannot thus
have my honesty called in question. In a personal

matter between us, I might extend mercy to the utmost, but in this case, I am but an officer of the law, and must fulfill its requirements.'

"'It was not my design to trespass on your feelings, much less to offer insult. Thinking you would admit the propriety of receiving a Divine precept in the express terms laid down, without weakening its force by reasoning on it, I appealed to you on the broad principles of the "golden rule." If you would wish to escape from my position, is it not your *religious* duty to aid me? What your *office* requires, must not come into the account, for the gospel does not allow any thing to sanction a wrong, and the application of the rule in question proves this thing must be wrong. Will you, then, grant me that aid which in my circumstances you would desire ?'

"In this dilemma the sheriff found himself compelled for the first time to reason, instead of yielding blind obedience to a hitherto undisputed law; and, though sensibly moved by the sophistry of the prisoner, his better judgment detected its fallacy. With some sternness, he replied :

"'You are an offender against both Divine and human law, and to allow you to escape would be a public evil. Your efforts are but loss of time: apart from other obligations, my bond, as well as oath of office, would not suffer me to connive at your escape. I entreat you, then, lay aside all worldly hope, and prepare for death.'

"The prisoner expressed himself as much concerned on this point, and extremely desirous of making proper spiritual preparation for his change; and, at his urgent request, was allowed for this purpose more freedom of his cell.

"The day of execution came, but no criminal appeared. Taking advantage of the sheriff's kindness, and disregarding his own solemn pledge of good conduct, he had contrived to escape.

"Suspicions of corruption on the part of the sheriff were entertained, and he was subjected to legal proceedings. The cost of his defence swept away the greater part of his remaining property, and, though acquitted, many of his former associates believed him guilty.

"For several years he labored under this additional burden, when happily the murderer was again arrested, and, before his execution, vindicated the character of Mr. Applewhite by a faithful statement of what had occurred."

Here Justus paused, remarking, "My narrative here ends, without relating further of this gentleman's history."

"Which I am happy in being able to supply,"

said the stranger. "Retrieving his character, he remained the same honorable and religious man; but his mind underwent a great change in relation to the rule of his past life. At first, he was inclined to think it a mistranslation, but his scholarship not entitling him to decide that point, he was quite bewildered. At length, as men are apt to do, he exchanged one extreme for another, and settled down in the opinion, that if the words were properly rendered into English, they were intended only for the apostles and other holy men, who had but little intercourse with the world.

"Thus privileged by his own interpretation, he set himself diligently to the task of recovering his own. Suits were instituted against his debtors, and no motive restrained him in pushing his claims to the utmost limit of legal exaction. His friends say that he is the reverse of his former self, and if in the way of securing his rights, he would not hesitate a moment to deprive widows and orphans of a shelter. 'Right wrongs no one,' is now his hobby.

"But *I* have a short story to relate, for the truth of every word of which I am ready to vouch."

Justus's manner indicated his surprise at the change affairs had taken, without noticing which, however, the stranger continued:

"It chanced on a certain occasion that a young gentleman on board a New Orleans bound steamer, belonging to the class known as abolitionists, was expatiating, as only such characters can descant, on the horrors his excited imagination connected with slavery.

"A young fellow from the South, who was present, ventured, at the risk of annihilation, to address the abolitionist during his rhapsody, and warn him against the danger of becoming himself a vile slave-owner. The manner of the philanthropist might entertain you, could I imitate it, as, with a lordly air and withering scorn, he scouted the foul insinuation; the remotest proximity to which he considered a degradation too infamous to contemplate.

"For years the paths of the abolitionist and Southerner were divergent. But, at length, on a bright summer's afternoon, as the latter was travelling near a farm-house, a disturbance in an adjoining enclosure attracted his attention. Judge of his surprise, when he found he had lived to see that same dignified, honorable abolitionist, engaged in the cruel task of mercilessly beating his own negro slave!"

It would be difficult to describe the feelings of Justus, as his former companion thus finished his story; mortification and anger for awhile predominated, as the Southerner with easy familiarity threw himself back, and gave way to a hearty laugh.

The first impulse of Justus was to eject his guest without ceremony, but, remembering the sacred demands of hospitality, he speedily recovered himself, and, imitating the manner of the other, joined in his merriment.

" Your prediction has been verified," said Justus, when quiet was restored; "but I presume at the time you meant nothing by it, having no reason for such a belief."

"A better reason, perhaps, than you think. I had seen too many with similar views become owners of slaves, to place much reliance on your protestations, and my observation further taught me such were not always the most merciful masters."

Justus slightly winced at this, but made no reply.

At length, the Southerner smilingly continued: " I had no idea I could play the abolitionist so well! No wonder though; I have just returned from a visit to my relatives in New England, where they preached this stuff to me almost incessantly. Parson Freelove, Uncle Hope, Aunt Charity, Cousin Faith, and all, so that I am now myself pretty well qualified for an abolition lecturer."

12

CHAPTER XXVIII.

CONCLUSION.

"The torch shall be extinguished which hath lit
My midnight lamp—and what is writ, is writ."

NOTWITHSTANDING the suspicious circumstances under which Sambo was found, he made a favorable impression on Southerner, who at once conceived the idea of negotiating for his purchase. Accordingly, on the following morning "a trade" was proposed, which, after some chaffering, was duly effected, Justus receiving for his bondman two negroes of less value.

A year or more had transpired since the date of the last transaction, when a traveller, driving a small two-horse wagon, entered a thriving village in one of the western counties of the State. There was nothing particular in the stranger's appearance worthy of observation, neither did he excite attention, save from a group of loungers, idly engaged in low witticisms and vulgar jests. Belonging to a class that infest our towns and cities, with no business of their own, these worthies found the more time to bestow on that of others. Known as loafers, and in most cases without visible means of support, they depended chiefly for this purpose on the dexterous dealing of spotted pasteboard.

The appearance of the traveller's equipage indicated a fatiguing travel over muddy roads. As the jaded horses slowly passed the street, the remarks their appearance called forth from the loafers were not designed for the exclusive hearing of their own circle.

"Don't he cut a *figger*! How much *furder* do you think his *hosses* will be able to drag that old v'icle, Bill?"

"That's mighty hard to tell, Bob, *shore;* they look like they might just a come from Californy, and the old wagin seems as near give out as them."

"Poor fellow!" responded Bill; "Jordan am a hard road to travel!"

The wagon was brought to a stand in front of the only hotel in the place, but, to the annoyance of the driver, this was found already crowded.

"I exceedingly regret it, sir," said the polite host; "but I fear I have already taken more company than I can render comfortable. However, I am satisfied you will lose nothing by it; for if you will but drive down the street to yon new-looking house, with the shade-trees in the yard, though a private residence, you will meet with hospitable entertainment."

"It's jog on, old fellow, is it?" he heard from Bill, as he again put his horses in motion. "Mine host does'nt like his appearance; you ought to have asked for the hay-loft, old codger! No doubt it would have suited you."

Disregarding this incivility, the traveller soon found himself at the designated dwelling, where, having made known his situation, he was cordially welcomed.

Being thus accommodated, he was disposed to rejoice at the fate which had driven him from the tavern; the quiet beauty and comfort of his situation more than compensating for the former disappointment.

A graceful air pervaded the house and its surroundings, indicating the presence of a cultivated taste in their well-planned arrangements. On a gentle eminence in the outskirts of the village, it commanded, from its cool and vine-embowered portico, a delightful prospect.

"You will please excuse me for a short time," remarked his host, "as necessary business demands my attention. Here are books and papers, with which you can beguile the time." But the traveller found occupation in other objects of interest, for the scenes around him awoke, somehow, strange associations, that sensibly affected him.

"I presume you have had a fatiguing day's drive, sir? you seem quite weary," aroused him from his revery, and notified him of his host's return, who had, unperceived, entered the room.

"Yes, sir; the roads are very heavy, and I have made a long drive."

The gentleman endeavored to draw his guest into conversation; but, finding him inclined to taciturnity, there was a mutual silence.

"I believe there is to be a sale of some 'niggers' in your town to-morrow, is there not?" at length abruptly asked the traveller.

"Yes, sir; there is to be an administrator's sale, and, I believe, among other things, there are some negroes to be disposed of. They will go high, too, as there will be much competition for them."

By degrees, a pleasant conversation sprang up, which was interrupted by the summons of the supper-bell. Before this, the new-comer had fancied his host's a familiar face, though unable to identify it as that of a former acquaintance. At the table, his notice was still more strikingly arrested by a member of the household, hitherto unobserved.

This was a child of some three years of age, whose features, even more strikingly than those of the other, prompted a recognition. But he could come to no more satisfactory conclusion than that he bore a striking resemblance to some one with whom he had been familiar. As he gazed in his eyes, he traced back the pages of memory for some record by which he could locate those who were now so strangely interesting him. The voice of his host, invoking a blessing on their repast, recalled him.

He now noticed the absence of the mistress of the dwelling, a servant in her stead doing the honors of the table. From his first arrival, he had felt a strange desire to see the lady whose tastefully arranged establishment, indicating the presence and skill of one of no ordinary capacity, had singularly impressed him with a vague and undefined remembrance.

"Carol's mother, while visiting the sick, has left him in my charge this evening," remarked the gentleman, as the child was seated by a servant near his father, "and I find him a little troublesome. He is our only child, and is very much of a pet."

"What did you call him?" inquired the other.

"I called him Carol. His name is George Carolus—rather an unusual one; but it was my wife's fancy."

The stranger, still complaining of fatigue, was early shown his room, where, in refreshing slumber, the events of the day were soon forgotten.

Early on the following morning, the traveller was invited by his host to join the family in their usual devotions. The servants were already orderly seated in the room, on entering which, he, for the first time, obtained a view of his hostess, who, suddenly rising, uttered an exclamation of surprise, and extended a cordial greeting to Mr. Justus, while that gentleman, with equal astonishment, ejaculated:

"Rosalind! Is it possible!"

"Mr. Burns," exclaimed the lady, turning to her husband, "allow me to introduce my particular friend, and tutor of former days, Mr. Justus. But I am surprised you have not sooner recognized each other."

"I see it now," remarked Mr. Burns, after warmly greeting his new-found friend; "your face, from the first, looked familiar; but I believe I would not have identified you."

Justus now recognized the gentleman as a minister he had formerly seen at Mr. Holmes's occasionally, and who officiated at "Sue's" wedding.

Notwithstanding his cordial welcome, and the evident pleasure his visit gave his friends, the guest felt ill at ease. The lady witnessed something of this, and was unremitting in her kind attention.

"Here is your namesake, Mr. Justus," she remarked, patting the curly head of little Carolus. "Is he not a handsome child?"

"A noble-looking fellow, indeed! It was his resemblance to yourself that first excited my interest, though, at the time, I could not satisfy myself whose features were reproduced in his."

By degrees, the conversation became very interesting; and, as much of the past had to be talked over, the gentleman took no note of time. As the clock told the hour of ten, he suddenly rose, and, looking at his watch, remarked:

"Agreeable society has caused me to overlook important business, and I regret that it becomes necessary to take my leave."

"Not so soon? We had hoped you would find it convenient to remain some days with us."

"It is necessary for me to return immediately. I will stop a few moments at the sale in town; then at once proceed on my way."

Mr. Burns here interfered; when, after arranging that Justus should remain until the following day, the gentlemen walked out to the place of sale.

They found business already in progress, a man,

with his wife and four small children, being put up together.

"Can't you sell them separately?" asked a voice from the crowd.

"No; they are to go together."

"You'll lose heavily on them, then; for I wouldn't give as much for the lot, and have them little niggers to raise, as for the boy alone."

"Can't help that, gentlemen. Who bids?"

"Five hundred dollars!" said an eager-looking individual, nervously looking around, as if thinking, by precedence, to escape competition.

"Six hundred!" said Justus.

"Why, the cussed fool!" muttered the first bidder; "ten dollars over my pile could a got 'em."

"Not exactly," remarked another. "Seven hundred!" and the bidding still went on.

"Look here, Bill!" said a seedy-looking character to the one addressed, "Ain't that chap biddin' so lively the one that druv' in town so grandly yesterday?"

"Yes, I'll be hanged if it ain't the same fellow! I reckon we mistook our man. We must keep an eye on him; he may be of our sort, and, if we can only get him in Fuller's back room, we'll be mighty apt to get our share of the funds he's so anxious to get rid of, if he's not biddin' only for a show."

"Yes; or if we can only git him to the bar in the *front* room, we'll git the good of a little of it."

"Gone!" cried the auctioneer. "Who's the purchaser?"

"Justus," answered that individual, advancing, pocket-book in hand.

"He's a heap better fellow, after all, than we took him to be, Ned," remarked the worthy formerly addressed as "Bill."

"Yes; he's a trump, certain!"

"I would remark before the selling is resumed," continued Justus, "that if the gentleman who was disposed to pay so much for this boy, is still of the same mind, he can have him for half of what the lot cost."

"Here's your man, and here's your money, too; just make me out a bill of sale and take it," said a coarse, rough-looking person, presenting himself.

"O, mastah!" implored the woman, "don't sell 'im; or if you does, sell *me*, too—sell *all* on us. But he's a good sahvant, mastah, an' ef you'll jis keep us together, you'll neber be sorry 'bout it." And she continued to entreat most piteously, while Justus proceeded to draw up the writings; the other party, in the meanwhile, counting out his money.

The woman's appeal being ineffectual, as a last

resort, the negro himself piteously entreated not to be separated; but, finding his petition powerless, he turned to the intended purchaser, and in moving tones remonstrated against the act, imploring the mercy of being allowed to remain with his wife, whatever else befell.

Here several of the bystanders interfered, and pleaded in behalf of the slave.

"Gentlemen," said Justus, quite coolly, "it does not suit my convenience, nor harmonize with my plans, to keep this boy; I bought him for the purpose of speculation, and one time to sell a *nigger* suits me as well as another, provided the price be good. It would soon be out of my power to buy a *nigger*, were I controlled by the little whims of each one obtained. But if the humanity of any one present will lead him to pay three hundred dollars over their cost to me, he can have the pleasure of keeping the family together."

"Well!" observed one of the remonstrants, "I have only this to say: the person who, under the circumstances, would sell that man from his wife, is simply a brute, and the purchaser no better."

"That's just my conclusion," said the harsh-looking man, thrusting back his pocket-book; "and if he still wishes to sell him, he must seek some one else to buy."

Justus turned on him a contemptuous glance, and would have replied, but at that instant, a gentleman exclaimed:

"I will accept the stranger's benevolent offer, and he may have the pleasure of making three hundred dollars by his first deal."

Quite a number of slaves were disposed of, Justus becoming the purchaser of the larger portion, for which the figures ranged quite high; his unfeeling conduct, and bold avowal of being a regular dealer, exciting much prejudice and competition.

The evening found Justus around the quiet board of his friends, the Burnses, who, if they had any unpleasant reflections on his extreme and discreditable change of principles, kindly withheld their expression.

Pleased with the result of his day's operation, the complacent slave-dealer was in an unusual flow of spirits, and, by his animated conversation, gave a zest to the mutual enjoyment.

Rosalind had never appeared so lovely. He had, indeed, known her gentle and amiable, but had never before formed a proper estimate of her character. He could not repress a pang of regret at the fatal misstep by which he had for ever lost a prize so desirable. And yet, it could not be said that his matrimonial connection was unhappy.

Possessing the affection and confidence of a devoted wife, though wanting to some extent in the congeniality and delicacy found to exist in Rosalind, on the whole he had not been disposed to repine at his lot. But this unexpected meeting calling up the contrast so vividly, revived his old passion with perhaps more than its former intensity, threatening to impair, if not altogether destroy, his subsequent happiness.

The class of feelings thus inspired, gradually changed the lively manner of Justus, until, ere the evening had far advanced, he became quite reserved and dejected.

This was in no wise lessened by a narrative of his host, given as an item of news recently transpired.

"A gentleman in one of the lower counties had occasion, some years since, to visit New York, taking with him one of his servants. While there, the boy was stolen by a mob, but subsequently made his way back to Texas. This, as you may suppose, was an unexpected event, especially to his wife, who, thinking him as one dead to her, had married during his absence. In view of this fact, and the probable trouble to which it might lead, his master was unwilling to receive him on the place again, though previously a favorite; and he was accordingly sold. This seemed to have an injurious effect on the negro's mind: he became dull and listless, and could never, except momentarily, be aroused from a kind of stupor. He was a faithful servant, obedient and industrious, but it seemed mechanical, and fears of insanity were entertained.

"At length, after being missed from his place, he suddenly entered the cabin, once his former home, haggard, and in a state of mental derangement. The sight of his wife seemed for a moment to recall his wandering reason. The woman, hearing her name pronounced in familiar tones, turned to observe; when, beholding the apparition, with a wild scream she sank insensible. Seizing a child she had held in her arms, with all the frenzy of madness, he exclaimed, 'This is one of the whelps,' and ended its existence by horribly mangling its throat with a knife. Attracted by its shrieks, the master now arrived, and the maniac was secured.

" The unfortunate woman awoke to consciousness to hear the most awful imprecations on her faithlessness; and, in the terror excited, imagined herself guilty to the full extent charged.

" The ravings of the madman were of short continuance. His mental tortures had consumed his vital powers, and death kindly ended his sufferings.

His wife did not long survive: the shock was too severe, and her reason was shaken. She died bemoaning her ingratitude to a kind and faithful husband.

"Such," continued Mr. Burns, "is the account I had from a neighbor, recently returned from that section; and though a shocking affair, it may nevertheless be true."

"A sad story, indeed!" replied Justus, whose excitement during its recital was quite apparent; and though his friend was deceived as to its cause, it awakened in the other a train of unpleasant and bitter reflection his blunted and hardened sensibilities could not stifle.

In a painfully disturbed state of mind he sought his couch, but weary hours passed before slumber visited him. Even then, his sleep was disturbed by frightful dreams, and the night passed in fearful agony.

First, he was in Boston—in Fancuil Hall, with "Mr. Clay" by his side; then he found the mutilated negro beside the lifeless body of his slaughtered foe. Once more, he was on the point of conveying to his desired servitude and home "Mr. Clay," now degraded again to simple Henry.

Again the scene changed: he had just returned from a successful and profitable tour of trading, and was occupying his couch at home. Suddenly the chamber-door flew open, and a huge dark figure entered, wildly advancing towards him, bearing a large and bloody knife; struggling to escape, with a yell of horror he awoke.

Drowsiness again stealing over him, soon a haggard woman entered the chamber, and took her silent stand directly in front of his bed. Her piercing eyes were fixed steadfastly on him, depriving him alike of the power of motion or of utterance. In her arms she held an infant, from a gash in whose throat blood was freely flowing. Silently a grim-looking man approached, and, taking the child, pointed to its bleeding wound, and laid it beside the terrified dreamer, who, with a more fearful cry than before, sprang to the floor.

His host, much concerned at his repeated alarms, now appearing with a light, Justus's mortification was complete. With many an apology for allowing himself to be disturbed by an idle dream, he reluctantly resumed his couch.

With joy the returning daylight was hailed, and at an early hour Justus took his leave, hastening to complete his annual round of slave-dealing.

THE END.